MW01223185

Fairhaven

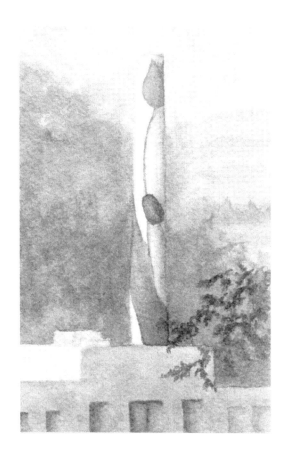

Other books by Ken Coffman

Fiction
Steel Waters
Alligator Alley (Ken Coffman and Mark Bothum)
Twisted Shadow (Ken Coffman with Mark Bothum)
Glen Wilson's Bad Medicine
Toxic Shock Syndrome
Hartz String Theory
Endangered Species
Mesh (Ken Coffman and Adina Pelle)
The Sandcastles of Irakkistan

Nonfiction
Real World FPGA Design with Verilog

STAIRWAY PRESS

Books can be ordered from:

Stairway Press
www.StairwayPress.com
1500A East College Way #554
Mount Vernon, WA 98273

This book is a work of fiction. Names, characters, places and incidents are the products of the author's fevered imagination or are used fictitiously. Any resemblance to actual events, locales or persons (living or dead) is entirely coincidental.

ISBN-13 978-0-9827734-2-0

The Armchair Adventure is an imprint of:

Stairway Press
1500A East College Way #554
Mount Vernon, WA 98273

Dedication

In memory of Lydia Braschler-Varo
October 1987 – July 2001

I used to live at Lake Cavanaugh in Skagit County and would regularly drive past Lydia's sad, informal memorial on Lake Cavanaugh Road. I never met Lydia or her family, but I'm saddened by her murder and the heartbreaking end of her short life. As of the moment I write this note, her murderer is still unknown and at large. As long as that remains the case, justice is not served.

I think there is still a reward offered for information that leads to the arrest of her killer. Stairway Press will add $1,000 to that reward.

Literary Inspiration

Once again and for very obvious reasons, I must thank Charles Willeford. When it comes to finely evoked characters, bizarre humor and outlandish plot twists, he is and always will be my master.

I thank my informal cadre of loyal supporters—for free advice, criticism, encouragement, guidance, proofreading and miscellaneous instances of discordant howling at my literary moon.

Judy Coffman, Stacey Benson, Pat Shaw, Adina Pelle, Eph Evans, Mark Bothum, Ken Lomax, Lisa Fredsti, Dr. Seymour Garte, Dock Brown, Gary Croft, Dale Edwards, Tommy Lee Bolser, Pat Bertram, Beth Hill, Wanda Hughes and Helen Verrall.

Author Notes on *Fairhaven*

First of all, though I live in Skagit County in Washington State and this book seems to be set in that magical place, I took liberties. Some of the places in this book either don't exist or were changed to support my artistic vision of the book. As an example, I know the Democratic and Republican offices are *not* near each other. It amused me to imagine them closer together, so that's the way I wrote this damned thing.

I don't know any policemen. I don't know any used car dealers. I don't know anyone in the local assisted-living facilities. I made a bunch of crap up. Don't walk around the streets of Mount Vernon and expect them to wholly match up with what I describe herein.

Well, there is one thing. The hostile bald eagle? I didn't make it up. Like flying weasels, those irritating and dangerous things are all over the place.

I would like to say something about the book's name and apologize to anyone who thinks my *Fairhaven* has anything to do with the lovely Fairhaven community a few miles up the highway. The name is a riff and reference to Charles Willeford's very dark unpublished novel called *Grimhaven*. Grimhaven. Fairhaven. See? My book is not so grim...you should, despite the ugly things described, find the book ultimately uplifting...a story about tough love, aging, euthanasia, family bonds, redemption and hope.

Email me at ken@stairwaypress.com if you have questions or comments. As always, online reviews, good or bad, are greatly appreciated. This is a tough business, please be my champion.

KLC – November, 2011

Introduction

Jake Mosby

THE AFTERNOON SUN broiled the beach. The olive-drab Skagit River, on the last lazy stage of its long journey from the Canadian Cascades, roiled and burbled. A little Mexican girl, dressed only in a sagging swimsuit bottom and dried mud, ran in tight circles, stirring up a cloud of choking dust.

Jake Mosby unbuttoned the bib of his patched and stained Carhartt denim overalls to expose his chest's thatch of gray hair; otherwise, he did not acknowledge the heat. He raised his fifth of Early Times bourbon in salute to a bald eagle lurking in a tree across the river. The eagle had been staring at Jake for an hour.

Why not make yourself useful and carry away this annoying child?

The eagle did not acknowledge this thought. Jake swirled the last swallow of golden liquid. Bright sunlight dancing on the river's ripples gave him a headache, but soon, nothing would matter.

Jake's skin was leathery...at 66, he looked 76. Folds of loose flesh, prickly with a week's accumulation of patchy stubble, hung from his jowly face. From under the brim of his floppy straw hat, watery, chocolate-brown eyes peered out with world-weary suspicion. He had a drinker's nose woven with red blood vessels and pasted to his face like an old potato.

A volleyball rolled to his feet. Tanned, fit college students, playing in a grassy area of the riverside park, yelled at him to kick it back. He ignored them. A willowy brunette wearing a tiny brown bikini top over teacup breasts ran over to retrieve the ball.

"Miserable prick," she hissed.

Jake, focused on an aluminum fishing boat idling slowly upstream past the old tulip-decorated smokestack, paid her no attention.

The alimony and child support payments he'd been paying had long since ended, but he was exhausted from stretching inflation-eroded law enforcement pension checks to cover the expenses of life in the twenty-first century.

His third-floor, walk-up apartment on First Street was scheduled to be demolished to make room for a luxury condo complex. Instead of looking for another cheap place to live, he decided to wade into the river and see if he could survive drifting downstream until the fresh water met the salt. Then, the eagles and sand sharks could have him if they'd take him. He imagined the predator-birds ripping his wrinkled, waterlogged skin. The image was vivid...he could almost feel cruel beaks and talons tearing at him. When the Early Times was gone and he'd smoked his last cigarette down to a stub, he'd wade in.

A red-faced, sweating man roasting in a dark suit blocked the sunlight.

"Jake? Jake Mosby?" he said.

"I'm busy," Jake replied.

Fairhaven

"You're not easy to find. If you have a phone, it's unlisted…and you didn't respond to our letters." The man held out a pudgy hand to shake. "A guy named Stonewall said I'd find you out here if you weren't hanging out on the stairs by the Jasper Gates statue. I'm Martin Grigsby with Grigsby, Hamilton and Smythe. I handled your father's affairs. I've been trying to reach you since your step-mother died."

Jake took his eyes off the nearly gone fishing boat and peered up at Grigsby.

"What? Betsy died?"

"They were on a Star Sun cruise ship off the coast of Brazil. Apparently, she ate a bad batch of polenta on a shore excursion and got sick. Weak from food poisoning, she caught pneumonia and died at sea. That was three weeks ago."

Jake never cared about Betsy one way or another. Like air, she just was. Around Jake's age, she was almost thirty years younger than his father, Chet Mosby. With extravagant taste, she did not veil her disapproval of Jake's threadbare overalls and bizarre frugality. At family get-togethers, Jake fought the impulse to tell Betsy that a fat ass covered in an expensive, tailored pantsuit—was still a fat ass.

"I'm glad you didn't find me. Even if Dad begged, I wouldn't go to her funeral."

"At your father's request, there was no funeral. She was buried at sea. It's unusual, but they can still do it in international waters. It's interesting…they shroud the body in a canvas bag and weigh it down with two cannon balls. As I understand it, with cannonballs being hard to find, they used dumbbells from the weight-training room, but never mind that. By tradition, the last stitch goes through the corpse's nose to make sure of death. It's quite a spectacle and cost your dad twenty-three thousand dollars. They did it at four A.M. to avoid upsetting the other cruisers."

"Is there a point to this ramble?" Jake said. "I'm on a tight schedule..."

"Right. Sorry. I shouldn't talk so much unless I'm being paid by the minute. Bad habit. To get to my point, we couldn't find you—though I admit we did not look very hard—so you missed Betsy's memorial service at Mother Mary's chapel two weeks ago Sunday. Other than Chet, the only people there were the ladies from her Tuesday bridge club. Her daughter was on a river cruise in Ireland, but she sent flowers. Jake, please. I'm dying in this heat; can we get out of the sun? I'll buy you a rum and Coke at The Trumpeter."

Jake carefully pulled a stub of a hand-rolled cigarette from a zipper pocket of his overalls. After straightening it, he put it in his mouth and lighted a match.

"Dad-burn it, Jake, I hate to tell you this way, but your dad died too. Massive coronary. Day before yesterday. He was having an early dinner at Il Granaio and pitched over in his clam linguini. The waitress said his last word on earth was 'tartufi'. Have you tried that? Gelato truffles. Magnificent. Perfect. My last word will probably be tort, not tart. I know...I should get to the point. Jake, can we finish our conversation in a more dignified manner? At the bar. Please?"

Jake let the words wash over him as he stared at the river until the match burned his fingers. The pain roused him from reverie. He extinguished the match in the sand and sucked his burnt fingers.

"I didn't see much of him the last few years, but I'll miss him," Jake said. "Betsy led him around by his dick, otherwise he wasn't a bad old guy. When's the funeral?"

"That's your call, Jake. It's up to you to make the arrangements for a memorial service. His friends are asking; that's part of the urgency to locate you."

"I don't have money for stuff like that."

"Your father had a funeral policy with deluxe coverage. All-inclusive. Per his request, he's already been cremated." Grigsby pulled a silk handkerchief from his coat pocket and mopped his brow. "Don't worry about the money. Jake, we need to talk. Get up, let's go."

He reached out his hand to help Jake up.

Jake thought about his determination to kill himself and end his dismal life. He was wrung out, used-up...depleted. Old, desiccated and useless. Ready to move on to the next world, if there was one. The only thing between him and oblivion was one final swallow of bourbon and the cigarette.

I suppose if I don't finish it, then I'm not breaking a promise.

After flicking the cigarette stub toward the volleyball players, he raised the bottle and stared at the unrelenting river through the dregs of amber liquid. He unscrewed the top and, with a pang of regret, poured the warm whiskey into the sand. With creaking joints, he took Grigsby's hand and lurched to his feet. After stretching his protesting back, he turned and walked along the soulless water toward the old Division Street Bridge.

"Bye-bye," the Mexican girl said.

Without turning, Jake grunted in reply while dropping the bottle into an overflowing trash bin.

They walked under the traffic-clogged bridge and along the riverside boardwalk. A backhoe worked at the demolition of an old brick building. Without speaking, they walked across an expansive parking lot.

The bar at the Trumpeter was dark. Tucked into a corner booth, Grigsby ordered iced tea while Jake ordered a double Captain Morgan, Coke and lime.

"Thank you, Jake. This is more a civilized place to talk than out by the river. As I said, we handled your mother and father's affairs. Betsy bequeathed everything—lock, stock and barrel—to her estranged daughter in Hoquiam."

"Dad told me. I know about that. She's welcome to it."

"But Jake, though she was much younger and healthier than your dad, Betsy died first. By state law, he got everything and now his will takes effect."

"His will was different than hers?"

"That's what I'm trying to tell you, Jake. In *his* will, her daughter gets ten thousand dollars and that's all. They didn't plan on *Chet's* will being the vehicle for distributing *Betsy's* assets. I suggested they account for this sequence of events, but no one took seriously the idea that Betsy might pass first. The bottom line? You get everything."

Jake drained his drink and waved his empty glass in the air.

"Another, sir?" the barmaid asked.

"Yeah, why not?" Jake said.

From his calfskin valise, Martin pulled out papers and spread them on the table. Jake's dad had organized everything neatly. The hand-written list of accounts and assets covered three fine-printed pages and included certificates of deposit, mutual funds, real estate holdings, stocks, savings bonds and several bank accounts. Then, his father had inherited Betsy's substantial holdings and his will passed them to Jake. They had lived a lavish lifestyle...now Jake could see how and why they could afford it. When Betsy's first husband had died, she'd invested the life insurance money in constructing an Alki Beach condo complex that sold to Windmark for twelve million dollars.

Jake felt guilty for thinking she'd been after his father's money. She'd been beyond wealthy on her own.

"I bet the daughter's pissed."

"She's displeased," Martin said, "but that's not your problem. Her husband owns a chain of plumbing-supply stores. She won't starve."

"I'm trying to live a simple life. This is too much responsibility. Got a pen?"

With a puzzled look on his face, Grigsby produced a walnut and gold pen from the inside pocket of his jacket.

Jake circled a listing for a used bookstore.

"Give her everything else," he said. The notation: *White Buick Riviera, 13,000 miles* caught his eye. He circled it. "I'll keep the car, too."

"Jake, sleep on this and think it through. With this news, you're in a fragile state…I've seen it a hundred times. Don't make important decisions until after the memorial. Things will look very different then, trust me. Also, you have your daughters' future security to think of."

"They're fine. You know what I hate most about being poor?"

"I wouldn't venture a guess."

"Rolling Red Man cigarettes like a dirty hobo…and I could never get the knack of rolling a pretty one." He gestured to the barmaid. "Miss, bring me a pack of Marlboros and another rum and Coke."

"I strongly protest—you're throwing away a small fortune," Grigsby sputtered.

"Write it up and get it ready for my signature. As long as I have a place to live and can smoke store-boughts, I have what I need for a simple life. I will not change my mind."

Grigsby sighed and bit his lower lip. "I haven't had a drink in ten years," he muttered. He waved a finger in the air. "I'll take a neat Glenfarclas, miss."

A handful of ancients from Peaceful Meadows Assisted Living Center came to Chet's memorial service. Peaceful Meadows was three blocks uphill from Mosby's Bookstore—across the I-5 freeway. Jake's daughters, Ellen and Eileen, would have come, but he refused to tell them. Standing in front of the small group gathered at the Vasa Hall meeting room, Jake read from a tattered paperback copy of Derrida's *The Gift of Death*.

> ...*that same "society" puts to death or allows to die of hunger and disease tens of millions of children without any moral or legal tribunal ever being considered competent to judge such a sacrifice, the sacrifice of others to avoid being sacrificed oneself*...

Afterward, Eleanor Bradley, leaning over a walker with yellow Wilson tennis balls attached as bumpers to the walker's front feet, gave Jake a kiss on the cheek and pressed a rolled-up book of Sudoku puzzles and a knitted hot pad—red and shaped like a heart—into his hand.

Puzzled, Jake examined the book and the heart.

"I need help with the hard puzzles," she said. "And—no one has too many hot pads."

"Thank you, I think," Jake said.

Martin Grigsby waited in the back.

"That thing you read?"

"Yeah," Jake said.

"It was an odd choice."

Jake shrugged. "I had to say something."

"In the future, if you need help finding something appropriate, let me know. Psalms from the Bible always works well." Martin sighed. "To get to our business, I documented your requests, but I'd like to take one last opportunity to talk you out of giving everything away. Not for yourself...your daughters deserve the benefit of the estate when you pass on."

"It's no good getting rich when someone dies. It's better knowing you get nothing. That way, the subconscious does not impatiently wish for a benefactor to expire. Besides, they're making their own fortunes."

Grigsby rubbed his temples with small, pudgy hands, and then proffered his expensive gold and black walnut pen. Jake signed by X's on the paperwork and it was done. While leaving, Grigsby allowed himself a small, satisfied smile. He'd done as Jake asked, but had taken advantage of 'wiggle room'. He'd transferred all the cash accounts to the bookstore bank account. The papers Jake signed approved the transfers. Jake wouldn't have to worry about buying store-bought cigarettes...they were more than covered for the rest of his life.

After refusing Martin's offer of a ride, Jake rolled up the sheaf of legal papers, the hot pad and Sudoku puzzle book, stuffed them in the hip pocket of his overalls and walked out of the building. He walked past the fairgrounds on the fractured sidewalks of Cleveland Avenue. In the sweltering August sun, listless traffic flowed past rundown houses. After half a block, his overalls glued themselves with sweat to his lower back. A Larouchey, set up in front of the post office with pamphlets spread across a card table, tried to make eye contact, but Jake ignored him.

Unaware, he passed a bank, the library and the Moose Lodge before finally arriving at Mosby's bookstore. He leaned against the adjoining brick building and looked over his inheritance. Three morose evergreen trees reached for the sky as if trying to escape an earthly prison. At their bases, bare patches of dirt were decorated with ugly clumps of dried dog shit and wind-strewn plastic grocery bags. An abandoned Ford Pinto, tagged with balloon-lettered graffiti, squatted on flat tires. Trash was strewn around the rear entry.

Behind a high window covered with wrought-iron bars, a storeroom had been converted to a small apartment. Jake intended to live there. It would be a simple life stripped of complications...run the bookstore and deal with the very few customers coming through the front door. An undemanding existence, that's what he craved.

With no fresh stock, no advertising and the addition of a sign saying I'm no longer buying used books, there won't be much business.

The store had been closed for a year. After Mrs. Wadsworth had passed away, his dad, ailing and uninterested, hadn't bothered hiring new staff or opening and closing the place while away on the long cruises Betsy scheduled. The last employee, José Rodriquez, had long since taken an assistant manager position at the Barnes and Noble store in Bellingham.

With darkened windows and flaking paint, Mosby's Used Books looked pitiful and desolate. Jake walked around the building. The front windows were streaked with pigeon droppings. Shielding his eyes, Jake peered inside...the sills were covered with lonely sun-bleached books, dust and dead bugs.

Fairhaven

In his way, he was happy—the rundown setting matched his pitiful internal wasteland. In this dust and rubbish, he was where he belonged. After sorting through keys on a massive ring, he found one that fit the front door. Inside, a rank odor made it clear something had crawled inside and died. Beneath the putrefaction, the building smelled of mildew and despair. After working his way through a tour of the building—stepping around black plastic trash bags and books spilled from their shelves—he returned to the front door and turned out the 'CLOSED' sign.

Once again, Mosby's was open for business.

Nort Spenser

Large for his age, Nort was gangly and clumsy.

In the current fashion, he wore a huge pair of farmer's jeans several sizes too large. His body drifted in the fabric like a stick in a bag. Scraggly sideburns and a thin mustache grew in patches on his pimply face. He wasn't stupid, but pretended to be in order to fit in with the Kool Boyz, his World of Warcraft posse. In a sweaty palm, he clutched a damp note delivered by a messenger…a sexy Latina named Olivia…on behalf of an even sexier El Salvadoran girl—Lucia Alvarez.

> *During first lunch, meet me by the ladies can next to the computer lab. I love you.*

The note was decorated with pink hearts and smelled of cologne. Her cologne. His heart pounded. Framed by bright sunlight from an outside door, Lucia approached. She wore short-shorts and a loose satin blouse over pushed-up breasts.

11

She boldly walked up and kissed him directly on the lips.

She tugged his hand.

"Come on," she said.

She stopped at a stub of hallway and slipped a key into a supply closet lock. For an instant, the cubbyhole was flooded with light and Nort could see cases of paper towels and toilet paper. When the door closed, the room was very dark—the only light was a faint stripe seeping under the door. Fabric rustled. She efficiently unbuttoned his jeans and pulled down his voluminous boxer shorts. She pressed him backwards—he fell onto a bundle of Scott Towels. She straddled him and worked his throbbing, over-eager erection into her moist heat. Overwhelmed, he came after a few strokes—less than thirty seconds—and filled her with molten globs.

In seconds, she was dressed again. Leaning over, she gave him a peck on the cheek.

"Thank you, baby," she said before slipping out of the room.

As his heart rate settled, he wiped a film of sweat from his brow.

What the fuck was that?

And...

Will my friends believe me when I tell them about it?

Lucia, uncomfortable with fluids leaking from her body, walked out the front door of the high school and slipped into her uncle's battered Nissan pickup. She handed him the closet key.

"It's done," she said.

While the truck maneuvered through Tacoma's rush hour traffic, she thought back to the family meeting—the night she confessed to her mother and father that she was two-months pregnant. The father was a twenty-year-old Oregon boy—a hookup while he was on leave from a tour in Iraq. Now, he was back in Iraq and had stopped instant-messaging her or answering her cell phone calls after she'd told him about the baby. While tears streamed down her mother's face, Lucia sat on their Salvation Army couch with her knees pressed together. After her father finished shouting and berating her, he cupped her chin to raise her face and spoke coldly.

"You will find a white boy from a good family and couple with him. We'll tell his family he's the father of the baby and ask for a thousand dollars for an abortion. They won't want anyone to know their son knocked-up a Salvadorian *puta* so they will pay to take care of it and keep it quiet. I will not have white-trash baby bastards in my house. Do you understand?"

She pushed his hands away and clenched her teeth.

"Yes, Papa. I understand," she said.

"Make sure it's a white boy. A Hispanic will want you to have the kid and collect the welfare money."

"I understood you the first time you said it, Father," she said through clenched teeth.

Charlie Fairhaven

Charlie had a childlike face and hazel eyes flecked with gold—eyes that seemed to change between green and brown. Over his plump body, his face seemed unnaturally thin and undernourished. Completing his youthful image, his cheeks were often pink with exertion or excitement.

There wasn't much to do on the graveyard shift at New Era Elder Care Center—he spent the night reading John

Ken Coffman

McDonald paperback mysteries on his Kindle and making sure clients didn't get lost on the way to the communal bathroom. He answered the emergency call button if someone heard a cat burglar outside their window or needed a paper cup of water.

Sleeping on the job was not an option. Every hour, on the hour, he made a round and looked in on patients—scanning a bar code with a portable reader on every floor at the end of every corridor so the nursing home management would know he was on the job.

The first client he killed was an old man...a former real estate developer named Barrymore Carter. For some reason, Barrymore went by the nickname Barnyard. He greeted everyone the same way. "Howdy, I'm Barnyard Carter from Olympia and I built Washington's first three McDonalds restaurants and I was a personal friend of Ray Kroc."

It was uninteresting the first time, and lost charm on repetition.

A private room at New Era was expensive...eight-thousand a month without extras like oxygen or low-fat, sugar-free meals. Barnyard's family was not poor, but his care, month-by-month, drained cash from his legacy.

Eight thousand a month while he watched Fox News on a flat screen TV and reintroduced himself to people who already knew he'd built the first three McDonalds in Washington and was a personal friend of Ray Kroc.

Most old people die between three and four o'clock in the morning. On the three o'clock round—standing like a ghost in dim light—Charlie stood over Barnyard's bed and watched him struggle for breath. Barnyard was already useless and dead, but, inexplicably, his body struggled on. The old man was a worthless burden sucking eight thousand dollars every month like a parasite.

14

Fairhaven

Slowly, without thinking it over—after lurking and listening for noise in the hallway—Charlie moved into position. With one thin hand, it was easy to clamp Barnyard's bulbous nose shut and cover the gaping mouth.

There was no struggle. Barnyard's eyes popped open and he stared until his chest stopped heaving and his eyes glazed over. When Charlie removed his hand, fetid air escaped with a feeble wheeze—and that was it. Dregs of life animated the old body and then they didn't. If a soul escaped, Charlie didn't sense it.

He didn't feel guilty...he'd done the family a service.

On the four o'clock round, Charlie filled out the death report form. Later, while ambulatory clients ate in the breakfast room and the doors for the room-bound were closed, paramedics on contract with the county wheeled in a gurney, body-bagged the corpse, and quietly hauled it away without upsetting the other patients.

Charlie stayed around after his shift and talked to Wendy Thomas—Barnyard's oldest daughter—in the employee breakroom. He handed her tissues to blot her eyes.

"I knew it would happen eventually, but I guess you're never really ready. He built the first——"

"I know."

"I'm sorry. I'm sure you've heard the story a million times."

And he'd still be alive if I wanted to hear it again.

"I hate to mention this," Charlie said, "but it's traditional for the family to leave a remembrance for the on-duty staff when a patient leaves us. A sort of gratuity—in tribute."

A tradition I dreamed up.

"Of course. I wasn't thinking."

She pulled a checkbook from a massive Coach purse.

"I'm not sure what's appropriate. Would five-hundred be all right?"

Charlie's cheeks glowed. Five hundred would nearly double his take-home pay for the week.

"Yes, ma-am, if that's not too much burden on the family," he said solemnly. He shot a glance at the check to make sure it was signed before folding it and stuffing it in the pocket of his scrubs. "Please don't mention this to anyone. Management frowns on the tradition because old folks generally die at night and the day staff rarely gets anything."

Wendy dabbed her eyes and looked at Charlie as if seeing him for the first time. She took a deep breath and steered her eyes toward the window.

"What about his things?"

"The staff will box up his stuff."

After going through everything and taking what they wanted.

But Charlie did not mention this.

"Come back at your convenience to pick it up," he said. "I'm very sorry for your loss, Mrs. Thomas."

"Thank you," she said. "I appreciate your kindness."

Eleanor Bradley

In her room at the Peaceful Meadows Assisted Living Facility—next to her twin bed—was a small bookshelf. This bookshelf was mainly occupied with Sudoku puzzle books, but also held a slim photo album. She wasn't the type to force it on anyone (like Mr. Albertson in Room 47 who made everyone look at photographs and newspaper clippings documenting his second place finish in the 154 pound weight class at the championship wrestling tournament in Pullman, Washington in 1953), so generally the pages went unseen. Sometimes, in the early hours of the morning when sleep evaded her, she'd open the book and relive her history.

In her day, she had been a radiant beauty. She won the Cinderella Queen contest—her foot fit perfectly into a triple-A shoe—and was the second-place winner in the Skagit City Carnival beauty contest in 1936. When she was twenty-three, she had a billowy polka dot dress that, on blustery days, made men trip over imaginary cracks in the sidewalk.

Those days were long past. Now she wore sensible shoes with crêpe soles. Cinderella's grandmother's shoes.

Slowly, she worked her walker up and down the hallways of the Peaceful Meadows facility, delivering her attention to one crisis after another. Dotty King could not find her glasses (hidden under a three-year-old copy of *Knitting Universe* magazine). She refereed William Corbin-Walter's argument over the rules in the 3:00 Pinochle game (10's-around are—and always will be—worth nothing). She fixed the TV when Beverly Thoms had the PVR programming hopelessly messed up. She found a marble to replace a blue one missing from the Chinese checkers game.

It was not the life she'd imagined when she was a young girl...the bright-eyed winner of the 1933 Talent Bee baton twirling competition for a routine set to a thin, scratchy version of The Dorsey Brothers *Coquette* playing on a rickety Victrola. Still, her boundless, irrepressible spirit radiated out through her washed-out, watery pale-blue eyes.

Ever perceptive, she was a legend in the facility. When Eloise Pemberton's prescription was filled improperly by Walgreens, Eleanor noticed and made sure Mrs. Pemberton got Aceon (for her hypertension) instead of dangerous Adipex (prescribed for weight loss).

In her down time, she liked to work on Sudoku puzzle books—but not the hard ones that made her feel stupid.

The easy ones.

Ophelia, the black dayshift Nurse-Practitioner—dressed in lavender scrubs—poked her head in Eleanor's room.

"I'm sorry to trouble you, Mrs. Bradley, but Omar locked himself in the visitor's bathroom and won't come out. He says he wants to talk to you. Only you."

Eleanor sighed and set aside her book.

"I'll be right there," she said.

1

Six Months Later...

Jake Mosby

THE OLD BRICK building housing Mosby's Used Books was one of the last remnants of the historic river town. Built in the 1920's on a then-muddy wagon road called First Avenue, it crouched like a canker sore between the Armageddon Coin and Collectables store and a squat, post-modern, glass-sheathed lawyer's office building. Down the street, like a cop holding screaming lovers apart, a day spa separated the Republican and Democrat party offices.

At least once a month, a lawyer or real estate agent would stop by and make an offer to buy the building. Jake would talk to them if they bought a book, but always said 'no' to any offer.

The city wanted to rezone to build a parking garage, but Jake had two friends on the city council; one a long-time friend of his father's, the other the oldest son of Tom Hiller, his boss when Jake had worked for the Seattle Police Department. Stubbornly, his friends refused bribes, ignored threats and vetoed eminent domain petitions. In addition, it didn't hurt that Hiller's brother-in-law was Mount Vernon's mayor, Bob Morris.

The situation would not last forever. When Sherman, his dad's ancient friend, expired, Tom Hiller, Jr. would then be powerless and the bulldozers would be unleashed. Until then, Jake was satisfied selling an occasional first-edition to a collector or a box of Harlequin romances to a lonely widow. Day-after-day, he sat at the counter and laboriously read and reread his tattered copy of *The Gift of Death.*

> *Let us note in passing that in none of these discourses we are analyzing here does the moment of death give room for one to take into account sexual difference; as if, as it would be tempting to imagine, sexual difference does not count in the face of death. Sexual difference would be a being-up-until-death.*

Jake was seriously considering tearing the pages out, soaking them with lighter fluid and burning them—when the door bells jingled.

A young man carrying a suitcase walked through the store's front door. After a few seconds of study, Jake placed the face in its proper context. His grandson. Norton. The husky young man was now seventeen—with a briar patch of dark hair on his head and a home-made tattoo smeared across his upper arm.

"What's the tat supposed to be? Jake said.

"Viper," Nort replied.

"Looks more like a coiled, steaming heap of brown shit."

"Fuck you too, Gramps."

After this warm reintroduction, Jake led Nort to the

bookstore's breakroom; a dark, cramped nook filled with plastic-wrapped stacks of Costco toilet paper, heaps of books and boxes filled with plastic retail bags. The printer had misspelled the bags—which read 'Moseby's' in fancy old-fashioned script—but refused to take them back. Jake was too cheap to discard them so he painstakingly, bag by bag, sat at the breakroom table and obscured the errant 'e' with an indelible Sharpie pen.

Unsure what to say in the awkward situation, Jake gestured for Nort to take a seat and lit a cigarette.

"Gimme a hit off'n that cowboy-killer, pops."

"Don't call me pops," Jake said. "And I don't want to be called grandpa either."

"Okay, G-P," Nort said while holding his hand out for the cigarette.

Jake pulled a notepad and stub of pencil from the pocket of his overalls and jotted a note.

"Cigarettes are a quarter each or five for a dollar," he said.

He pulled a pack from a zipper-pocket. After extracting a cigarette, he carefully cut it in half with a pen knife and nudged the stub across the table. The other half he worked back into the package.

"That's half a cigarette."

"Around here, that's a cigarette. You want it or not?"

"You're the Mayor of Cheap. The president of Idiotistan…the governor of Fuckton," the kid grumbled while lighting the stub with a match.

He dropped the match on the table where it burned a black mark before dying. The ancient wooden table top was covered with similar black marks.

Eileen—Nort's mother—was Jake's younger daughter.

Instead of sending Nort back to school after the Christmas break, she'd put Nort on a Greyhound bus with a suitcase and a one-way ticket from Tacoma to Mount Vernon. He'd gotten a 16-year-old girl pregnant and had been arrested twice for jacking cars. The pregnancy, after cash changed hands, ended at a crisis pregnancy center, and the car theft charges were negotiated down to probation, but Eileen had seen enough to know how this movie ended…and she didn't like it.

"I can't stop you from flushing your life down the toilet, but I don't have to watch you do it," she'd said.

She was married to an orthodontist named Hayward Spenser and they lived on a tree-lined suburban street in an upscale Tacoma neighborhood. Hayward wanted to send Nort to a boot camp for troubled teenagers in Wyoming. They could afford it, but Eileen protested at the waste of money.

"For that much money we could pay off the X-ray machine," she'd said.

"But your dad——," Hayward had said.

"I know Dad's certifiably insane, but I turned out okay, didn't I?"

Eileen raised a hand, flicked a wrist and struck a pose. With a mane of dark, sculpted hair and long, slender legs, she was sexy and beautiful, but had a hot temper and cruel sense of humor. She was both much better and much worse than okay, but Hayward, knowing the borders and landscape of treacherous territories, did not directly answer her question.

"Whatever you think is best, babydoll," he said.

"What's there to do around here?" Nort asked.

"Nature's way is to work or die. Every man chooses."

"Half the time, I have no clue what you're talking about.

You're a fucked-up old fossil. Got an Xbox?"

"Never heard of it."

"Shit. Playstation? Wii? Atari?"

"No. No TV, no world web or Internap or whatever it's called. If you want something to do, sort out the Westerns. The Louis L'Amours and Zane Greys are all mixed up on aisle three."

"This sucks ass. You suck ass. I'm not staying."

"Good. I didn't ask you to come. Fuck off and have a great life."

Nort stood. He took a last drag off his cigarette and, with a defiant look on his face, stubbed it out on the table.

"I don't have scratch. Gimme some money and I'm dust."

Jake chuckled. The sound emitted from his chest as a phlegmy rumble.

"I'll pay you five bucks an hour. Payday's on Friday. You can sleep on a bedroll here in the breakroom for twenty bucks a week. I'll pay for food, but cigarettes, booze and sodas come out of your pay. After a few weeks, if you don't piss your money away on candy bars and reefers, you'll have enough for a bus ticket. Maybe your aunt in Hoquiam will take you in."

"Five bucks an hour's not even minimal wage."

Jake, gingerly holding his cigarette stub, drew a final toke before dropping it on the table. He extinguished it with a blackened thumbnail.

"Around here, you're paid what you're worth," he said.

"And don't say reefer. That's old. Say toot or S-G."

"S-G?"

"Yeah, SG. Spiderman's Girlfriend. It's math…logic. MJ, Mary Jane. Get it? Mary Jane? Marijuana? That's what we say."

"Coming up with stuff like that means you kids have far

too much free time on your hands. You're going to toughen up like a Spartan. Have you heard of the Spartans?"

Nort shook his head.

"When I was in school, they told us the story of the Spartan kid who never complained…even when a fox ripped open his stomach and shredded his guts, the boy said nothing. They didn't have Xboxes or any of that stupid shit back then."

"That's gaylord. I'd shout bloody murder if a fox bit my guts."

"The story is allegorical. Not to be taken literally, get it?"

"Whatever," Nort said. "And gimme a nip off that rot-gut."

Jake rinsed out a water glass in the utility sink and placed it on the table. "Good idea," he said. He poured a slug of Early Times and pushed the glass across the table.

"To the good times," Jake said.

Grinning as if he was getting away with something, Nort tapped his glass against Jake's and drained it. Nort choked…tears spouted. For a moment he couldn't speak.

"Damn, that's smooth," he finally said while pushing his glass across the table for a refill.

After an hour, the bottle was empty. Nort was fully inebriated…reeling and slurring.

"My p'rents suck ath. They won't let me drink anything, not even a flippin' beer. My friends have to bribe a bum to get wine at the Circle-K. If they could see me now, they'd be all 'Fuck, Nort, you got a fucking cool granddad who lets you drink all you want'. Awe…some."

Nort's head sank to the table. He drooled on its surface and mumbled some more, but it was incomprehensible. Jake got up and staggered back to his apartment. He mixed three raw eggs with two tablespoons of salt and looked at the foul mixture for a full minute before guzzling it. It worked almost immediately; he vomited everything from his sour stomach into the sink. He was left with a taste of bile and a throbbing headache. He drank a large glass of water, swallowed a couple of aspirin tablets and sat at his table for a few minutes feeling sorry for himself.

Then he found a dirty sock and filled it with a cup of granulated sugar. He weighed the makeshift sap in his hands. Staggering a little, he made his way back to the breakroom. Nort had not moved. Jake arranged a towel under Nort's head and gauged how hard to hit him. He didn't want to cause permanent damage, but wanted to add memorable pain to Nort's hangover headache. Jake swung the sap and whacked Nort on the back of the head. Nort grunted and gasped, but did not wake up. Leaving Nort with his head twisted at an unnatural angle, Jake walked back to his bedroom.

In the morning, Jake felt somewhat the worse for wear, but not too bad. Nort, still collapsed over the breakroom table, snored like a camel. Jake made coffee and slid a cup up to Nort's nose. He jostled the kid's shoulder.

"Time to get up," Jake said.

"Unghh," Nort groaned. "I feel like a mule kicked me in the head. Give me something for the pain."

"Aspirins are a quarter each," Jake said. "Drink your coffee—it's time to go to work."

Later that morning, while Nort haphazardly made cloudy circles on the counter glass with a dirty cloth and spray from an antique bottle of Windex, Jake offered Nort a drink from a bottle of Maker's Mark he'd found in his father's office.

"Come on, kid. It's five o'clock, have a drink."

"Shit, no," Nort said, "drinking with you hurts like hell. Maybe later."

Jake grinned and swirled the whiskey in the bottom of his glass.

"Some people are born to drink and some people aren't," he said.

He drained his glass and smacked his floppy lips.

Charlie Fairhaven

Charlie switched to a contract position with an agency called Temporary Medical Professionals. TMP took a 15% commission and deducted taxes from his paycheck and assigned him temporary and fill-in work around the county. Slowly, his reputation grew. It was unspoken, but if a patient or family wanted termination service, then quiet, childlike Charlie landed a shift.

Over time, he grew to crave the power of life and death. He'd look into the eyes of the client and let them know.

Tonight or tomorrow night?

Next week or never?

Sometimes the client would be resigned and ready—other times there would be fear and uncertainty written in their eyes.

The morning after, he'd ask for a private moment with family members. Almost always, he got a tip. Sometimes a hundred dollars, sometimes a thousand. Once a grieving widow with a shaking hand and nearly illegible handwriting wrote him a check for twenty-five-hundred dollars. Twenty-five hundred tax-free, commission-less dollars for providing a service many needed but did not know how to ask for.

Charlie was a loner, so he didn't care that the nursing

home staff looked at him with veiled derision and avoided socializing with him— as if sensing the aura of death surrounding him like a miasma. They pretended not to know, but it wasn't true. They knew him and the others like him…others that came before and would come after. Catholic nurses crossed themselves after passing him in the hallway. They didn't think he noticed, but he did. He saw everything.

Sometimes, he'd wake the clients and tease them. In the dead of the night, he'd touch their hairy noses and pat their wrinkled cheeks. Their bodies were weak and their attachment to life was tenuous…but still, they clutched at overripe, ready-for-harvest lives.

Some were ready—as they imagined things, they would expire peacefully into the loving arms of the Lord. They were no fun. The fun ones were the stubborn, spirited oldsters grasping at their pathetic little lives as if they were the most valuable treasures on earth. They were the ones that made Charlie feel alive and powerful. They safeguarded tiny flames he lived to extinguish.

At Peaceful Meadows, Eleanor Bradley's room was filled with handmade crafts. A knitted doily rested on her dresser. A knitted duvet covered her guest chair. To ward off the air conditioning system's eternal chill, her bed was covered with knitted afghan blankets. Over the years, she gave away knitted items by the hundreds. Nurses and maintenance staff nodded politely, and then dropped them in a Salvation Army donation box on their way home. In every spare minute—when she wasn't working on Sudoku puzzles—with click-click-clicking needles she industriously cranked out one item after the other.

She knitted with mad intensity and focus.

It was midnight when Charlie poked his head into her

room.

"You're up late, Mrs. Bradley. Can't sleep? I could get you a pill."

"I knitted you a hat."

"I don't want it."

"No one has too many hats."

"I do."

"What happened to Billy Porter in twenty-two?"

Charlie looked up and down the hallway before entering the room. He held the door so it closed quietly behind him.

"Poor old guy. He's no longer with us...he passed on."

"When?"

"Between my three and four o'clock rounds. He was okay at three when I checked on him."

"I heard something."

Charlie remembered.

Billy had struggled and knocked a plastic cup of water from his nightstand. Charlie had to use a hair dryer on his scrubs so it wouldn't look like he wet his pants. And, Billy was toothless, but he tried to bite anyway. Unconsciously, Charlie rubbed his guilty right hand. In spite of several hot-water scrubs, it felt slobbery and unclean.

On quiet soles, he walked to Eleanor's bedside.

"What did you hear?"

"It was three-thirty. I know because I looked at my clock. It was a gift from Ollie, my grandson. It's a nice clock...expensive. He used to make a lot of money working for the Jewish Lehmann Brothers. I don't remember when he gave it to me—after the Reagan years, I'm sure. It keeps great time and the hands glow in the dark so I can see them."

"What did you hear?"

"Billy whispered to me…he said you murdered him."

Charlie tilted his head back and laughed.

"I've been around the dead a lot. They never talk to me."

"I know you have. Death follows you around like a lonesome dog."

"What I mean, Mrs. Bradley, is I work in a lot of old folks homes—"

"They're called 'assisted living facilities' now."

"I know, Mrs. Bradley. I work in many assisted living centers and naturally, I see a lot of dead people. It's the nature of my job…like a convenience store clerk sees a lot of the cheap beer, men's magazines and cancer sticks customers drop on the counter."

"The 7-Eleven clerks are all Asians and Pakis now."

"I know, Mrs. Bradley." He bent over her bed. "What I don't know is why old folks cling so hard to shitty lives. You can't love Oprah, Cream of Wheat, lime Jell-O and watered-down orange juice that much."

"Everyone is different. God wants me to knit and help my neighbors and solve number puzzles. And I will until he calls me home to rest. When he wants me, he'll take me himself. If you come around here late at night and try your tricks, I'll scream loud enough to wake the dead. Try me and see if I won't."

Charlie laughed.

"You would. I don't doubt it," he said.

He turned to leave.

"Don't forget your hat."

Charlie, with a cheerful, innocent grin plastered across his face, held out his hand to stop her.

"I haven't earned it yet," he said.

2

Jake Mosby

JAKE WAS IN his usual place—perched on a stool behind the cash register working on the Sudoku puzzle book Eleanor Bradley stopped in each week and left him. Jake thought the puzzles were a stupid waste of time, but he dutifully and methodically worked at the numbers until the puzzles were done. He didn't think Nort noticed, but if Eleanor was a day late in delivering a new book, Jake fretted.

"I'm not doing anything," Nort said.

"That's nice," Jake replied while filling in a number on the puzzle. His face was scrunched with concentration.

"I'm bored."

"That's because you're not doing anything."

"And you can't make me."

"Right," Jake said. "Exactly."

"I'm not going back to school and I'm not staying here. I'll beg on the street."

Jake looked up.

"Used to be that a man would rather die than be a beggar or take charity," he said.

"Things are different now."

"I can see that. Good luck out there."

"What's wrong with you? You don't care about me at all."

Jake licked the tip of his pencil.

"When I was in Da Nang, I was stabbed in the gut with a rusty knife by a starving eleven-year-old who wanted the three dollars in my wallet." He lifted his shirt to show a twisted scar. "After I killed him with a brick, I realized God didn't exist or was the biggest asshole of us all. I care about you, but out in the world you'll die of AIDS or get stabbed in an alley by a cracked-out whore. It doesn't pay to get emotionally attached to the doomed."

"You're a sick, twisted, cheap old fuck and I hate your guts. I should kill you and put you out of your misery, old man."

"If you killed me, who would you have to talk to?"

"I don't like talking to you. It's depressing and useless."

"Then you should stop it."

Jake grinned. His brown, horsey teeth created a grotesque spectacle. Before Nort could dream up a response, the bells over the front door tinkled. Jake leaned over to see who entered. A thin, jittery Mexican wearing a do-rag over short-cropped hair stood in the doorway. A jagged scar trailed down his neck into his shirt. Jake reached down and pulled out his sawed-off 12-gauge shotgun and dropped it noisily on the scarred countertop.

The young man made a series of gestures ending with a flourished middle finger before stepping back outside into weak sunlight. Nort walked up to the counter.

"What was that?"

"They test me once in a while."

Nort peered at the ugly weapon.

"Are those things legal?"

"They're legal if you don't get caught. It's the kind of thing better to have and not need than need and not have."

"Whatever. Can I touch it?"

Jake scratched his head and sighed. He put the puzzle book aside, picked up the gun and cracked it open. After ejecting the two cartridges, he pushed it across the counter.

Nort picked it up cautiously.

"It's heavy," he said.

He held it out, aimed and dry-fired. The hammers clicked loudly in the quiet store.

"Hold it with your arm locked up like that and it'll tear you up...it kicks like a drunken mule. This ain't a TV western gun. Hold it down and use your arms like springs to absorb the shock."

"If I keep it low, how do I aim it?"

"That's the point of a gun like this—you don't have to aim. Point it in the general direction you're interested in and let 'er rip. Make sure you're close; it's no good beyond ten or twenty yards." Jake sighed. "And, don't fire it at all unless you absolutely need to. Showing it should win an argument without leaving a bloody mess to clean up."

"It's fucking awesome."

Jake impatiently gestured for Nort to return it. After reloading it, he put it back on its hook under the counter.

"Those are not exactly the words I'd use," he said. "Now get back to the sweeping. I'm not paying you to fuck around all day."

"You're hardly paying me at all."

"What you're doing can hardly be called work, so it all evens out. Go."

Charlie Fairhaven

Charlie waited. Until his next assignment, it was his last night at Peaceful Meadows...the Canadian orderly he was replacing was returning from visiting his family in Coquitlam. At four o'clock, he poked his head in to check on Mrs. Bradley. Tired of the Sudoku puzzles, she was knitting furiously—wide-awake and listening to the snoring and other routine sounds of the night.

"Can't sleep?" Charlie said.

"Billy said you'd come."

"The ghost of Billy Porter is still hanging around? I figured he'd be long gone by now. Don't the sleeping pills work? If you'll pardon the expression, you should be dead to the world."

"I don't take any of the pills you give me."

"That's too bad, Mrs. Bradley, 'cause I give you more than just sleeping pills. You'll probably die from arrhythmia. Once you start taking Digitek, you're not supposed to stop."

"I don't care."

"Then I don't either." He winked at her. "One way or another...I just stopped by to say goodbye for now. I'll be back, but I don't know when. I hope to see you then, Mrs. Bradley. In the meantime, I'll miss our chats."

"Don't smooth-talk me, I see what you are. Behind those pretty eyes, you're an evil insect. You have a dead soul."

"I can't help what you think, Mrs. Bradley. If you still have that hat, I've changed my mind. I'd love to have it."

She looked at him suspiciously for a moment before eagerly sorting through items in a large cloth bag.

"I saved it special for you," she said.

"And I appreciate it very much, Mrs. Bradley."

Without coming too close, he took the hat from her outstretched skeletal fingers.

"Do you need placemats for your dining table?"

"No thank you, Mrs. Bradley, this is enough."

He placed it on his head. Red with a jagged green horizontal pattern, it had hanging earflaps and an absurd fuzzy dangling ball hanging from its floppy peak.

"It looks good on you."

Charlie smiled and eased the door closed behind him.

This souvenir represents an unfulfilled promise.

Fairhaven

3

Jake Mosby

THE MORNING SETTLED into a routine. At eight A.M., Jake turned the front door sign to 'OPEN'. Then, three of the more-mobile clients of Peaceful Meadows strolled down the street and came in for coffee. On stools, they huddled around a barrel used as a table, played dominos and talked about the weather.

"Coffee's a quarter a cup," Jake said the first time they showed up.

"Your dad gave it to us free. It's tradition."

"Are there any other expensive traditions I should know about?" Jake complained.

Nort hollered from the back of the store.

"Look what I found…"

He threw a handful of mouse-nibbled magazines on the counter. Jake looked them over…they were nudist magazines filled with men and women playing volleyball and horseshoes. Some of the women were pretty, but others were dumpy; overweight and plain. In the action shots, the men's limp cocks flopped absurdly.

"Where'd you find 'em?"

"Stuffed behind a board by the circuit breakers. Think they were great-granddad's?"

"Nah, probably not. These are from the Fifties...from before he had the store. What do you think?"

"This isn't what I've seen in Hustler."

"Those magazines are fantasies. This is more like what real women are like. You knocked up a chick, so the plumbing shouldn't be too much of a surprise."

"It was dark when we hooked up...I couldn't see nothing. This is what men jerked off with before the Internet?"

Jake nodded.

"Can I keep them?" Nort said.

Jake considered.

"Leave one, you can have the rest," he said.

"Good afternoon. I'm Sarah Goodwin from Century 21. Are you the owner?"

She was dressed in a cream-colored business suit over a lacy, red camisole. Jake put his puzzle book down and leaned over the counter. Her legs, encased in smooth, shiny nylons, were trim and firm with muscle. She wore scarlet pumps that matched her camisole and fingernail polish.

"I'm the owner," he said.

"And your name?"

"Mosby, like the sign outside. Odd coincidence, eh? Let me guess, you're new."

She flushed, but her cheeks didn't quite reach the shade of her undergarments.

"I didn't want to make an incorrect assumption, Mr.

Mosby."

Nonchalantly pushing an ineffective broom, Nort worked closer.

"This is my horny grandson, Nort."

"I'm very pleased to meet you, Nort." She held out her hand for a shake. "That's an unusual name."

"Short for Norton," Nort said. "Can I call you Sarah?"

Jake rolled his eyes. "Give me a break," he muttered.

"I stopped by because I have a well-financed, very-motivated buyer keenly interested in your property, Mr. Mosby."

"Of course you do."

Nort leaned on his broom and looked over her chest.

"It wouldn't hurt to hear the lady out, G-P."

"For Christ's sake," Jake said. "All right, tell me all about it."

She put her valise on the counter. "It will take work, but I'm sure I can table a cash offer of two-million. And, Mr. Mosby, I'd have to talk to my boss, but I believe we could take a very skinny seller's commission, perhaps as low as two-and-a-half points. If we set up a real estate investment trust, the proceeds are essentially tax-free. I took the liberty of drafting a binding letter of intent which dissolves if I've misled you in any way. You have nothing to lose and the world to gain, Mr. Mosby. Can I get a no-obligation signature?"

She placed a substantial bundle of paperwork on the counter and dropped a silver pen on top.

"You're smooth, I'll give you that. What was the name of that asshole from Century 21 that was in here last week?"

Nort pried his eyes off Sarah's blouse and glanced at Jake.

"Alvarez?" he said.

"No, he was from RE/MAX. I remember now...Cantrell was the Century guy. The cheap fuck bought a copy of John Saul's *Comes the Blind Fury* for fifty-five cents." Jake tapped a thumb-tacked, hand-written sign.

If you want to talk about real estate, buy something.

It was below an accompanying sign.

We care about your business, but not so much about you.

Sarah looked confused.

"I live in a new condo out in Burlington. I don't have room for any books."

"Then you have no business in a bookstore, do you?"

"We have Avon romances, three for a buck," Nort said eagerly. "They don't take up much room...and they're very popular with real estate agents." He placed a rubber-banded bundle on the counter.

Jake swiveled on his stool and pointedly reopened his puzzle book.

"I'll take the books," she said.

She opened her pocketbook...pulled out a dollar and slid it across the counter. Without looking up, Jake took it, hit a key on the old cash register to open the cash drawer, and slipped the bill in.

"I put a nice, big sign in the front window. Perhaps you saw it. It says this property is not for sale. The message seems unambiguous to me, but still, a couple of times a week, one of you assholes stops by to offer up a sleazy developer's pretty package. I'll take your card and," he pulled open a drawer stuffed with business cards and dropped hers in, "put it with the rest. I'll call one of you if I change my mind, otherwise, take your books and flitter off. I'm busy."

"Don't mind the old man, I know how to handle him." Nort smoothed thin hairs on his upper lip. "You look uncomfortable in that jacket, Miss Sarah. Come back to the breakroom and have an RC Cola. We can get to know each other and talk about your proposal. Do you have an Xbox in your apartment?"

Jake snorted and returned his attention to his puzzle. Sarah slipped the paperwork back into her valise.

"I guess I should be going. Please call me on my cell phone…"

"I'm sure your proposal is amped," Nort called after her. The doorbells tinkled as she exited. "Frag me, Jake. I wanted to see what was under that jacket. I'll bet she has sucklicious udds."

"Udds?"

"Like udders, under a cow? Tits? Boobaloyas? It's English, don't you know any? And, she was totally tuned in to my vibe."

"At least pretend to sweep, will you?"

Nort dragged the broom toward the back of the store.

"I'd like to plunder her hope chest," he muttered.

The breakroom had a hot plate. Jake showed Nort how to make Mulligan Stew with a large can of Dinty Moore stew as base.

"Are you paying attention? Half a can of water, half a can of instant rice, chop in extra carrots, celery and whatever else is around. Cook on low for an hour and its ready."

"I'm sick of eating your dog food. You have cash, ya cheap

fuck, let's order something real. Dominoes will deliver a pizza and Cinna-sticks."

"What's a Cinna-stick?"

"Pizza dough with sugar and cinnamon on it. They're good."

"You shithead kids will eat anything advertised on TV if it has sugar on it."

"It's better than eating homemade Alpo all the time."

"Besides, how are we going to call anyone? The phone hasn't worked for a year."

Nort beamed with pride. "The phone works fine. It just needed to be turned on at the Frontier office. The phone works now."

"Why did you do that? Now people will call us."

"Everyone has a phone, it's like a basic human right. I saw it on Current. They even have phones in Bangladesh."

"Then go to Bangladesh and leave me in peace."

"Speaking of cash, it's payday. Time to cough up some scratch, chigger."

Jake sighed and pushed away the Sudoku puzzle he'd been agonizing over.

"Okay."

He pulled out his notepad and looked through the entries. His forehead crinkled with concentration as he added and subtracted numbers. Then he unzipped the rear pocket of his overalls and pulled out his wallet. He extracted a twenty and two ones and pushed them across the table.

"That's it? I worked my ass off for almost a week and I get twenty-two bucks?"

"Twenty-two dollars, twenty-eight RC Colas, forty-three cigarettes, three meals a day and a cot. The way you play at working, *you* should be paying me. In fact, maybe I added wrong and you owe me twenty-two bucks."

Nort stuffed the money in his pocket while blinking away tears.

"You're a horrible old cheap bastard. I hate you and I hate it here. Fuck you, old man."

"I didn't ask you to come and I'm not making you stay. Come or go…I don't give a corn kernel shit."

"You should die and make room in the world for someone useful."

"Whatever you do, do it quietly. I'm trying to think."

He erased a number from the Sudoku and tried another. Nort slammed the front door when he left.

Ninety-eight minutes later, Jake still worked on the same puzzle. It was the last one in the book and devilishly tricky. Nort came in. After walking by Jake, he pulled an RC Cola and a bowl of leftover stew from the little fridge, and then sat down and started eating.

"Broke so soon?" Jake said.

"There's a video arcade at the mall," Nort replied, "with an old Battlezone console. If you don't mind, I don't want to talk about it."

Nort shot rubber bands at a dead spider.

"School's a waste of time."

"It's wasted on you. I agree with that. But, someone has to design the stupid, useless electronic gadgets your generation is addicted to. Education probably isn't wasted on them."

"So, you think I'm stupid?"

"That's not what I said. But, you *are* stupid. You and your whole spoiled generation of iPod-addicted, video-game-playing, reefer-smoking, MySpace sex-addled morons stuffing your faces with candy bars, fast food and Ritalin."

"You don't even have a computer. And, how do you know about MySpace?"

"Oliver told me about it."

"So, we agree, I'm not going back to school after the Christmas break."

"Talking to you makes my hemorrhoids hurt. Why do you think that is?"

"Well, I'm not going to school."

Jake squirmed on his stool. "I think I need one of those inflatable donut things for my ass," he said.

Nort fashioned a slingshot from a Y-shaped branch and a giant rubber band. He flicked marbles at a pile of discarded books. Jake tried to ignore the racket. On the wall behind the cash register, the old-fashioned Princess phone was attached to the wall. It rang. Startled, Jake stared at it.

"You pick them up and talk into them," Nort said.

"I know how a phone works. It's just that…once they start ringing, they never shut up. I prefer to be left alone. I never told you to fix this one."

Nort hauled himself off the floor and darted over. Before he could grab the phone, Jake picked up the receiver.

"Mosby's," he said. He listened for a moment. "Eileen? How'd you get this number?"

"It's great to talk to you too, Daddy. How's the kid doing?"

"I haven't killed him yet, but it's early in the day."

"So, you two are getting along?"

"No."

"Good. Daddy, I'm sorry about sending Norton, but I

didn't know what else to do. Do you think there's any hope for him?"

"I'm not sure what you mean. We all end up the same. Rotting corpses. Dead meat. Worm food. Unless we're cremated like my Dad—then we're ash and bits of ground-up bone in a cheap Chinese urn on a dusty shelf."

Eileen laughed. "Hayward thinks *my* sense of humor is weird. I wish I'd known about granddad, I would have come down for the memorial service."

"Dad doesn't know the difference. He's dead."

"I know that. Mom says you gave away everything to Betsy's daughter. She's mad as hell about it. She thinks you should have given it to us, but I don't care, Daddy. We sold the Ferrari."

"You wanted one since you were a snot-nose."

"I know, Daddy, but it wasn't practical. Hayward bought me a BMW SUV. It's way better for carrying our golf clubs. Ellen will probably call. She signed a million dollar contract with J. Crew."

Nort poked Jake's arm.

"Tell her to send the Xbox," he whispered.

Jake held his palm over the receiver.

"Go ring the doorbells."

"Why?"

"Just do what I say."

Nort sauntered toward the front of the store. He stared back at Jake for an insolent moment before reaching up and jiggling the bells.

"Great to hear from you, Eileen, but I got a customer."

He cradled the receiver.

"I thought she'd never shut up."

"What about the Xbox?"

"Fuck the Xbox. If you're bored, go sort out the sci-fi books on aisle four."

Charlie Fairhaven

At home, a third-floor condo in Everett, Charlie had a locked trunk pushed far back in his walk-in closet. In the trunk, he stored keepsakes. Billy Porter's blue plastic cup. A scarf worn over the bald head of a cancer patient from a hospice in Arlington. His first kill was special; from Barnyard Carter's bedside shrine, he kept a little plastic hamburger complete with a flaking decal of the McDonald's golden arches. He buried his face in Mrs. Bradley's lumpy hat and breathed deeply of its old-person scent before placing it gently on top of the treasure trove.

There were others who needed his service. He'd seen them on the street holding crude cardboard signs:

Will work for food

Stranded, need gas

One memorable sign said:

Why lie, need weed

Hopeless human trash.

The world would be better without them, but no one had the courage to do anything about it.

Day by day, Charlie felt strength and resolve gathering.

Fairhaven

Commoners lacked the will to do what was necessary, but Charlie was different. His duty would be his pleasure.

He opened the curtains. Outside, close enough to nearly touch his little balcony, sodden evergreen trees swayed in the wind. Around the complex, Christmas lights glittered. An inflated Santa, straining against guy wires, flopped back and forth. Low clouds drizzled cold rain.

One day, I'm moving to Florida or Arizona. There are lots of customers there.

As dawn broke against the south-eastern sky, he pulled the curtains closed and fell into bed.

4

Jake Mosby

PETE HUTTON WAS out of his jurisdiction. He worked as an apprentice homicide detective in the neighboring city of Everett. He was tall with bushy black hair and long sideburns. Thick around his middle, he tended towards fat. His mother, Rose Hutton, had been Jake's housemate and partner in the Seattle PD when he worked in the Homicide Division. Her lavish, home-cooked meals could be blamed for much of Pete's weight problem. He wore a light-blue, cotton-polyester leisure suit over a pink, open-collar shirt.

"Pete," Jake said.

"Jake," Pete replied.

Nort, carrying an armload of old *Life* magazines, appeared from the back of the store.

"What's this?" Pete commented.

"Eileen's spawn. Nort."

A broad grin spread across Pete's face.

"I remember you, Norton. The last time I saw you, you were about three. You bit my leg. I still have the scar if you want to see it."

46

"Some things don't change," Jake said. "Don't get too close, or he'll bite you again."

Nort dropped the magazines.

"What kind of gun is that?"

"Glock, 40 caliber."

"Ever kill anyone with it?"

"Not yet."

"Jake has a sawed-off shotgun under the counter."

A pained look spread across Pete's face.

"I don't want to know anything about it."

"If Rose sent you to check on me, tell her I'm fine," Jake said.

Pete walked down the aisle in front of the cash register.

"Mom didn't send me. I'm looking for...a book on do-it-yourself plumbing."

He plucked one from a shelf and dropped it on the counter.

"Right," Jake said. "Need an electrical code book to go with it?"

"No, this will do."

Pete reached for his wallet.

"Your money is worthless here. Me casa, tu casa all the way to soup kitchens and bankruptcy."

"You know the way. Stop by around dinnertime and mom will feed you. It's no big deal, don't agonize over it, just get in that Buick and drive over." Standing by the front door, Pete waved before walking out. "Thanks for the book."

"What does a guy have to do to be left alone?" Jake complained after Pete was gone.

"I'm sick of your dog food. Let's go there tonight."

"Fuck me blue," Jake said.

At Rose's ranch-style house in Stanwood, the scene was mayhem. She raised endlessly yapping miniature terriers. One, wriggling under her arm and lapping at her face, kept her company while she stirred a massive pot of chicken and cornmeal dumplings. Her son's teen-aged friends laughed and played a first-person shooter video game on a huge flatscreen TV.

Rose was a massive woman with huge breasts and meaty thighs covered by an acre of flowing, tie-dyed muumuu. Her hair was elaborately swept up in a lacquered wave and her fingernails were painted with miniature flowers. Her husband, Donald, was even larger—a walking mountain of a man. He pressed a drink into Jake's hand and returned his attention to the Seahawks playing Oakland on a tiny TV screen mounted under a kitchen cabinet.

After a few minutes of shyness, Nort succumbed to the inexorable attraction of giggling teenage girls huddled on a couch. He accepted the proffered plastic gun and was soon shooting aliens on an eerie spaceship...with a sweating glass of icy lime Kool-Aid at his side and a wide grin on his face.

The racket was relentless. Jake had a favorite quiet place far from the madness of the main house. At the end of a long corridor, a makeshift sewing room was attached. Warm, it was sheltered from the backyard by an out-of-control cluster of rhododendrons. One of Rose's sons, Alexander, reclined on a futon with his hand urgently working under the t-shirt of a red-haired, freckled girl.

"Beat it," Jake said.

Embarrassed, the girl stood. Looking at the floor, she rearranged her clothing before escaping down the hallway. The boy, with hormonal juices flowing and skateboard shorts tented, scowled.

"We were here first."

"Want your mama to know what you're doing? Vamoose, amigo."

"I'm not afraid of you, old man."

It had been twenty years since Jake had been in a fist fight. He sighed before putting down his glass and taking a stance.

"The first blow is yours, shit-bird," he said.

The boy laughed at the absurd spectacle.

"Mom would kill me if I touched you, Uncle Jake. I'm just making sport. Don't rile yourself up."

"Good, because you'd get an unforgettable ass-whuppin'."

Alexander's laughter echoed down the corridor as he walked away.

Except for weak, lackluster sunlight oozing through the shades, the room was dim. The rhododendrons rustled in a breeze. A heater in the corner, set to low, whispered. Ice rustled in his glass as he sipped. Donald only drank good stuff. Chivas. Smooth.

After a few minutes, with his head tilted back and his mouth wide open like a corpse, Jake slept. He often had the same dream.

He was in a filthy, stifling old house by the Fir Island slough. Roger Thompson, holding a .38 clasped in both hands, fired at Jake— twice—at short range. Roger, mean as a junkyard dog, bleeding from a nose crushed with a monkey wrench, must have been disoriented and seeing double when he aimed carefully and killed Jake's doppelganger twin. Jake was dazed and deafened by his shotgun's return fire while acrid cordite smoke seeped from the barrels. Phil Donahue kissed celebrity ass on an over-loud TV. A ten-foot cougar skin nailed to the wall. The sting of Jack Daniel's on the back of his throat. Looking down the black barrel of a .38 revolver and knowing...time's up. C'est fini.

The ghost of the dead twin haunted Jake.

A girl, perhaps six, with dark, curly hair and wide, curiosity-filled eyes, stood over Jake.

"Are you dead, Uncle Jake?"

He sat up and wiped moisture from the corners of his mouth. He'd either spilled his drink or pissed in his overalls. He clasped his hands on his lap to hide the stain.

"Not quite," he said.

"I brought you dinner, Uncle Jake."

"What's your name?"

"I already told you. Anna-Marie."

She held out a heaping plate of steaming food. Noticing a quart can of Old Style tucked under her arm, he worked it free and popped the tab. After a long drink followed by a satisfying belch, he put the can on the floor and took the plate.

Anna-Marie giggled.

"You're supposed to excuse yourself when you burp."

"Excuse me. Are you the youngest?"

She giggled. "No, Diana is the baby, not me. She's three. Alexander says mama has another baby in her belly, but I'm too young to know about it."

"So am I. Run back and see if there is another can of Old Style. If there is, bring it. Can you do that?"

She nodded solemnly. "You can count on me," she said.

Jake smoked half of an American Spirit cigarette and watched the sun dissolve to the west. The outside door at the end of the hallway was rarely used—its hinges complained loudly as he tried to slip out quietly. He cussed under his breath at the noise. A crushed rock walkway hugged the house and weaved through a moss-covered rock garden to the front. In a private corner, he took an endless piss against the concrete blocks at the end of the house, and then worked the latch on a massive wrought iron gate and walked to the Buick. Under a dripping carport, Nort flipped pennies against a wall with a tall blonde boy.

"What are you doing?" Jake asked.

"Figured you'd try to leave without me."

"You figured right. You could stay here and no one would even notice the extra mouth to feed."

"You're not half as clever as you think you are."

Nort gathered pennies and exchanged a complex battery of hand gestures with his penny-pitching partner.

"You've had a snoot full. Can I drive? It'll be safer."

"Got a license?"

"No, but neither do you, pop. It don't matter if you got a license as long as you don't get stopped."

Jake grinned.

The kid was a moron, but he had a point.

He tossed the keys in Nort's general direction. After settling behind the steering wheel and carefully adjusting the seat and the mirror, Nort backed up.

"This time of night, it's quicker to take the Pioneer Highway."

"I was paying attention, so I know the way. Shut up so I can concentrate on the road."

Jake leaned against the window and soon snored like an asthmatic bear. Scanning the road for police cars and driving with hands positioned at textbook 10:00 and 2:00 positions on the steering wheel, Nort, vigilantly and without attracting any unwanted attention, drove back to the bookstore.

Charlie Fairhaven

The car, a white Toyota Corolla with dented fenders and cracked windshield, was the plainest he could find. One day, after a long shift in Mount Vernon, he paid cash for it at a Little Stevie's Pre-Owned Auto Emporium. Little Stevie was truly little—a shriveled, brown raisin of a man with scrawny arms and caved-in chest. For a hundred-dollar 'expedite fee', Charlie drove off without filling out any paperwork.

On the streets of Skagit County, the car was unremarkable. Nearly invisible. Charlie wore wrap-around sunglasses and a faded Swinomish Yacht Club hat pulled down to his ears. A girl lounging by a bus stop caught his eye as he drove by. He turned around for a second look, then pulled over twenty yards past her.

She casually strolled up and leaned in through the passenger-side window. She might have been very young...under the thick makeup, it was impossible to tell. Meth head. Her eyes were sucked back in head as if her brain pulled a vacuum. Loose skin drooped from her face. Jittery and twitchy, her fingernails tapped on the car door with an arrhythmic beat. Filthy hair flopped around her face like damp moss.

"You wanna party, sugar?" she asked.

"How much?"

"A hundred for an all-nighter."

"No."

"I'll polish your knob for twenty."

"Hop in."

"Let's see your money first."

Charlie handed over a bill. She examined it in the dodgy street lighting, and then slipped into the car.

"I know a place we can go," she said.

The 'place' was a stub of alley behind a Chinese restaurant. Glass from a broken floodlight glittered and crunched under the Corolla's tires. As soon as the car was stopped, she fumbled with his zipper.

"Wanna smoke some crystal first?"

She pulled back and looked at him with suspicion, but couldn't resist the idea.

"You got some?" she asked with uncontrollable eagerness.

"Medical grade. I'll pour you a drink, then get the stuff from the trunk, okay?"

She searched his thin face for trouble, weighed the decision and made a judgment call.

"Sounds good," she said.

He turned on the radio. It was preset to a noisy pop music station…a funky beat throbbed. From a thermos, he poured an orange juice-Everclear cocktail into a plastic cup.

"Go easy, this packs a punch."

"I can handle it," she said.

She guzzled the drink and held out the cup for more.

Charlie chuckled.

This is too easy.

He refilled her cup.

"Give me a minute, okay?" he said.

He got out and scanned the area. It was a perfect

location—dark and isolated. Traffic on First Street echoed. It might as well have been two million miles away. In the distance, from the gang-controlled part of town, he heard a muffled gunshot or low-rider backfire. In the trunk, a tank of CO_2, connected by a hose to the car's cabin, rested on the floor. He slowly turned the valve. The hiss of gas was faint.

From his calculations, she'd be unconscious in a minute and dead in five minutes. It would be a painless death; she'd get sleepy and drift into oblivion—a far more clean and humane end than she deserved, but Charlie was a nice guy. He didn't want her to suffer through her hopeless life any longer. His goal was the opposite...to peacefully end her suffering as an act of mercy.

He watched through the passenger-side window, but her passing was uneventful—slowly, with her eyes closed and she slid down on the seat...boneless like a ragdoll. Her shallow breathing was imperceptible, so he could not mark her passage.

When he was sure, he turned off the gas and rolled down the windows to air out the car. Then he walked around the car, opened the door and pulled the body out. He gently placed her in a barred-shut doorway and arranged her limbs for comfort. For modesty, he tugged her denim skirt to cover her gray, pasty thighs. She wore a cheap bracelet made of white seashells and elastic string. He carefully removed it and slipped it in the pocket of his scrubs before driving away.

Noticing hunger gnawing at his belly, he drove along the freeway bypass and pulled into the line at the Dairy Queen drive-through. The manager's special was chicken salad and fries. He ordered it.

"And I'll take a large diet Pepsi with that," he said into the microphone, "with lots of ice."

Fairhaven

The cashier was a plump Indian woman wearing a syrup-stained smock over blubbery rolls of fat. She had a resigned look of despair in her eyes. Her graying hair was covered by a hair net.

Idly, Charlie wondered why she wasn't working at the Indian casino down the highway.

Maybe she wasn't really an Indian...maybe she only looked like one.

"Ya want ketchup for the fries?"

"Yes, please," Charlie said politely.

Her soul cried for release, but Charlie squelched the impulse to help.

A man can only do so much for a chosen few.

The rest were on their own.

5

Jake Mosby

JAKE LOOKED AT the old men playing cards and scratched a boil on his neck.

"I'm worried about Eleanor," he said. He sat behind the counter reading his falling-apart copy of *The Gift of Death*. "You guys seen her?"

"We already told you, Jake. She lives at Peaceful Meadows up the hill. We don't like the game room, so we don't go up there."

"Yeah, their puzzles are missing a bunch of pieces and they don't even care."

Jake frowned and returned to his book...only to be interrupted by a large woman buying five Johanna Lindsey paperbacks for $2.75.

"If you can find a first edition of *Captive Bride* in good condition, I'll give you ten dollars," she said. Jake grunted and slowly pushed her quarter across the counter with his index finger. "It's about a beautiful rich English woman," the woman continued, "named Christina who is kidnapped and held hostage by Sheik Abu. She's not only pretty, but really smart."

"Of course she is," Jake said.

At eleven o'clock, the old men suspended their card game to walk down the street to get the senior special at the Mount Vernon Café. As they left, they argued.

"It's Tuesday and that means liver and onions."

"Fried chicken."

The door bells tinkled behind them.

"Fred was right, today is liver day," Jake said.

Nort looked up from sorting *Star Trek* novels.

"Who gives a fuck? And how can you read the same book over and over?"

"One good book is all a man needs to live a simple life."

"I'm tired of your simple life. Nothing exciting ever happens around here."

"When you've lived as long as me, you'll see. Excitement is very overrated."

Nort dropped a batch of papers on the counter.

"Is this true?"

"What?" Jake said.

"I found some legal papers and it looks like—if you drop dead tomorrow—I get a check for a hundred-thousand dollars. Is that true?"

"You just happened to stumble over these papers?"

"Yeah."

"Stumbled over them in a locked drawer in my desk…"

"It wasn't much of a lock. I worked it open with a letter opener and a paper clip. If you were serious about security, you'd use a better lock."

Jake snorted. "That's one way to look at it," he said.

"Is it true? Your lawyer will write me a check?"

"Yes, it's true."

"That's a lot of money."

"In some ways it's a lot…in some ways it's nothing at all."

"I could do a lot with a hundred G's."

"And, all you gotta do is patiently wait for me to keel over."

"Patiently?"

"Yeah. Patiently."

While they stared at each other, the door bells jingled. They looked up. With glacial slowness, Eleanor came in. She wore dark sunglasses resembling welder's goggles. Her tubular body was encased in a shapeless cotton dress bearing a faded floral print. Her thin, gray hair was plastered to her head in brittle-looking, hairsprayed ringlets. Like many older women, she smelled of old diapers and cellar rot.

"You can quit fretting," Nort said. "Your girlfriend is here."

Jake shot Nort an annoyed look.

"Go piss up a rope," he muttered. Then he spoke more loudly—with artificial cheer. "Good morning, Mrs. Bradley." He pulled a limp puzzle book from under the counter. "I finished the book for you."

She grunted impatiently as she worked her way up the aisle.

"We have no time for 'good mornings' or puzzles."

Nort cocked an eyebrow at Jake. His thought was evident.

This from a woman who needed ten seconds to travel six inches.

Jake, with a stern look, warned Nort against saying anything. Eventually, she stood at the counter and pierced Jake with an intense stare from washed-out blue eyes.

"You think I'm an addled old bag, but I know things."

"I'm sure you do, Mrs. Bradley."

"You used to be a homicide detective with the Seattle police…you were in the *Everett Herald* all the time wearing a

black suit and paisley necktie. No offense, but at Peaceful
Meadows, we called you the black lizard on account that the
black ones are the mean ones...and you had a hard look in
your eyes."

"No offense taken, Mrs. Bradley. That was a long time ago.
They put me on disability after I killed Sergeant Wilson. I'm
retired."

"Pardon me, but the lizard don't change its stripes.
'Specially the ugly black ones," she said solemnly. "You're a
homicide detective and we have a homicide to solve. There's
murder afoot."

"Murder?" Nort said. He dropped a falling-apart copy of
Star Trek Vanguard: Harbinger and stood up.

Jake sighed and set aside the Sudoku book.

"Come back to the breakroom and have a seat. We'll have
a cup of coffee and talk about it, okay?"

"Coffee will kill you quicker than a viper. I brought my
own hot drink—herbal tea," she said. "It's not poison."

After looking around the dirty, cluttered room with
undisguised disgust, Eleanor settled in a folding chair. Sensing
a long story, Jake—hiding the bottle from her—poured two
fingers of Makers Mark into his coffee. She removed a dainty
china cup, saucer and crocheted coaster from her bag—each
delicate item was protected by a custom-knitted pouch. After
the table arrangement was adjusted properly, she waited while
Jake topped off her cup with hot water.

"Charlie Fairhaven. They call him Fairhaven the Finisher.
He acts all 'Good morning, Mrs. Bradley' and 'How is your
tapioca pudding, Mrs. Bradley,' but I'm not fooled. I wasn't
born yesterday, Jake."

"We can see that very clearly," Nort said.

Jake shot him a look of warning.

"Shirley Wilkins was going to be married on Valentine's Day. Her fifth, the groom's third. He's in a wheelchair, but his mind is sharp, thank you very much. She ordered a wedding dress online—it was white with an apricot sash. If she wants to wear white, that's her decision…it's not our business to say anything about it."

Nort fidgeted in his chair with impatience.

"What about the murder?" he said.

"Mrs. Pearson made fun about the white wedding dress. Said Shirley had entertained more peders than a sports bar urinal, but I don't tolerate crude talk like that. You can be assured—I gave her a piece of my mind."

Nort closed his eyes and sat back in his chair.

"As you can see," Eleanor continued, "Shirley had everything to live for. She was happy. Nearly giddy, or as giddy as a woman in her seventies with bad gout and diabetes can be. But…" Jake and Nort waited with anticipation. "…she made Charlie angry. He doesn't like being called a murderer."

"So he killed her," Nort said.

Eleanor gave Nort an impatient look.

"We need to go through this methodically, young man, but, yes, he killed her. Two nights ago. At 3:15 in the morning. And that's not the only one. He killed Billy Porter too. And who knows how many more? The man is not a human being—he's death with legs."

"How do you know all of this, Mrs. Bradley?" Jake said.

"The walls are like paper, so everything could be heard."

"And you have the room next door?"

"No," Eleanor said sharply. "Mr. Champion is next door.

Fairhaven

He doesn't see well and thinks it's 1973, but his hearing is keen like a dog—he hears everything. He can hear Mrs. Chesterton's radio across the hall and three doors down. Complains all the time and she doesn't play the radio loud at all. Just a whisper. She likes the late-night talk radio shows. The ones about Mars people and sea monsters in the Bermuda Triangle. I don't care so much for those programs myself, but Mrs. Chesterton doesn't sleep much so she has to do something to occupy her mind. Her husband was a preacher, but he died in 1998. God rest his soul. Church of the Nazarene in Covington."

Nort opened his mouth to speak, but Jake raised a hand to stop him. Nort got the message: if you distract an older person, you'll inspire a long ramble and it will take a long time to return to the point.

"What did Mr. Champion tell you he heard?" Jake said. His voice was gentle.

"Shirley told someone to stay away. Then the bedding rustled and the springs complained."

"Maybe she had a lover come for a visit," Nort said.

"I know that sound, young man, and that's not what Mr. Champion heard. He described a murder. A cold-blooded murder. Fairhaven suffocated her. He's a nursing home terminator, everyone knows that. He kills the hopeless and the ill. Shirley called him a murderer and he killed her. And now he's going to kill me."

"Why do you say that, Mrs. Bradley?" Jake said. She averted her eyes and took a sip of tea. "Ah. You said something to Fairhaven."

"When I have something on my mind, I come out and say it," she said.

"Yeah, eventually," Nort said.

Eleanor poked out her bottom lip and glared. Jake scowled.

"He told me I'm next," she said.

"You should talk to the police about this," Jake said.

Eleanor snorted. "They won't do anything. They're too busy writing tickets and playing with their laptops at Starbucks. My step-daughter got a hundred and forty-four dollar ticket for doing forty-five in a thirty-five speed zone. Greedy jackbooted, fascist bastards. A hundred and forty-four dollars. She's a cashier at Safeway, she can't afford that. The police are less than useless." She glanced at her watch. "Pinochle at three o'clock. If I'm not there, Cathy Sinclair fills in and she couldn't win a hand if it held nothing but trumps. So, you'll take the case. Charlie Fairhaven needs to be caught and prosecuted to the fullest extent of the law. If you don't help me, I'll take care of it myself. I'm old, but I can stab a man in the belly with a case knife."

"Please don't talk like that, Mrs. Bradley," Jake said. "I'll poke around a little and see what I can find out." He took out his notepad and pencil stub. "Tell me everything you know about Fairhaven and I'll take a look at him."

"Now we're getting somewhere," Nort said.

Eleanor smiled. "I watch the cop and lawyer shows on TV. I like *Law and Order* and *CSI* and *Bones*, so I know how to run background. I already did all the work for you," she said.

She pulled note paper from her bag and pushed it across the table. The paper was covered with cramped, spidery handwriting.

"He works for a temporary services agency. I even got his social security number, which was not easy, let me tell you." She lowered her voice. "My daughter brings tins of Toll House chocolate chip cookies and I share them with the Chinese girl who does the Peaceful Meadows bookkeeping. You have everything you need to get started and take this murderer down. He'll get fifteen-to-life in the state penitentiary not the death penalty, not in this liberal state, but that's good enough. At least old folks can go to bed at night without worrying about being murdered in their sleep."

Jake's eyes flicked between Eleanor and the notes.

"Holy crap, Mrs. Bradley, you're awesome," Nort said.

"Uh," Jake said.

"Make this creep face justice," Eleanor said.

She drained her tea, then wiped the cup and saucer with a handkerchief, put them back in their pouches and stored them away in her voluminous bag. They watched her arrange herself behind her walker and work her way, slowly, out of the store.

After she was gone—leaving behind the scent of cologne and old flesh—Nort looked at Jake with eagerness.

"Finally. Something interesting will happen around here," Nort said.

"No."

"What do you mean, no? We have a mission. A case. A murderer to take down."

"There is no case," Jake said. He pressed his palms against his temples. "The woman still thinks Reagan is president, for Christ's sake. Women are always imagining things and senile old busybodies are the worst. Just nod your head and let them talk, but don't pay any attention or you'll end up believing all kinds of crazy shit."

"I can't believe there isn't a hint of curiosity hiding in your cold-blooded, evil little lizard heart. Not a speck? Not an iota?"

"Stop reading my Derrida book after I go to bed. It's not good for your undeveloped mind."

"Don't dodge my fucking question. You must be curious, even if just a little."

"Thirty years of crawling through the dark, stupid little crevices of the human psyche is more than enough for an old man. I paid my dues. I'm retired. Done. Finished."

"You're a fucked-up, hopeless relic. *You* should kill yourself and leave a little extra room in the world for the young and useful."

"Now you're catching on," Jake said.

"I'm going to look into this."

"No you're not. You have a job and you're on the clock. Go sort the graphic novels."

"I did that yesterday."

"Good. Now that they're all sorted out, you can re-price them… bump them up a buck each."

All through the afternoon, Nort shot disgusted looks at Jake. He lurked nearby when Jake gave up and cracked open the phone book—then picked up the Princess telephone to make some calls. Nort grinned when Jake scribbled down where he was told Charlie was working that night.

Stanwood Retirement Villa.

"Now what?" Nort said.

"Now nothing," Jake replied. "Go sweep the breakroom."

Charlie Fairhaven

In keeping with its low-budget nature, the owners of Stanwood Retirement Villa did not bother dreaming up a more relaxing, creative name. It was a one-story, white-painted concrete building on the highway behind the Scandia Coffee Shop and a nail salon. Charlie did not like the depressing nature of the place and resolved to turn down future assignments there. For the upcoming week, the temp agency had him scheduled for the much larger Peaceful Meadows which he liked much better.

He'd been assigned to Peaceful Meadows many times…he was comfortable there. It was much bigger—with five hundred 'guests', the old folks died regularly and it was easy to slip in additional victims without anyone noticing.

There were many souls ready for harvest at Peaceful Meadows.

And, they had Starbucks coffee in the breakroom.

After checking in, he clipped a temp badge onto his scrubs and walked to the breakroom for a cup of coffee. A plate of snickerdoodles sat on the communal table. He helped himself.

"Mr. Fairhaven?" Charlie turned. "I'm the day supervisor, Marian Wells. Welcome to S-R-V."

Marian was short and stocky and compressed into a nurse's white uniform like an overstuffed pillow. Her hair was dyed dark, almost black. Scraggly hairs bristled from a mole on her chin.

"Thank you," Charlie said.

"I talked to the family of Mr. Waters in Room Four. They can't afford to keep him here, so they're taking him back home in a few days. They have young kids and no room for him. The doctor is sure…he's not going to get any better. It would be a blessing if he moved on."

"Moved on? You mean if he died? The family would be fortunate if he assumed room temperature? He'll be a huge burden if they take him into their home."

She stared at him boldly. "Yes."

"Why are you telling me this?"

She licked her lips and averted her eyes to a corner of the room. "Shall we simply say...your reputation precedes you?" Charlie took a bite of his snickerdoodle. "I'm not judging, Mr. Fairhaven. If my comments are inappropriate, I apologize."

"If the need is so clear, why don't you take care of it yourself?"

"I'm Catholic," she said as if it explained everything. "If anything happens, I will say a prayer for Mr. Waters' immortal soul."

Charlie finished the cookie and licked cinnamon and sugar off his fingers. He hated weak people...people who dodged their responsibilities. People who couldn't or wouldn't do unpleasant tasks, no matter how clearly they were necessary.

"Yeah, you do that," he said.

Despite vowing he would not do Marian's dirty work, Charlie relented during his four o'clock round and released Mr. Waters' spirit from its earthly bounds. Waters wore an elastic medic-alert bracelet.

Do Not Resuscitate.

Charlie worked the bracelet off Waters' skeletal wrist and slipped it in his pocket. He stood for a minute looking at the body. The old man's face was tortured and unattractive...with gaping mouth, greasy, tousled hair, half-lidded dead eyes and slack, gray cheeks. The old man's bowels rumbled...his belly quivered and jiggled as if something was burrowing deep inside.

There would be a mess to clean up later, but that was not Charlie's problem. There was a cleanup crew for those dirty jobs.

Charlie was still angry and disgusted with Marian, but otherwise, it felt wonderful to be doing what he was born to do…act as a tool of an angry, impatient God. He felt great in all senses of the word; satisfied and filled with well-being like a giant standing astride the world. Powerful and delivering peace and relief to the worn out and hopeless.

It felt great.

Really great.

With an indescribable lightness of being, he finished the round of the facility looking in on the sleeping clients, and then, in the cluttered front office, thumbed through the old metal filing cabinet for the proper Death in Facility form.

It was two pages printed on cheap paper, streaky from a malfunctioning copy machine, and stapled together. He'd filled out the form many times before. It was like an old friend.

Is the cause of death unknown or uncertified by a medical practitioner?

That would be a 'no'.

Has the death or does the death appear to have occurred in suspicious circumstances? Has the death possibly resulted from a criminal act?

Charlie laughed.

No, not at all. No way.

Some parts of the form were not his responsibility. The day staff would notify next of kin and then check off the appropriate box. An area at the top of the form required a stamp and a signature…that was for the facility manager. He looked it over…everything was filled out neatly and properly…there would be no suspicions raised. Just another routine night in the old folk's home…and another body for the mortuary.

He leaned back in his chair and turned on his Kindle. He'd read this book before, but it was good every time.

"It's the power of God working in you," she said. "It's a great responsibility, Johnny. A Great trust. You must be worthy."
—Stephen King.
The Dead Zone.

You know it, Steve.
Testify.

6

Jake Mosby and Charlie Fairhaven

JAKE WOKE UP early and angled his Timex in the room's dim light in order to read the digital display.

5:30.

He listened, but the store, except for the clattering and clicking of a tired exhaust fan, was quiet. After tip-toeing down the back hallway, he stopped and looked at the door to the storeroom where Nort slept. He heard nothing. The side door was rarely used and Jake made a mental note to oil the creaky lock and squeaky hinges.

Even after the racket, Jake heard nothing from the storeroom.

The hinges protest loud enough to wake the dead, but not an idiot teenager.

He walked to the carport and pulled open the driver's door of the Buick. A figure moved and Jake, startled, hopped backwards.

"Hey, G-P," Nort said, rubbing sleep from his eyes.

Jake pressed a clenched fist against his chest.

"You can kill an old man with a scare like that. What're

you doing out here?"

"I figured you'd be up to something."

"Where'd you get a key?"

"From Lowe's. They make copies."

"Get out. I'm taking the car."

"No, you're not, G-P. You're a hazard on the road. I'm driving. Go around to the passenger side."

Jake considered, and then sighed. He walked around the massive car and settled in the passenger seat.

"Drive," he said.

"Stanwood Retirement Villa?"

Jake wondered if Nort might be slightly less stupid than he appeared.

"Yeah, I want to get a look at this Fairhaven character."

"Park under the evergreen tree," Jake said after scanning the SRV parking lot.

Three other cars were in the lot—a monstrous gray Cadillac Coupe de Ville with 'Stanwood Retirement Villa' written in fancy script on the doors was parked by a ruby-red 1968 Camaro with a black racing stripe on the hood. The third car was a nondescript white Toyota.

"Which car is his, would you guess?" Jake asked.

"How the fuck would I know?" Nort said. He sat in silence for a moment. "Oh, he'd want a car that wouldn't draw any attention…"

"Right," Jake said. "You stay here."

"What are you doing?"

"I told you. I want to get a look at this asshole," Jake said.

Jake strode across the parking lot and walked around the Toyota, trying the doors and peering in the windows. After his inspection, he faced the assisted living center, leaned against the car, and waited. At 6:10, a round man in hospital scrubs waddled over.

"That's my car."

Jake waved an American Spirit cigarette. "Got a light?" he said.

"I don't smoke."

"That's not what I asked."

Charlie extended his hand to shake.

"Charlie Fairhaven. And you?"

"Jake Mosby, Detective-Lieutenant with the Seattle Police Department."

Charlie looked over Jake's threadbare canvas overalls and laughed. "I heard about the budget cuts. They must be getting really desperate."

"I'm retired."

"I see. To what do I owe the pleasure of meeting you on this fine morning?"

"As unofficial liaison to the Mount Vernon Police Department, I'm looking into a string of nursing home murders and I wonder if you'd be willing to answer a few questions?"

"I'd be happy to, but I don't know what I can do to help you."

"That's easy. Keep your eyes open. Poke around and let me know if you notice anything out of the ordinary. Report rumors. Pass along any useful gossip."

"I don't see how a guy like me could possibly be of use, but, if I do hear something interesting, how do I get in touch?"

"Come down to Mosby's Bookstore. I'm always there."

"Mosby's Bookstore. I'll remember that. Now, perhaps

you'll get your scrawny, retired ass off my car so I can go home, Detective-Lieutenant. It's been a long, exhausting night."

Jake pushed away from the car and brushed off the seat of his overalls. Without saying another word, he walked back to the Buick and settled into the passenger seat. Charlie stopped at the edge of the parking lot and turned on his turn signal before merging onto the road. Nort and Jake watched him drive slowly away.

"How much of that did you catch?"

"I'm young. My ears work good. What'd we learn?"

"Fucker's cold and focused like a fellow I met once…a guy named Wilson."

A long silence stretched in the car.

"Is there a point, old man? What's *Wilson* supposed to mean to me? Did something interesting happen? Is there a lesson?"

Jake turned his liquid-brown eyes on Nort.

"That was a long time ago. Never mind."

While he worked his car through the unsynchronized stoplights on Riverside Drive, Charlie's mind raced.

The old man wants to play. Okay, we can play.

When he considered everything he'd done over the years, it seemed inevitable that one day he'd make a mistake and get caught. Then, he should be hailed in the press as a hero for providing a needed service to the public, but he knew the law saw things differently.

Truth-be-told, deep in his heart, he *craved* the attention of the public. A trial with a jury of his peers might be fun. He imagined it like *Boston Legal*; quick-paced and witty—with sexy lawyers and snappy dialog. The end-of-life moral issues could be aired and the feeble arguments of religious fundamentalists would be shredded by *Boston Legal*'s wise, liberal screenwriters. They used cases from real life…he imagined bold newspaper headlines. At the end, perhaps he could be freed with one of Alan Shore's gymnastic, bombastic legal maneuvers.

One-hundred yards from his turn onto La Vista Avenue, he flicked the turn-signal lever.

I might get caught…that's part of the challenge and a big part of the fun.

But, it hadn't happened yet and Charlie always stayed alert and ready for anything the world might throw at him.

To win the game, he'd have to stay smart and be careful.

Very careful.

Jake Mosby

Nort placed Jake's chipped mug on the counter. It steamed. Jake put down his paperback book and looked at the coffee suspiciously.

"Did you find the rat poison in a cupboard under the sink?"

"Shut up. I'm trying to be nice." Nort dragged over a stool and settled on it. "What's the plan?"

"The plan?"

"What are we going to do about Fairhaven?"

"We?"

"I've been playing at stupid my whole life…I know the drill, Pops. We'll play it your way. Rainy for this time of year, ain't it? How about those Mariners? Think they fixed their relief pitching problem?"

Jake sipped coffee and tented his book.

"You're very annoying." They sat in silence for a couple of minutes before Jake spoke again. "Bring me a roll of duct tape and that box of spikes from the junk drawer."

Nort hopped off the stool and hustled away. The nails were long and thin—an eighth of an inch in diameter and six inches long. Jake carefully wrapped the tacky gray tape around a nail's head. Nort aped the action. When the wad of tape was about an inch-and-a-half thick, Jake studied it and massaged it into shape. Then, with a fast motion, he stabbed it into the counter. It sank in the wood with a solid thunk.

"So, G-P, we're making shivs for the relics."

"How do you know about shivs?" Jake asked.

"*The Sopranos*." Jake looked at Nort with a vacant expression. "You been living under a rock? It's a cable TV show about gangsters."

"Oh," Jake said. "After the divorce, my ex got the TV and I didn't have the money to replace it. I'm way behind on TV culture."

The tape on Nort's shiv was not as neatly wrapped as Jake's but Jake nodded—*okay*—after inspecting it. Making more, they worked in silence for half an hour.

"How many are we making?" Nort asked.

"How many nails do we have?" Jake replied.

Jake pressed bags of shivs on Fred and Karl.

"I'm not sure we need this," Fred said.

"If you don't need it, you don't need it. No problem. But you guys lying in your beds at night are defenseless. That's no good. Tuck it under your mattress where you can reach it." With a stabbing motion, he demonstrated its use. "See? Easy."

"Okay," Karl said.

Fairhaven

When the old men left for the café, they carried heavy paper bags.

"That was cool," Nort said after they left. "Fairhaven's going to mess with the wrong coot and get one in the gut. Blammo. Welcome to a very rude surprise."

"It's better than doing nothing," Jake replied.

That afternoon, Eleanor brought a Sudoku puzzle book. Jake paged through it before hiding it under the counter. He showed her a shiv and she immediately grasped the concept. Leaning over her walker, she didn't have much strength, but poked the counter a few times with surprising vigor.

"Pig sticker," she said.

"Aim for something soft, like the gut."

"I wish I'd thought of this when my first husband cheated on me with that Monkey Wards sales clerk," she said dreamily. "The fool never could never resist a huge pair of knockers and a zipper that came down easy."

Her handbag rested in a wire rack on the front of the walker. When she left the store, it was stuffed with shivs.

At three o'clock, Jake locked the front door and turned the 'CLOSED' side of the sign out. Nort was already in the Buick with the engine running and the air conditioner blasting.

"You're a presumptuous little shit."

Nort grinned. "I try," he said. "Where to?"

Jake sighed and scratched his bulging belly.

"Mount Vernon Police Department."

The Police Department was housed in a three-story concrete building. It was time for the afternoon shift change—dark blue cars streamed in and out of the parking lot alongside the building. Jake got out of the car.

"You can stay with the car if you want."

"Right," Nort said, "like that's ever gonna happen. We're partners. Inseparable, like Booth and Brennan."

"More like a racehorse with dung stuck in its tail. And, you should stop watching so damned much television. It turns your brain to mush. Obviously."

Inside, Jake had nothing in his pockets, so he walked through the metal detector without hesitating. Nort had change in his pocket…as well as car keys, a heavy chain dangling from the belt loops of his over-sized, drooping skateboard shorts and a belt with a lurid, metal red-eyed pirate belt clasp. While Jake waited with a lopsided smirk on his face, Nort was cross-examined, inspected and carefully hand-wanded before being allowed to continue.

Irritated by the delay, Nort said, "What are you grinning about?"

"Nothing," Jake said.

In the elevator, competing attorneys worked out a plea deal for a second-degree assault charge.

"More law gets practiced in coffee shops and elevators than in the courtroom," Jake commented.

"What does that mean?" Nort asked.

Jake sighed. "Forget it," he said.

They walked down an industrial, green-painted hallway and entered the homicide office. An older woman with painted-on eyebrows which made her appear perpetually startled, looked up from her desk. She looked intently at Jake for a moment, and then put aside her can of Diet Pepsi. After holding up an index finger to ask for a moment, she hurriedly pulled a lipstick tube and compact mirror from her top desk drawer and touched up her lurid lips. After dabbing with a tissue, she smiled to expose a mouthful of crooked, yellow smoker's teeth.

She was the rare kind of woman who looked better when she *didn't* smile.

Before discarding the tissue, she dabbed at moisture between her ample breasts.

"Jake Mosby, as I live and breathe. You used to visit here."

Myopically, Jake stared at her.

"A very long time ago," he said.

"Well, *I* remember you. Maureen Olsen—I was McCormick back then. I had such a crush. You helped me get rid of McCormick, remember?"

"Sure, of course. It's coming back to me," Jake said unconvincingly.

"We almost had a thing."

"I wouldn't forget something like that."

Nort snorted and rolled his eyes. "Give me a flippin' break," he muttered.

"I have a name and a license tag number I'd like to run down."

"It would be impossible for me to say no to anything you want, Jake. Anything at all. Can I ask you a personal question, Mr. Mosby? Are you still married?"

"No, not for a long time. Divorced. She married a baseball player and moved to California."

Maureen fluffed her hair and grinned.

"That was my lucky day," she said. "Give me a minute." Delicately—to avoid breaking her long fingernails—she typed in the numbers. She scratched her chin. "Registered to José

Hernandez of Concrete. Last title change was four years ago. Want me to run a background check on him?"

Absently, Jake scratched his ear.

"No, don't bother," he said. "It won't lead anywhere. I have the sense that Fairhaven is a careful one. Something about him really bothers me…for a heavyset guy, he's got grace. It will bug me until I figure it out. Run Charles Fairhaven and variants, please."

"Skagit County or state?"

"Both."

"Two minutes," she said.

They looked over her shoulder as she quickly and efficiently clicked through screens and menus.

"He looks clean, Jake. A traffic ticket three years ago. That's it."

Jakes twisted his face into a sour expression.

"I was afraid of that," he said. "Try the FBI database."

"If he had a file, the system would have flagged it. There's nothing."

"Crap," Jake said. "I was hoping this would be easy."

Maureen fluffed her hair.

"Jake, we should get together for a drink and catch up on old times. I'm free tonight, or tomorrow if tonight doesn't work."

Jake looked her over. She pressed her knees together and sat up straight in her chair with her chin in the air.

"Sure, Maureen, that sounds good. Friday night would work fine."

She cocked her head as if puzzled. She frowned, and then smiled. Moisture glittered at the corners of her eyes.

"That's a yes," she said under her breath. "A yes."

Fairhaven

"Yeah, why not," Jake said with a little more certainty in his voice.

Hurriedly, she scribbled her address on a scrap of paper and handed it to Jake as if wanting to close the deal before he changed his mind. Jake folded the paper and slipped it in a pocket of his overalls.

Jake and Nort walked back to the car. Under misty skies, the Buick dripped. A rainbow-tinted trickle of oily water oozed toward a storm drain.

"You can't be serious about tapping that ancient piece of ass."

Jake looked at Nort for a few seconds before answering.

"A woman like that would be very tolerant of a man's foibles, faults and weaknesses. At my age, that's nothing to take for granted."

Nort started the car and adjusted the vents to clear fog from the windows.

"I'll take that as a 'yes', loser."

"Take it any way you like, twerp."

Later, they sat at the breakroom table and Jake poured a few ounces of Maker's Mark from a dusty bottle hidden behind the little black-and-white television.

Nort pushed his glass over. "Gimme two bucks' worth."

Jake pulled out his notebook and made a notation before pouring one finger in Nort's glass.

"If *you* ask, I'll bet mom would send my laptop computer. There's a lot you can do on the Internet…looking up public records and then there are maps and shit. Satellite photographs. All kinds of stuff. Don't you want to try something new?"

"There ain't nothing new. Everything is made of the same old shit. Sometimes it smells a little different, that's all," Jake said.

"Trust me, G-P, we need it."

"You're an ignorant, spoiled pip."

"And you're a washed-up, obsolete Stone Age relic. So fuckin' what? Call mom. Tell her to send my computer."

"I'll think on it."

Nort sipped the whiskey and made a face. "This stuff is disgusting."

"I'm not the one who just spent his last two dollars on it," Jake said.

7

Jake Mosby

AFTER SEVERAL ERASURES and scribbled trial entries, Jake finished a Sudoku puzzle. He put the book away and stood up to stretch his aching back. The door bells jingled. Nort looked up from counting Nancy Drew mysteries. A man wearing sunglasses and dressed in a leisure suit and Birkenstock sandals held the door open for a teenage girl.

The girl was waiflike—about sixteen, thin as a rail and dressed all in black…long-sleeved shirt, jeans and massive boots. Her skin was covered with white powder with black sprayed around her eyes. She looked like a ghostly raccoon and she'd either been dining on human blood or her mouth was decorated with red food coloring; her smile was ghastly. Resting between the small bumps of her breasts, a desiccated hairy claw hung on a leather string.

"Honey, see if they have any Raymond Chandler," the man said.

"They're on aisle…", Jake said.

"I'll help her," Nort interrupted. "Follow me," he said to the girl.

Jake and the man watched them.

"Raging hormones," the man said.

"Tell me about it," Jake replied.

"I'm going to come right out and tell you I'm a real estate agent, but don't get excited. I was a friend of your father's."

"Old Fred had a lot of friends."

The man stared at Jake.

"Your father's name was Chet. We were in the Rotary Club together for twenty-two years."

"No offense…"

"None taken. Herb Meyer."

"Jake Mosby."

They shook hands.

"Your father was a clever man—careful with his money. He owned this whole block and leased space to the lawyers and all the other businesses on this block. Except…"

"Go on."

"The corner with the party rental place was owned by an Armenian couple."

"Was?"

"They died. Maybe you don't walk by there much? The place has been closed for three months. The heirs are willing to sell for a reasonable price. Cash only. Your dad wanted to renovate the place and open another professional center…lease out space to a veterinarian or dental office."

"I've never had any cash in my life."

"Well, you do now."

"I do?"

"Don't be coy, Jake. I know Martin Grigsby. Your dad's lawyer?"

"He wears heavy clothes on a hot day."

Herb laughed. "That he does, but he's a good lawyer anyway."

"I don't like lawyers."

"I know, and insurance agents, bankers, tax collectors and real estate agents. Did I forget anyone?"

"Union organizers, bitter widows and baseball players."

"Okay. Fine. The tax assessment is four-hundred and eighty-four thousand. I could sell it with conventional loan terms, but it would take four to six weeks before the estate gets the money. Pay cash and they'll take four-hundred grand."

"Your commission?"

"I shouldn't take a seller and buyer commission at the same time, but I think charging full commission to the seller and a one-percent finder's fee to the buyer is fair. Cash, of course—we don't need any paperwork for that part of the transaction."

"I'm trying to live a simple, unencumbered life."

"One of the papers you signed and notarized was a general power-of-attorney. Tell Martin to make it happen and it's done. That's pretty simple."

"What's he charge?"

"I don't know, but it's reasonable. One-fifty-an-hour? I have no idea."

"I used to live on one-fifty a month."

"That's irrelevant to what we're talking about."

"I suppose." Jake sighed and looked around the store. Everywhere he looked there were unwanted complications. Ceiling tiles were stained from a leaky roof. A group of fluorescent lamps needed replacing. The walls needed paint. "Okay, tell Martin to go ahead," he said.

"Shake on it?"

"I'd rather drink on it." Jake pulled the bottle of Maker's

Mark from under the counter…followed by two cloudy water glasses.

Herb looked in his glass, blew it out and set it back down.

"Hit me," he said.

After Jake poured, they tapped their glasses together and drained the whiskey.

"Betsy's daughter listed your dad's house with me," Herb said. "She's in no hurry…she'll hold out for a good price."

"Good for her."

"I spent many happy hours drinking beer on his deck. On a sunny day, Krista would run around the yard for hours and hours. He was proud of you, Jake. Somewhere in that house he had a folder filled with your newspaper clippings and your pictures on a wall of fame. We'd go through them sometimes."

"I never craved attention. I just wanted to do my job."

"When you shot Lefebvre, the newspapers went crazy with the story. We always wondered what really happened."

Jake stared into his empty glass with a head filled with restless, unbidden memories.

Lefebvre laughed.

"Put your gun down or I'll kill the kid."

He stood in a doorway framed with blood-red light from the setting sun. The little naked girl's head flopped loosely.

She was already dead.

Isabella Koontz was her name. She'd been abducted from Chuck E. Cheese while celebrating her eighth birthday with a pizza party. Lefebvre shook the girl—her slack limbs flopped like a puppet.

"Ah, can't fool you, can I, cop? She's already dead." He threw the girl toward Jake. She hit the floor with a sad, solid sound. "What about you, cop? Are you dead too? You can't be doing too well with a steak knife in your ribs."

Jake's limbs were leaden...too heavy to move. Blood crusted where it flowed down his side. The knife was not in his ribs because he'd pulled it out. It lay ten feet away with thick blood dripping from the blade. A fly, buzzing, tested it and found it to its liking. Buzzing. The sound filled his head. He'd heard it before. In the bad neighborhoods of south Seattle, it was the ever-present sound of death. Jake wanted to let go. He was tired and deserved a long rest. An eternal rest far away from pain. With no more dead little girls lying on a filthy floor like a forlorn, out-grown Raggedy-Ann doll.

Buzzing.

Lefebvre nudged Jake's gut with his foot.

"Cop? Still with me?"

As Jake rolled over he pulled the trigger on his nearly antique .25 automatic...his throwdown weapon that was stuffed in his sock. He had no idea where it was pointed, but it took the toes off Lefebvre's left foot like a chainsaw. Lefebvre screamed. He sat down and bent his leg to pull his foot close. The end of his canvas deck shoe was shredded. Blood erupted.

"Ooohhh," Lefebvre moaned.

Jake could not raise the weapon, but he scooted it across the floor until it pointed in Lefebvre's direction.

"No," Lefebvre said.

With energy Jake didn't know he had, he pulled the trigger again. The bullet ripped a gash through the right cheek of Lefebvre's ass. He sprawled on his back. Still alive, Lefebvre writhed and screamed at the ceiling. Jake willed his arm to move and slowly, as if through telepathy, the small gun rotated. Like passive spectators, they watched it move. The last bullet ripped through Lefebvre's shoulder blade and lodged in his spine.

Lefebvre's mouth worked, but no sound came out. He blinked as if confused by what had happened, and then, after bleeding out for a few minutes, died.

Okay, God. No more dead girls at this creep's hand. I'm done.

He relaxed and waited for death to claim him.

But, he lived. The paramedics plugged the hole in his chest and the press went crazy for a week before another blood-drenched atrocity claimed the front pages. While Jake was still in his hospital bed, the police commissioner pinned a citation to his thin hospital gown.

"You okay, Jake?" Herb said.

"There's not much to tell. The fish-wrappers blew it all out of proportion. I shot the guy and he died. That's it."

"Okay, whatever you say, Jake," Herb said. He called out to his daughter. "Come on, Krista."

She and Nort approached.

"I told you, Herb. Call me Talon." She waved the claw. "Talon. You should be able to remember that."

"Cute," Jake commented.

"Last year she insisted on being called Moonflower Pixiedust."

"My daughter, Eileen, dyed her hair blue. Now her husband is an orthodontist and she manages a chain of car washes down in Tacoma. Go figure."

"So, you're saying there's hope for the next generation?"

"I wouldn't go that far," Jake said.

"G-P, Talon and I were talking," Nort interjected.

"That's nice."

"She needs a summer job and has good ideas how to increase business around here."

"I don't want any more business. I'd be happy if I never saw another customer walk through the door."

"Too bad, I already hired her," Nort said.

Jake sputtered. "On what authority?"

"Mine. I'm assistant manager, right? I have authority to hire and fire."

"I gave you the title to shut you up about asking for a raise." Nort looked at Jake sternly.

"It would be simpler for you if you went along with my decisions and let us do what we want."

"Oh, for the love of Judas Iscariot. I need a drink."

As the kids walked off—chattering with their heads close—Jake gestured with the bottle.

Herb nodded.

"Sure, Jake. One more for the road," Herb said. "What do I owe you for the books? Out-of-print Chandler paperbacks are almost impossible to find these days."

"Give me a buck and we'll call it even," Jake said.

Herb laughed.

Jake hesitated, and then added another splash to his glass.

"Don't laugh at me…I was a cop not a businessman."

"Fair enough," Herb said.

They saluted with their glasses before draining them.

"Krista? Let's go," Herb called out.

The kids appeared from the back of the store.

Nort walked stiffly…as if trying to appear taller than he really was.

"I'll see you tomorrow, Talon," he said.

"Yeppers," she replied.

Jake and Nort watched them exit.

"I can't decide if you'd like it better if I hated her or if I liked her," Jake said.

Nort considered.

"I want you to like her. I really do," he said. "She might look like a freak to you, but she's really smart. She likes Halo and Marilyn Manson and hates Miley Cyrus."

"You learned all of that in such a few minutes? Outstanding. You explored and catalogued all of the vital points of her personality."

"You're a relic...a useless remnant of obsolete, discarded history. You don't know a single fucking useful thing about anything important in today's world."

"And I thank Thor for that," Jake said.

Charlie Fairhaven

On the drive back to his apartment, Charlie thought about the Burtons.

They lived in his condo complex as Charlie...one floor down. They had a sad situation. Their twelve-year-old son, Kelly, had Down Syndrome. He was a good-natured kid—bubbly and excited about everything—but, he was as mentally developed as he ever would be. For the rest of his life, he'd be a burden. This was an easy problem to solve and Charlie detested the Burtons for not having the gumption and will to take care of it themselves. Like the services he performed for other weak people, he would have to do it for them.

It would be easy. Kelly was allowed to walk the grounds and play with their Scottish terrier (Scottie) as long as he stayed in the fenced recreation area and away from the swimming pool. Charlie planned to mix powdered sedative in ice cream. No kid could say 'no' to ice cream. Then, behind a hedge after Kelly passed out, he'd hold restaurant-grade plastic wrap over the 'tard's fat face. After removing the plastic film, no one would be the wiser. The cops wouldn't do an autopsy or open a murder investigation for a useless feeb.

When Charlie arrived at his home, he thought back to his encounter with the old cop and was antsy and anxious. When he saw Kelly—throwing a red plastic ball for Scottie in his clumsy, underhanded manner—he instantly felt better. In his freezer, the Rocky Road ice cream mixed with sedative was already prepared. He had the plastic wrap…there was no reason to wait. He was ready. His mood turned cheerful as he scooped doctored ice cream into a sugar cone.

Downstairs, he looked around for witnesses. There were none. It was early in the afternoon, so no one sat on their postage stamp decks. The pool area was deserted. He lured Scottie with a dog biscuit. Kelly, predictably, followed. With his friendliest expression, Charlie held out the dripping ice cream cone.

A storm flew across Kelly's face.

"Not from strangers," he shouted while knocking the cone to the ground. "Papa says."

Charlie was outraged. A red border framed the world and he could barely restrain himself from knocking Kelly down and stomping on his stupid, vacant slobbering face until he was dead. Scottie licked at the mess on the grass.

Go ahead, eat the whole thing. Knock yourself out.

Scottie would have, but Kelly picked him up and hugged the squirming body tightly to his fat chest. Charlie took a deep, calming breath. Once his heart rate settled, he used the plastic film to pick up the ice cream mess. He threw it in a trash bin. Kelly shot suspicious glances over his shoulder as he walked to the building.

Live another day, another week, another month, but sooner or later, I'll get you.

Charlie assembled his most innocent, cheerful smile on his face and waved.

"See you later, Kelly," he said.

Later, Charlie sat on his bed looking through his treasures. Handling them calmed him. When his doorbell rang, he shut the lid of the trunk and slid it into the closet. Unnoticed, an onyx turtle still lay on the bedspread. He opened the door to find Lorena Burton holding a ring-shaped pudding cake.

"Kelly was upset. What happened this afternoon?"

Charlie laughed.

"It was nothing, Mrs. Burton. I offered Kelly Rocky Road ice cream and he slapped it out of my hands. It was my mistake. You have him well-trained."

Mrs. Burton peered around Charlie—into his condo.

"We feed him well, Mr. Fairhaven. He can't hold a complex thought in his head, so we raised him with simple rules. Don't get in a stranger's car. Stuff like that. I apologize if he upset you. I brought a peace offering."

Charlie took the cake and hefted it. Heavy and dense, it had cherry frosting drizzled on it.

"Can I come in and chat for a minute?"

"Oh, the place is such a mess. I wasn't expecting visitors."

From Mrs. Burton's viewpoint, the condo was immaculate and spotless. Uncluttered and austere. Clinically clean.

She sighed. "We'd given up on having children...Kelly

came to us late in life. He's God's blessing. You might think of him as mentally challenged, but to us he's eternally childlike and sweet. His heart is filled with love, Mr. Fairhaven. Overflowing with God's pure, sweet love. Do you understand?"

Sure, I understand. Kelly is not the only one in your family incapable of complex thoughts.

"Thanks for the cake, Mrs. Burton," he said.

"I work part-time at Seattle General Hospital."

"That's nice."

"In the geriatrics department. Cognitive health. It used to be called the memory center."

"Good for you."

"I heard stories about a nursing home attendant called Charlie Fairhaven. Disturbing stories."

"I can't be held responsible for the way people flap their jaws about stuff they know nothing about."

"I suppose," she said.

After studying his face, she took a last futile peek around his substantial body as if seeking something in the condo, and then walked out and toward the elevator.

In his kitchen, he scraped the cake into his garbage pail and scrubbed the plastic plate with soap and hot water until it glistened. He dried and arranged it in the precise center of his counter. It was decorated with the cartoon image of Sleeping Beauty. If he could figure out a way to kill the three Burtons—and the stupid little yappy dog too—the plate would make a great souvenir.

He walked to his bedroom and saw the onyx turtle lying on his bed. Instantly, he was filled with fury.

The turtle was not in the lockbox. It was not in its place.

He threw it at the mirror over his chest of drawers. After fracturing the glass, it bounced off and landed on the carpet. Charlie, through force of will, calmed himself. He picked the turtle up, placed it carefully in the trunk and slid the trunk into the back of the closet where it belonged.

Then, with a blank look on his thin face, he methodically and mechanically cleaned up the broken glass.

8

Jake Mosby

IN A NEGLECTED corner of the bookstore, Nort and Talon chattered and scribbled on a large piece of construction paper. From his perch, Jake could see the bobbing tops of their heads, but could not hear what they talked about. They all looked up when the doorbells tinkled.

A bicycle messenger, with an aerodynamic helmet clamped on top of snaky dreadlocks, walked in. He wore a tight, black Lycra racing suit and bike shoes that looked suitable for ballet. With earbuds jammed in his ears, he walked with a dance-like rhythm. Without saying anything, he left after Jake scribbled where indicated on a receipt form.

Nort and Talon got up off the floor and walked over.

"What the fuck was that creature?" Jake asked rhetorically. "Mount Vernon used to be such a sleepy little farm town."

He unzipped the packet and pulled out a sheaf of legal papers. Held by a rubber band, a note was enclosed with the papers.

Call me, Jake. Everyone says I'm a good cook. Breakfast the

morning after is my specialty.
—Maureen

She included her home phone, cell number and e-mail address and, in case he'd lost her note, repeated her street address.

"Huh," Jake grunted.

"Gross," Nort said while watching Jake fold the paper and stuff it into the pocket of his overalls.

In turn, they passed around and examined the papers. It was a collection of Charlie Fairhaven's public, police and FBI records. A Department of Motor Vehicles form listed his home address. His criminal record was clean except for a charge of animal cruelty when he was thirteen which Maureen, digging deep, had found. The penalty had been twenty hours of community service and a mandatory evaluation from a child psychologist.

"Not much here," Nort commented.

"Well, now we know where he lives, that's something." Jake pressed the papers back in the packet. "While we're gathered, I have something to say. I can't sleep for thinking about this. We're having a grand old time with drinking and smoking and playing little games with each other. But, this thing with Charlie Fairhaven is different. I know his type. If you mess around with him, he will kill you. I won't leave you out, but I don't want you anywhere near him unless I'm around. You're both going to look me in the eye and tell me you understand and you won't do anything without me knowing about it. Okay?"

Anger flared in Nort's eyes. "I don't like orders from a smelly, broken-down old drunk."

Talon tugged Nort's arm. With a serious expression, she

94

sent Nort a message with her eyes before turning back to Jake.

"I understand and will respect your wish, Mr. Mosby. And so will Nort. Right, Nort?"

Nort, looking at her, calmed. He glanced at her hand as it stroked his arm.

"Okay, G-P. Message received."

"I want to hear you say it."

"I won't sneak around or do anything about Fairhaven unless you know about it and give the okay."

"I'll take you as a man of your word," Jake said. "We'll get him, but carefully and cautiously." Jake rubbed his aching temples. "Your hair looks nice today, Talon."

Under the corpse-like white makeup, she beamed and patted at the spiky tufts.

"My secret is cornstarch," she said proudly.

Jake searched the kid's faces.

"I don't know what you kids are up to, but you should know my plan. Beyond dealing with Fairhaven, I'm going to sit on this stool, work on Eleanor's puzzles and sell off Dad's stock of old books until the coroner's van hauls off my cold, lifeless body. As long as what you're doing does not interfere with that simple plan, then I don't care what you do."

Talon pulled Nort away from the counter and they conferred in whispers for a full minute.

"Okay, G-P, we agree to honor your wishes."

"I wasn't asking for permission, I'm telling you the way things will be. I'm the boss. I give the orders."

"Absolutely," Talon said sweetly, "and we're giving your plan the green light for go-ahead."

Jake took a deep breath.

"You kids are killing me. Get away. Scoot."

"As you wish, sire," Nort said.

Talon curtsied.

Jake settled back on his stool while the kids went back to their construction paper sketches. Nort was happy when, later that afternoon, the brown-clad UPS delivery man dropped Nort's laptop computer on the counter. After opening the shipping box, Nort showed the battered, stickered old Dell to Jake.

"Three-G, four-G, twenty-G," Jake said. "Don't need it, won't use it, don't care. Get the ugly thing away from me."

"You'd love the Internet if you gave it a chance."

"No, I wouldn't," Jake said.

"I got an I-M from Dad. He's turning steak into charcoal on the barbeque tonight," Talon said to Jake. "You're invited."

"I already have a date," Jake said.

Herb Meyer pulled up to the back of the bookstore. The Pinto carcass had been hauled away by the city after Nort called every day and made himself a pain in their butt. A street sweeper took care of most of the scattered parking lot trash and a crew of Mexicans, hired from a day labor agency, took care of the rest along with weeding and replanting foliage. The broken windows had been replaced...the store no longer looked abandoned. Martin Grigsby paid the bills from the bookstore bank account. Jake didn't seem to care as long as he didn't have to see the invoices or deal with the workers. He'd grunt whenever he saw something new or repaired, but it was impossible to tell if the grunt represented gratification or displeasure.

The kids climbed into the back of Herb's Yukon and immediately began adjusting the passenger-cabin heater controls.

The Meyers lived in a suburban neighborhood threaded with golf course fairways. Across the backyard, tall, green trees were stirred by the chilly wind. The Weber BBQ was a stainless steel, propane-fueled monstrosity. Herb put on a red apron that said 'Don't molest the cook, he likes it.'

"Don't bother telling me how you want your meat. I overcook everything to perfection," he said.

Mrs. Meyer was a sturdily built woman half a head taller than Herb. She pressed a cold can of root beer into Nort's hand.

"Krista told us all about you," Mrs. Meyer said.

Krista made a slashing motion to cut off this line of conversation. "Call me Talon," she said.

"When she was three, she wanted us to call her Buffy, like the TV show. We prefer to stick to the name on her birth certificate."

"When I'm 18, I can petition the court and change my name."

Mrs. Meyer smiled. "Of course you can, dear. Nort is an odd name."

"Short for Norton."

"Ah," Mrs. Meyer said. "Do you play golf, Nort? We play a lot and are always looking for a fourth."

Talon gave her mother a withering look and dragged Nort away.

"Golf is for fogies," she said. "My parents are embarrassing."

"Mine too," Nort said. "They're golfers and talk about it all the time. It's weak. Eagles and birdies and putts-for-par. Makes me want to hack up bile."

Soon, after Herb had decorated the neighborhood with smoke signals, the table, shielded by a green and white Campari umbrella, was covered with a platter heaped high with steaming steaks. Mrs. Meyer finished tossing a green salad and handed out honey-wheat rolls.

"Do you say grace?" Mrs. Meyer asked.

Nort shook his head.

"I hope you won't mind if I say a few words," Herb said.

Talon and Nort exchanged shrugs.

"Lord bless this table and the fruit of your bounty that we will enjoy. Amen."

"Amen," Mrs. Meyer said.

"Dig in," Herb said.

They devoured mass quantities of food and eventually, the pace slowed.

"I have a Granny Smith apple pie for later," Mrs. Meyer said.

"I couldn't eat another bite," Nort groaned.

Mrs. Meyer grinned. "That will last about three minutes. So, Nort. What are your plans for your life?"

"Here comes the cross-examination," Talon muttered.

Nort put down his knife and fork.

"I was going to bail on my high school senior year. School is a waste of time and Jake can use me around the store…but, Talon and me've been talking…"

A skeptical look flicked across Mrs. Meyer's face. "Yes?" she said.

"Maybe I'll transfer and get my diploma here. That way, I can work with Talon on her business."

"Oh, shit," Talon said as her parents swiveled their heads and looked at her.

"Language, dear," Herb said.

"Business? Herb, do you know anything about this?"

"First I've heard. What kind of business, sweetie?"

"Unfortunately, due to competitive threats, the nature of our business must remain confidential for the near term," Talon said formally.

"Are you going to say anything about this?" Mrs. Meyer asked Herb. He shrugged.

"As long as they're not doing anything illegal, I'm pleased the kids are showing initiative. You're not selling crack, right, baby?"

"Right, Dad, we're selling crack. That's why we're calling the business *The Filthy, Disgusting and Illegal Crack House*."

Herb laughed.

"Besides, that would be a stupid business because not many people smoke crack anymore."

"Relax, honey," Herb said to his scowling wife. "These kids are hilarious."

Maureen lived two blocks from a convenience store decorated with Mexican ads—*Cerveza del Pacifico*, *Modelo* and Western Union *Donaciones de Caridad al Mundo*. Jake, driving the Buick, stopped at the grocery and bought a pineapple upside-down cake and a cold six-pack of Milwaukee's Finest. As he cruised through the neighborhood, brown-skinned kids stood at their sagging fences and watched with wide eyes. The white-giant Buick was unusual amid the oil-burning Hyundais and battered Ford pickups.

At the address—a ramshackle duplex—overgrown grass was dead in scabrous patches. After studying the address to make sure there was no mistake, he heaved himself out of the car. He opened a corroded gate and kicked a broken Big Wheel off the walkway. Fumbling with the grocery bags, he tugged at a squeaky, sagging screen door and raised his fist to knock on the door, but the door flew open. A younger version of Maureen stood in the doorway with a brown-skinned, brown-eyed baby resting on her hip. The baby sucked a filthy thumb and looked at Jake with guarded misgivings.

"What's the baby's name?" Jake asked.

The girl ignored him and spoke over her shoulder.

"I'll be next door playing 'Oh Hell' with the neighbors for a couple of hours," she said. "Then I'll come back."

Jake handed her the pineapple cake.

"See if they want some of this," he said.

She took it and walked off. Jake watched her large buttocks jiggle in tight Capri pants.

Inside, the lights were off. The curtains were pulled closed and a portable heater emitting lukewarm air provided dim illumination with its orange filaments. As his eyes adjusted to dimness, he looked around. A broken-backed couch lurked under the front window like something long dead. Maureen stood in her bedroom doorway wearing a flimsy wrap.

"Jake, I hope you don't mind. I figured we'd have sex first, then I'd scramble you up some eggs."

"Nice place," Jake commented.

"Don't play with me, Jake. I should have made a move like this a hundred years ago when I was pretty, but I didn't have the guts. Oh, how I remember. You were magnificent—like a god treading the hallways of the police station. When I saw you again the other day, I thought it was another chance. But, people like me don't get second chances. We don't even really get first chances. We get brown shit on a stick...this was a mistake."

"Before you get wound around the axle, let me try again."

"Huh?"

"I like you fine, Maureen. If we can stir up an erection, I'll be happy to share it with you. But this place…it stinks. Why are you here?"

"My daughter's old man—I sold my house to pay his lawyer, but he was found guilty and the judge put him away for ten-to-twelve at McNeil Island prison. Hell, Jake, I don't mean he was just found guilty, he was guilty, but wouldn't cop a plea, so the judge made an example of him for wasting the court's time. This place looks bad, but it's only temporary while I save enough for a down payment on a new place. In the meantime, I know what this looks like, but we're saving a lot by living here. The police station job is part-time and the baby…"

"Okay, enough already, I get it," Jake said. "Get dressed and throw a few things in a bag, we're leaving. My apartment at the bookstore stinks, but it's better than this dump."

"Don't tease me, Jake. I can't leave my daughter and grand-daughter."

"Yes, you can. You've done enough. No one can save the world. Sink or swim, your daughter needs to fend for herself. I'll give you two minutes to make up your mind."

"What about all my stuff?"

"We'll send someone around later."

She nibbled a cuticle.

"I feel horrible and guilty and I haven't even left yet."

"Good. Feel guilty all you want, but do the right thing for yourself for a change. Or not. It's your call."

Jake left the house. Sitting on a step, he lit a cigarette. Out of habit with moistened fingers, he made sure the match was completely cold before throwing it into the wet grass. He popped the top on a can of beer and sipped. The neighborhood seemed quiet, but there was activity. A pair of Popsicle-licking teenagers strolled by. Occasionally, a neighbor's window blind twitched as someone checked on Jake.

After six minutes, Maureen appeared. She was dressed, but her unbrushed hair was lumpy and asymmetrical—queerly pressed over to the side. She carried an old-fashioned leather suitcase.

"I can't believe we're doing this," she said.

"If we're going to live together, I want to get one thing straight from the get-go. I don't like scrambled eggs," he said, "but poached is okay."

At the bookstore, Jake parked under the carport and killed the engine. Immediately, the temperature in the car grew cool. It was a cold and windy day. Regardless, a film of moisture decorated Maureen's furry upper lip.

"When you worked in Internal Affairs, you had a reputation for being a cold-blooded asshole. A snake. But, I always saw warmth in your eyes, Jake."

"You don't survive on streets of the Rainier Valley unless you're an asshole. I didn't ask for the job, but I got it anyhow—and outlasted three commissioners before they put me back in Homicide. When I was with the Seattle P-D, I'd look down your blouse and I'd want to put my hand down your shirt and play with your big jahoobies."

"They're still real big, Jake, though it's been a long time since a man touched them. I never thought I would, but I miss that. Go ahead."

"It's too cold out here. Let's get inside."

The apartment, though only one room attached to the back of the bookstore, was surprisingly large and lavish. One side was taken up by a kitchenette, the other by a large bed. Jake adjusted the thermostat…the heater thrummed and complained, but eventually warm air poured out.

"Don't tell Nort how nice this place is—I make him sleep on a bedroll in the breakroom. He's never been back here. The bathroom is that way." Jake pointed.

"Should we have a drink before we get busy?"

"I have a better chance of getting hard if we try before I get too drunk. You get undressed and I'll go to the bathroom to try to get something started."

"Sure, but let me use the toilet first. At my age, bouncing on a full bladder is a bad idea."

Jake pulled a beer can from its plastic ring and put the remainder in a compact refrigerator.

When Maureen returned, she handed him a tiny tube of lubricant. Jake looked at it. *Slippery Sensations, Safe with latex.*

"Things will work better if you lube up good. Hurry back."

After pissing, Jake slipped off his overalls. He massaged and stroked his flaccid penis, but wasn't able to get much reaction. He slathered goo and looked at the wreckage of his body in the mirror. His arms and neck were brown and leathery, but his body was pasty and white with a tangled tracery of blue veins. His gut and ass sagged. He considered taking out his teeth, but decided to leave them in.

Naked, he padded back to the apartment. She was in the bed with a sheet drawn up to her chin.

"I'm shy, Jake. It's been so long, this is like my first time. Go easy, will ya?"

"Right," he said.

He tugged down the sheet. Long years are never kind to a woman's body, but while looking over her secret flesh, Jake felt a twitch. A small awakening.

"It might be better if you turn off the light, Jake."

He grinned. "You're probably right," he said.

He wasn't sure he'd achieved much in the way of penetration, but after working over her for a few minutes, he came. After she went to the bathroom to clean up, he fluffed up the pillows and lighted a cigarette. She came back after flushing the toilet.

"Scoot onto the other side so I can have the side closest to the bathroom," she said.

After moving over, he handed her the cigarette. She took a drag, then stole a sip of his beer.

"That was real good, Jake."

"Let's not kid ourselves," he said. "I was what it was."

Charlie Fairhaven

Charlie's next fill-in job was at the Wind in Willows hospice. He was assigned for a week to replace a care-giver taking an extra week of maternity leave.

There was no hurry. There were so many in need of being taken, he would study them and set priorities. It wasn't practical to kill everyone, but the thought thrilled him.

What if I go down the corridor, room-by-room, and reap them all?

As he made his rounds, he imagined it.

Goodbye, Mrs. Carter.

So long, Mr. Harris.

Have a nice trip, young Betty Travis.

Fairhaven

It would be a glorious night, but he needed to exercise patience and restraint. A large number of deaths would attract attention he was not ready for yet.

In Room 27, Harold Peterson did not stir. There was a familiar odor, but that was never a sure thing—many of the very old emitted the smell of death. Charlie put his fingers on Harold's neck. It was cool.

Good one, God. Took one yourself, did you?

To remind me of my place?

There was paperwork to fill out and a couple of phone calls to make, but Charlie didn't mind. He appreciated God's sense of humor. Charlie would get his turn. He was filled with good cheer for the rest of the night.

Ken Coffman

9

Jake Mosby

FOR A CHANGE, Jake slept well. He woke to the smell of brewing coffee. Maureen, wearing a silken wrap, stood by the single-element burner watching the coffee percolate in an old-fashioned campfire coffeepot.

"Good morning, Jake." She put a cup of coffee on the nightstand for him and loosened the tie on her wrap. "I didn't get completely dressed in case you wanted to have at me again."

He scratched his stubbly chin and considered.

"We'd better wait a few days so I can charge up," he said.

Naked and scratching his paunch, he walked to the bathroom to wash up. She couldn't hide a smile as she watched him hobble. He was old and broken-down, but he was a man.

Nice to have a man around again.

When he came out, she placed a poached egg on his plate.

"Will you give me a ride to work?" she said.

He dipped a piece of toast in watery egg and examined it.

"Take the bus," he said.

"Will you meet me for lunch so I can show you off?"

He looked her over and considered the question while

running a finger across his furry teeth.

"Okay," he said.

When Nort finally appeared, yawning and grinding his fists in his eyes, Jake was at his station counting the change in the cash register.

"How was dinner at the Meyers?"

"Fine," Nort said. "They're old. They play golf. How was your date?"

"Fine. Maureen lives here now. We're sleeping together."

Nort mulled over the idea.

"Okay," he said. After a few moments of thought, he continued. "That's disgusting."

Maureen, with her hair covered against the wind and intermittent rain by a scarf, walked a few blocks to catch the bus at the Skagit Station. She didn't plan to say anything to the other ladies until lunch time, but she could not resist. She stood before Alma Johnson's desk and did a slow circle.

"Notice anything different?" Maureen asked.

"Let me get my spectacles," Alma said. She peered through thick lenses. "Did you buy a new scarf? I've seen that dress a hundred times, so that's not it."

"Is there any color in my cheeks?"

"No, not that I can tell."

"I have a boyfriend. Jake Mosby, remember him?"

Alma thought about it. "I think so. He's still alive?"

"Oh yes, Alma, he's very much alive. We mated like newlyweds all night."

"I sincerely doubt that," Alma said.

Just before noon, Jake parked the Buick in a disabled parking spot and walked into the Mount Vernon PD stationhouse. He stood before Maureen's desk. She gathered her purse and made a show of taking his arm.

"Don't wait up for us, kids," she said cheerily to her coworkers peering from their cubicles.

As Jake escorted her out of the building, she waved and greeted everyone she saw.

"Where shall we go?"

"Does the Big Scoop still make a milkshake for a buck ninety-nine?" Jake said.

"It's two ninety-nine now. I was thinking we could go somewhere nicer..."

"You're buying, so we can go wherever you want."

She considered.

"Big Scoop is good," she said.

After waiting a minute, they were given a booth by large picture windows looking out over the parking lot.

"There's one thing I should tell you if we're going to be a couple," Jake said, while looking over the menu.

She shuddered. She'd been happy for eighteen hours; now it would end. She knew it. There was always some cruel twist of fate that popped up to derail her dreams. "Okay, Jake. I understand."

"When you order a sandwich, go ahead and order it just the way you like it. But, when it comes, don't take it apart and inspect it. And, for damned sure, don't change it by taking anything out or adding anything. I hate that. Just eat it the way it comes."

"Can I add mustard?"

"If you want mustard, order it that way."

Tears collected at the corners of her eyes.

"I'll try, Jake. I'll really try."

"You can do it. I know you can."

She ordered a bacon and tomato sandwich with extra mayo and onions and salt and pepper. After it was dropped on the table in front of her, she looked at it wistfully.

"Not even a peek," Jake said around a mouthful. "Just eat it."

"Okay, Jake," she said. She took a test nibble. "My daughter called three times already. She wants to know how she's going to pay the rent. She has a little bit of savings, but it's harder for her to make ends meet with the baby."

"It's not your problem anymore. Keep propping people up and they'll never learn to stand on their own. Let her fall on her face."

"It seems so cruel."

"I didn't invent the world—I just live in it. Tell her you love her and wish her well, but you're moving on with your life."

"I don't have to go back there if you'll let me spend some of my savings on clothes. She'll hand me the baby and break my heart and talk me into coming back."

"Do what you want with your money. How's the sandwich?"

"I usually take the pickles off and eat them separately."

"I knew it would be something like that."

The kids met Martin Grigsby at the abandoned party supply store. Across the boardwalk, the green Skagit River boiled and hissed around pilings. Gang signs and graffiti were scrawled on the store's outside walls. After Martin had sorted through a motley collection of keys, he opened the front door. Inside, quite a bit of old stock had been left behind, including rolls of colorful crepe paper and rental punch bowls. The back wall was painted with the clown logo and store name: Party Central.

"The rental place on College Way offered five hundred bucks to haul all the old party supplies out," Nort said. "That's a fair deal…we should take it."

"We'll make more money by selling the stock on eBay or Craigslist. Or, we could clear out a corner at the bookstore and make our own party supply section. No one buys old *Life* magazines and *National Geographics*. The old man might not even notice what we're doing."

"The old coot sees everything."

"He won't say anything because it would complicate things."

"Maybe," Nort said.

"Then it's settled. We'll create a party supply section. The old folks like parties, they'll buy this stuff."

Martin, listening in to their conversation, smiled.

Nort doesn't have a chance with this clever girl.

"We'll get a day labor crew to help with the clean-up. Are you sure Jake gave the okay to buy three cargo containers?"

Talon looked at Martin with a cool, bemused expression.

"Sometimes it's simpler if we don't tell him everything," she said.

Talon stayed at Party Central to supervise the cleanup crew while Nort filled a large box with crepe paper and party favors and then carried it back to the bookstore—following a path that led from Party Central across a wild patch of briars along a fence at the back of the Moose Lodge to the rear of the bookstore. After walking through the carport and coming around to the front, he found Jake sitting behind the counter with a pained expression on his face. Jake pressed a fist into his solar plexus.

"What's with you, pops?" Nort asked.

"Too damned many onions on my burger. My stomach can't take it."

"Why didn't you just pick them off?"

Jake stared. "Shut the hell up. Insolence is unattractive. Sometimes you milk the goat and sometimes the goat milks you."

"We should take you to the doctor and get your senility looked at."

Jake looked the boy up and down. Nort wore mid-calf shorts hanging so low his boxer shorts showed—and lurid yellow Converse high-top sneakers. His shirt had a bizarre clown face with Incubus scrawled across the top in bloody red script.

He shook his head with wonder.

"Never mind. What's in the box?"

"Oh," Nort said, "nothing…nothing you need to worry about."

"Good," Jake said.

Talon and Nort busied themselves all afternoon playing with a clattering label-printing machine and putting new prices on books. They used an eBay database to figure out prices. Some of the stock was junk and the prices were reduced, but some stuff went up. Some, a lot. The really odd-lot stuff was put up for sale on Craigslist.

"I'm never going to get rid of this stuff if the prices jump to the moon," Jake complained.

"Pricing authority is part of the responsibility of your assistant manager," Nort said with a defiant set of his jaw. "You can fire me, but you can't micro-manage me. Besides, things would be simpler around here if you let me do what I want."

Jake grumbled. "You think you have me all figured out."

He returned to his Sudoku puzzle.

Later, Nort came out to see what Jake was discussing with an angry customer.

"Two hundred and fifty bucks for a 1966 Pontiac sales manual? Your dad sold me a Studebaker manual a couple of years ago for twenty-five dollars."

"I agree, it's an outrage. Go buy a cheaper one up the street. Try Easton's or the Tattered Page, or maybe Village Books in Bellingham has one. Ask for Chuck when you're there…if he has it, he'll find it for you."

"You know full well they don't—never mind, just give me the goddamned thing."

As the customer left, Jake called out to him. "Come back and see us again real soon."

"That manual was marked at ten bucks this morning," Nort said.

"Nobody likes a wise ass," Jake responded.

Charlie Fairhaven

He reported for his overnight 10:00 P.M. to 6:00 A.M. shift at the Wind in the Willows. The outgoing supervisor was a black-haired Italian with a thick accent. He put a hand on Charlie's shoulder.

"I understand you lost one last night. It's always sad when a patient passes on our watch."

It is?

"Yes, it is," Charlie said. "Very sad."

"Keep a close eye on Mrs. Templeton in Room 19. She's hanging on bravely, but doesn't have much left to give."

"I'll give her special attention," Charlie said.

At 3:15, he stood over Mrs. Templeton's bed like a specter. She was awake…her cloudy eyes glittered in the dim light. A black woman, her loose skin was a dusty ebony in color. She clutched wooden rosary beads in her fist.

"Do you have any last words before you go, Mrs. Templeton?" Charlie asked with a gentle, soothing voice.

"Thirsty," she whispered.

Charlie shrugged. "You might have come up with something more interesting, but who am I to judge? I'm thirsty too, but there's a difference between us."

He pinched her nostrils closed and covered her mouth. Her eyes stared at him. Beyond a few twitches, she did not struggle and soon the feeble light in her eyes died.

"The difference is, my thirst will be slaked," he whispered to her dead body.

He took her beads and slipped them into the pocket of his scrubs. Then he walked down the hallway to the breakroom to buy a Coke from the vending machine, before tackling the required phone calls and paperwork to report Mrs. Templeton's sad transition.

The rest of the long night was uneventful.

Eleanor Bradley

She was interested in the man in Room 24. Malcolm Smith.

He was a tall man with thick eyeglasses wearing a neatly trimmed white beard. He sat in a wheelchair and read thick books while recovering from knee-replacement surgery. It was out of her way for her trip to the breakfast room to pass by his door.

"Good book?" she said.

"O'Brian. *The Reverse of the Medal*. I've read it before, but it's just as good the second time around. Aubrey is sent to the Marshalsea prison. Today, the only thing left of that prison is a wall. Charles Dickens said that prison, where his father was sent for a debt, was filled with 'the crowding ghosts of many miserable years'."

"Fascinating," Eleanor said. "I've seen you in the hallways. Are you supposed to be walking?"

"Yes, it's part of my PT regimen. Every day I'm supposed to walk farther."

"Okay. Good. Get up and I'll walk with you."

Malcolm chuckled. "You're bossy."

"None of the staff around here cares about us as long as we are quiet and don't bother them when they're watching *American Idol*. They're not even supposed to be watching TV, but they do it anyway. *They* don't care if you walk or if you sit in your chair and drool all day, but I do. You have a chance to get out of here if you work at it. Most of the people are here until they die, but you can escape."

"That's true," Malcolm said.

"So, let's get to work."

He slipped a bookmark into his book and closed it up...then dragged his walker around to the front of his wheelchair.

"Okay," he said. "Let's do it."

10

Jake Mosby

FROM WORK, MAUREEN brought home a CD-ROM collection of death reports. Nort used an Excel spreadsheet on his laptop to sort out the data. Skagit County was an elephant's graveyard—attracting retirees who dutifully transitioned into elderliness and death.

"We can sort the data on any column and make charts and graphs with animation and color," Nort said. "Want to see how the death locations look in a pie or scatter chart?"

Jake, looking over Nort's shoulder at the screen, threw up his hands.

"This is all garbage. We're not going to find out anything with computers," he said. "Nothing replaces footwork."

With a sad, resigned look on his face, Nort closed the spreadsheet. "If you don't think computers are any good, then what the hell do you suggest?" he said.

"Do they have maps on that thing?"

Nort brightened. "Yeah, sure, of course." Nort pulled up Google Maps and found Charlie's condo complex in Burlington in both street and satellite view.

"If you need a computer to find an address on a map, then there is no hope for your generation," Jake said.

"If we had a printer, I could print this out."

"Just what we need, more electronic crap to break down and drive me crazy."

With the Princess phone, Jake made a few phone calls and found Pete Hutton at home. Pete had just finished his shift, but agreed to put his police uniform back on and meet them at Charlie's condo.

At the condo complex, Jake spoke briefly.

"See if you can get the building manager to give you a key to B533 to check out a disturbance."

"What if he insists on a warrant? That's his right."

Jake put his hands on his hips and scowled. "Ask to see his elevator inspection records," he said.

Pete laughed. "I see where you're going with that…might work," he said.

A few minutes later, Pete came out with the key.

"Drop it in the manager's mail box when you're done. Can I go home now or do you need me for your breaking and entering? Mariel is making meatloaf. By the way, mom says 'hey'."

"Tell her I said 'hey' back. Yeah, we can take it from here. Thanks, Pete, I owe you one."

"I'll add the favor to the list," Pete said.

After listening at the door for a minute in the quiet corridor, Jake used the key to open the door. He and Nort entered and looked around. The place was immaculate and sparkly clean. There was little décor.

"You could learn something about housekeeping from this

guy," Nort said. "Everything seems just-so. Should we rearrange his furniture? That would piss him off."

"No."

"What are we looking for?" Nort asked.

"There's always something," Jake replied.

They looked under the couch cushions and behind the frozen foods in the freezer. They looked through the garbage can under the sink and clothes folded neatly in the dresser. Then, in the back corner of the closet, Jake found the chest. After throwing it on the bed, he flicked the lock.

"Shall we break it open?"

"No," Jake said, "let's take it with us. It's heavy, you carry it."

While Nort lifted it, Jake took a final look around the place, and, after making sure Nort was not watching, tipped a painting hanging on the wall so it was a little crooked.

"That's better," he muttered.

Nort struggled with the weight as they worked their way down the stairs. Jake dropped off the key and rejoined Nort in the car.

"Let's go," he said.

Back at the bookstore, Nort put the trunk on the counter.

"Grab the bolt cutters from the carport, will ya, kid?"

In a minute, the padlock was sheared and they flopped open the lid. Nort picked out items and looked them over.

"Trophies," Jake said. "I'll bet there is a story—a dead body—associated with each item."

"Holy shit," Nort said. "You think each one is from someone he killed?"

"Yeah."

"This is creepy, there must be a hundred or more things in here." Nort examined a plastic McDonald's hamburger. "It's a lot," he said.

"Yes, it is," Jake responded.

"But, it's just a bunch of stuff. It doesn't really prove anything."

"It's close enough for me," Jake said.

"What are we going to do with it?"

"Tonight? I'm going to have a drink before turning in. How about you?"

Unconsciously, Nort rubbed his temples and considered. "I'll have an RC," he said.

Jake grabbed a handful of the trophies and took them back to the breakroom. After pouring a drink, he looked through the collection.

"Are you awake enough to get back in the car and run an errand?"

"Sure, pops. What do you have in mind?"

"Drive out to Wind in the Willows...find Fairhaven's car and put this on his radio antenna." Jake held out the loop of rosary beads. "If he's around, just drive on. Don't wait around and don't let him anywhere near you. If he's in his car or watching the parking lot, then come straight back. Don't interact with him in any way."

"Consider it done," Nort said.

Charlie Fairhaven

Dawn broke as Charlie walked to his car. He settled in his seat and yawned. From the corner of his eye, he noticed something wrapped around his antenna. He got out and pulled off the rosary beads. Back in the driver's seat, he clicked the beads together and coolly considered the situation. He wasn't angry or scared.

He was being challenged.

A thin smile decorated his lips. Slipping the beads around his neck, he felt as if he was up to the game.

He was ready. There was nothing in his condo he would miss except his treasure chest and that was likely gone. He hummed along with the radio as he drove. In the adjoining county, in Stanwood, he had a long-term storage unit rental. In the unit, he kept cash and a second car—a beige 1994 Ford Taurus with a primered fender and cracked windshield. A car that was nearly invisible in Skagit County.

Eight blocks from the storage unit, he left the Corolla keys in the ignition after parking at a 7-Eleven. A group of day laborers—sitting on the curb and observing the world with passive eyes—waited for someone to come by with a job. They watched Charlie walk away.

The car would be gone in an hour.

He walked to the storage unit and unlocked it, then rolled up the garage door. He looked around for witnesses, but the complex was deserted. He went in, rolled down the door and flipped on the overhead lights.

He'd installed a large mirror on one wall. He looked at himself. Fat, cheerful Charlie Fairhaven. He worked off his hospital scrub shirt and t-shirt. Underneath, his body was swaddled in cotton wrap. Often, it was hot and uncomfortable, but day after day, in readiness, he wore the padding.

First, he pulled out the Teflon inserts that rested above his back teeth and made his cheeks look over-stuffed. They were uncomfortable and made his speech labored and difficult. Of all of his disguises, he hated them the most...they made him seem stupider than he wanted. Always struggling with his words, he spoke as little as possible and he knew that many people thought his intellect rested on the sad border of stupidity. Slow in speech and slow in thought. It was a prison. He didn't know how truly dumb people could stand it...why they didn't all kill themselves rather than endure the chains of idiocy...the insult of a molasses-slow mind.

He looked at the slimy Teflon inserts before dropping them in the trash.

No more and never again.

Now for the rest of his body.

Like a butterfly emerging from a cocoon, he worked himself free of the thick wrap and emerged as a new man—thin, muscular and fast like a viper. On an exercise mat, he did a fifteen minute Tae Kwan Do routine until his lithe body glistened with sweat. After toweling off and putting on tan slacks and a long-sleeved white shirt, he looked very different. He added a gold chain around his neck, black and white shoes and a pair of gold-accented sunglasses. He imagined how the picture of the unveiled, reborn and handsome Charlie Fairhaven would look in the newspaper.

The Taurus started immediately. He drove many miles down the freeway to the next county—south of Everett to a strip mall beauty shop, for a haircut. Blonde highlights were added to the bristly cut that replaced his floppy surfer dude style...he was a new man. He rented a room in an extended-stay hotel and stood, daydreaming, on the microscopic balcony overlooking the pool.

This was the end game. Soon the public would know of his achievements. After all the years of hiding behind uncomfortable camouflage as fat, dumb Charlie Fairhaven, the cops would handcuff him and haul him to jail—and then the media frenzy would begin. People from coast-to-coast would know his name. They'd know he killed hundreds...but was it enough? How many had the most prolific serial killer taken? 1,000? He'd need a miracle...divine intervention...to get there. It was almost time to come out of the shadows and bask in the spotlight. It was almost time for the world to know his name. But, there was one last question.

How many can I reap first?

As an artistic gesture, he was determined to take all fifty-four lives at the Wind in the Willows, but how many more than that could he get?

Can I get all the old folks at Peaceful Meadows? 500 souls? It would be a truly grand finale. A perfect end to my lifetime of creating magnificent murders.

He needed a goal—a quota. Could he get one hundred in a week? That sounded like a nice, round number. He'd call in sick for the Wind in the Willows job and visit other nursing homes all week. Then, on Sunday night, he'd create his masterwork—a glorious geriatric holocaust at Peaceful Meadows.

To the bizarre old man with huge, yellow teeth and tan overalls—who had pushed him from complacency into action—he owed a huge debt.

Needing rest, he closed the curtains and collapsed on the hotel's king-sized bed.

He slept.

Ken Coffman

Jake Mosby

"G-P, there's something you should see," Nort said.

Jake, though hunched over a Sudoku puzzle, had drifted off to sleep with his head propped up on his hands.

"You can kill an old man by waking him up too fast," he complained.

He'd been dreaming of the pair of feral pit bulls he'd killed in rural east King County many years before. The woman who ran the dog fighting ring had set them on him. The dogs had ruby-red eyes and were covered with bloody, half-healed wounds. In his dream, greasy black smoke stained the sky. The dogs ran at him with silent intensity.

He shook his head to clear the disturbing images. "This better be important."

Nort looked sober: pale and ashen.

"What?" Jake said.

Nort handed over a keychain. It was a cheap, black plastic give-away with Mosby's Used Bookstore silkscreened on it. A single key emblazoned 'BUICK' was on the ring.

"I checked the key, G-P. It starts the Buick."

Jake's thoughts, still scattered from sleep, refused to embrace the significance.

"You found Dad's spare key…"

Jake put it on the counter and pushed it across to Nort. With a shaking hand, Nort pushed it back.

"I don't want it, G-P. The key was in Fairhaven's trunk. It's one of his trophies. I called the temp agency and asked them to check the log book. Fairhaven had a temp gig at Seattle General. Grigsby told me that's where great-granddad died. I think—"

Fairhaven

"Don't say another word, kid." Slowly, after rubbing a hand across his face, Jake stood. "Goddamn it," he said.

Stretching, he reached for a key hanging on a wire from a nail high on the wall behind the counter. With the key, he opened a drawer beneath the counter and pulled out a squat, ugly, snub-nosed revolver. He dropped it in the pocket of his overalls.

"When they question you, tell the truth as much as you can, but don't mention you saw the gun. In the District Attorney's world, that would make you an accessory."

"What gun, pop?" Nort said.

"Say it just like that and you'll be fine," Jake said.

"I'll use your script, but don't even think about leaving me behind. It's not going to happen. I'm your driver."

Jake pressed on his temples as if hoping to keep his head from exploding.

"Okay," he said. "So be it."

While Nort drove the Buick across town to Fairhaven's condo, Jake was silent. He lit an American Spirit and blew the smoke out of the window.

"How many people have you killed, G-P?"

"That's a hell of a question, kid. I think about it all the time. I don't know any more. Some I dreamed I killed, others I don't remember so clearly. More than ten, but it's nothing to be proud of. If you can get through life without killing anyone, that's the way to do it."

"Do you regret any of them?"

"The only one that bothers me is the kid in Da Nang. He didn't deserve to die, but I was young, drunk and callous. I left his body buried in a heap of trash in an alley. That was wrong.

123

The rest of them had it coming. Most of them would have killed again, so killing them was a valuable public service. On the other hand, a man can justify anything. Take Fairhaven, for example. He probably thinks of himself as a brave hero granting mercy to the doomed. And he's right, to a point. The problem is: you can't exercise the power of life and death without growing to love it. Then, you go too far...it happens every goddamned time. God is the master of ending human life, he doesn't need our help."

After arriving at the condo complex, they waited in the parking lot. They needed a keycard to enter the building, but Jake did not want to bother the complex super again.

"What're we gonna do?" Nort asked.

"Wait for inspiration," Jake said.

Inspiration took the form of a Down Syndrome afflicted boy, wearing a sloppy, dopey, crooked grin and carrying a yapping little dog.

As he came out of the building, Jake called out to him.

"Hold the door!"

They stood outside Fairhaven's door on the fifth floor. Jake checked the load in his revolver.

"Are we waiting for inspiration again?"

Jake looked up. "I told you, the world hates a smartass," he said before turning around and pushing hard on the door with his butt. The flimsy wood around the lock splintered and the door popped open.

"Okay, that works," Nort said.

Holding the gun in front of him, Jake entered the condo and looked through all of the rooms. He stood in front of the crooked painting.

"Fairhaven hasn't been here." Jake sank down on the couch. The revolver, pointed at the floor, hung between his legs. "I screwed up when I told you to mess with him. He bolted."

"Maybe he stopped for breakfast after his shift?"

"It's possible, but I don't think so. I think he's gone."

"I'm not sure I understand what you're saying. We can hang out here and wait for him to show up."

"I could be wrong, but I *know* this fucker. Once he knew we'd been in his treasure chest, that was it. This game moves to the next stage."

"What do you think he'll do now?"

"It could be anything, but I think he'll kill...kill as many as he can before we catch him. This has gone as far as we can take it. We need to talk to the police." Jake sat on the edge of the couch and ran his hands over his head. "I fucked this up. It's more than we can handle on our own."

"What can the pigs do?"

"Not much. It's a big, dumb machine. But I don't see another way through this."

The Mount Vernon police department was housed in a squat two-story building by the railroad tracks. At the visitor's metal detector, Jake put his gun in a plastic basket. The bored cop manning the station looked at the gun and at Jake. Instinctively, her hand drifted toward the Glock automatic on her belt. She took in Jake's tan overalls and Nike running shoes.

"Got a permit for that thing?"

Jake grinned. His false teeth in the fluorescent lighting looked like antique, urine-stained bathroom ceramic. He pulled out his wallet. In the last few hours, his hands had picked up palsy and he was clumsy when offering a laminated card for inspection; it was a permanent concealed-carry permit with an embossed seal—signed by the former governor of Washington State.

The cop looked it over carefully, both sides. "There used to be a cop around here named Mosby," she said.

"Yeah, and I used to be him," Jake replied.

After glancing at the trunk, she shrugged and made up her mind.

"Okay," she said.

She made up visitor's badges and handed them to Jake and Nort.

"He's a living legend," she told Nort.

They took the elevator and walked down the gleaming floor of a long corridor until they came to a door labeled 'Homicide'. Jake pressed a button and the lock buzzed. He held the door open for Nort to pass through.

A pretty, black woman with close-cut hair and mottled purple birthmarks on her skin sat behind a desk. Her garish nails were painted with elaborate tableaus; sea, sky and orca whales. Across the entry area, an angry-looking, dark-skinned Latino, dressed in orange overalls, was handcuffed to a steel chair. He glared at them with unveiled hostility.

"I'd like to talk to the shift supervisor," Jake said.

"Do you have an appointment with Captain Greenburg, sir?"

Jake didn't answer. He turned and walked across the room, settling slowly in a guest chair as far away from the prisoner as possible. Nort, lugging Fairhaven's treasure chest, chose the chair next to the Latino, but Jake shook his head slightly. Nort slid over to leave an empty chair between himself and the snarling prisoner.

"Sometimes they bite," Jake commented.

The shift supervisor appeared twenty minutes later. He was a tiny, Jewish man—dapper in a three-piece suit—wearing a flashy silk necktie decorated with a race car bearing the number '3'.

Greenburg's oily, dyed-black hair was swept back from his square face making his large nose more prominent like a ship's prow. Behind trendy, no-rim eyeglasses, his eyes were active and intelligent. They flicked from Jake to Nort, to the treasure chest, the prisoner and back again.

"Jake Mosby? *The* Jake Mosby?"

"No, the other one," Jake said acidly.

"Ha, that's funny. I recognize you. It's an honor and privilege to meet you, sir. Your deeds and service are folklore around here. I'd assumed you were no longer among the living, but here you are, alive and breathing."

"Barely," Nort muttered.

"Please, come back to my office, sir."

They walked through the common area where plain-clothes officers stared at computer screen and tapped on keyboards. All the desks were clean. No loose papers were lying around—they were either in baskets or folders. They arrived at Greenburg's office and went inside. The office was dominated by a huge walnut desk. The only things on its gleaming surface were a laptop computer, a silver-framed photograph and a model racecar emblazoned with promotional decals.

#3, Dale Earnhardt.

"I see a family resemblance, young man," Greenburg said. "You are a relative?"

"The old man is my grandfather. I'm staying with him and helping at Mosby's bookstore."

"Ah," Greenburg said. "Mosby's bookstore. I never put that together. Admirable. Most young people don't get the opportunity to learn the value of hard work, so I despair when I consider their future. But, you're not here to philosophize. To what do I owe the honor of your visit?"

Jake rubbed his stubbly jowls. "On a tip from a resident of The Peaceful Meadows Retirement Community, we instigated a private investigation…"

Greenburg listened intently and patiently while Jake told the story. After Jake was through speaking, he leaned over the desk and poked through the trunk, and then looked over the papers Maureen had printed. Finally, he leaned back in his chair and steepled his fingers.

"Well, Jake, this tale is most interesting, but you have not given us anything we can go to the DA with. I can't validate the chain of custody on this evidence and by rights, you should be arrested for breaking and entering. Fortunately for you, burglary is not part of my purview. That is to say, it's not my department." He emitted a short, barking laugh at his witticism. "What evidence do you have that would hold up in court, Mr. Mosby? This type of case—rest home euthanasia—is notoriously hard to prosecute. Plus, you know how it is, there's murder and then there's murder. There's no upside to looking at hospices and nursing homes very closely."

Jake leaned forward and held out his hand.

With a questioning look, Greenburg tilted his chair forward and stretched out his palm. Jake dropped his father's key ring into it.

"That's my father's key ring. It was in Fairhaven's collection. This is not the kind of case that's going to court," Jake said.

Greenburg examined the key ring and took a deep breath. He pursed his lips and stared into a corner of the room. Jake opened his mouth to speak, but Greenburg held up a finger to silence him.

"Give me a minute to work through this," he said.

He took off his glasses and rubbed the bridge of his nose.

Making a decision, he leaned forward and put his elbows on the desk.

"I have managed my career very carefully, Mr. Mosby. I make only the right enemies and run a disciplined department in accordance with the precise letter of the law. Everything is clean—straight-up and by the book. One day, I will be assistant Mayor, perhaps even Mount Vernon's Mayor if the Jewish vote gets a little stronger. From there? Who knows? A statewide office? Maybe even governor someday? Who is to say?"

Jake's shoulders slumped.

"However, I am unable to resist the temptation you present me." With an index finger, he rolled the model racecar across the desk. "Dale Earnhardt didn't become a champion by avoiding all hazards. He took calculated risks. The opportunity to work with the legendary Jake Mosby...I have a small budget for consultants. I'm going to write up a backdated temporary duty assignment to cover your activities thus far and give you special Deputy status.

"Dealing with other jurisdictions will be your problem, but I'll make a few phone calls on your behalf. You'll get a badge and an office. I can't give you any officers to use fulltime, but I'll ask the team to give you as much priority as possible without jeopardizing their other cases. All I ask is: keep us fully in the information loop. Let's be clear, Mr. Mosby. I don't want a complex and unorthodox case like this in the system. You said this case will not go to court and I intend to hold you to your word on that. I don't think anything more needs to be said about it. Do we understand each other fully and completely?"

"Yes," Jake said.

"Good. Come back in a couple of hours, sign the paperwork, and pick up your badge. I'll introduce you around. Okay?" Greenburg handed the key ring back to Jake and shook his hand. "I can't get over it. The legendary Jake Mosby. Is there any chance I could talk you into changing your wardrobe for this contract? I saw pictures of those shiny black suits you used to wear. Are any of them still around?"

Jake looked down at his belly pressing outward on the thin, tan fabric. A brief flash of stubborn anger hardened his face, but was then it was gone. He chewed his lower lip and raised his huge hands in supplication.

"I'll see what I can do," he said.

A big grin spread across Greenburg's face.

"Oh boy, I just had a thought," he said.

Jake exchanged a look with Nort.

"What?" Nort said.

Jake sighed and scratched the loose flesh at the jowly corner of his jaw.

"Pay close attention, kid. This is going to be some seriously twisted shit."

"You worked Internal Affairs for a few years in Seattle?"

"Yeah," Jake said. "They were some of the ugliest and most fucked-up days of my life. I survived, but only just. Barely."

"And the black cop who committed suicide? The one who killed the Asian family in the International District and burned down their store. What was his name?"

"Jackson," Jake said.

"I wouldn't expect you to actually *do* anything, but it would be helpful if the word was spread around the water cooler that you're helping me with an I-A investigation. Maybe something would shake loose. I don't think we have anything out of hand going on in the department, but sometimes it's difficult to know what you don't know. See? Would you mind?"

Jake sighed.

"I don't give a shit what you tell people," he said.

Nort, not quite following the implications, looked from Greenburg to Jake and back again.

"Can I get a badge, too?" Nort asked.

Greenburg laughed. "Dale Earnhardt took risks, but none of them were unnecessary and stupid," he said.

Nort and Jake walked to a BBQ place several blocks away and Jake ordered a pulled-pork sandwich and a beer. Nort ordered a grilled cheese sandwich and a root beer.

"That was interesting," Nort said. "Greenburg seems smart."

"Most times—smart people are more trouble than they're worth."

"Did that meeting turn out like you expected?"

"No," Jake said.

When the sandwiches came, Jake looked around furtively before opening his for inspection. With a fork, he picked out slices of Jalapeno pepper and stacked them on a napkin.

"If you don't like peppers on your sandwich, tell them to make it without them," Nort said.

"Shut the hell up."

"What's next?"

"We'll get a hotline phone number and a police artist sketch on a flyer to blanket every hospital, nursing home and hospice in the area. Then hope our luck changes. I doubt that we'll find it, but we'll put the car on the regular patrol search list."

"We have a picture of Fairhaven. Why not use that?"

"I don't think that Fairhaven exists anymore."

"What does that even mean? Half the time, I don't understand the shit you say. We're looking for Fairhaven but he doesn't exist anymore. You're addled, G-P."

Jake chewed on his sandwich and looked at Nort with passive, watery eyes.

"Here's the bottom line, kid—the police artist will emphasize features not easily disguised." Jake stole a look at the restaurant clock. "Finish your beans...we have a stop to make on the way back to the bookstore."

There was a bustle of activity around Chet and Betsy Mosby's ranch-style brick house. An 'Estate Auction' sign had been stabbed into the front lawn and a truck labeled 'Mack's Estate Sales' was parked in the driveway. Mack was a fireplug of a man—short and stocky—smoking a cigar and yelling at his moving crew of young, tank-top-wearing Hispanics.

Nort parked on the street and they walked up to talk to Mack.

"Don't bang up the shit, you knuckle-dragging morons.

That scratch cost me five hundred bucks, asshole."

"How's it going?" Jake said.

"Fine. I'll make a butt-load of money at auction if these dickheads don't ruin the inventory. Whoever owned this place had good taste in furniture. Hardwood stuff you can't buy anymore. Stuff that lasts forever. The Italian leather chairs are going to my house."

"What about the rest of the stuff?"

"I paid an all-inclusive price. Some shit, like the kitchen stuff, will go to the Goodwill and I'll claim a tax deduction. The rest goes to the landfill and I'll pay by the ton to get rid of it. What's your interest, pal?"

"This place was my dad's"

"Mosby? Right. Mind if I see some ID?"

Jake grinned without humor. He pulled his expired driver's license from his wallet and showed it.

"Sorry about that, Mosby. I get people trying to pull shit on me all the time."

"I understand."

"Are you here to supervise, Mr. Mosby? I'm not taking any fixtures or anything. I'll leave the house in saleable condition, just like the contract says."

"I thought some of my old clothes might be here. Can I go in and take a look around?"

"I should have recognized you. There's a room in back that has a lot of your pictures. When you were a younger man, of course. Cop, right?"

"Yeah."

"Fine, but don't take anything without telling me. It's all mine. But, I'll make you a good price on odds and ends." Mack winked. "You get a family discount."

Weaving through the house, they dodged workers carrying chairs and framed art. Down the long hallway past the bathrooms they found a bedroom used for storage. The workers had not gotten there yet; it was untouched.

Inside, there were framed articles from the newspaper and a display case filled with awards and citations.

"Wow," Nort said, "you have a wall of fame."

"I can't believe Dad kept all of this crap," Jake said.

He walked to a closet and rolled the door aside. The closet was filled with clothes on hangars, including blue police uniforms and even an olive drab Army uniform from his Vietnam years.

"You didn't know about any of this?"

"I would've made him get rid of it if I had," Jake said. "All this stuff represents parts of my life I've worked hard to forget."

He gathered an armload of black suits and walked back toward the front of the house. Nort looked at all the stuff hanging on the wall and picked off a framed citation which he tucked under his arm. They walked back through the house and showed Mack the clothing.

"Shit, you're doing me a favor. Get it out of here," he said.

"There's a glass display case in the back room. Filled with medals. Deliver that to Mosby's Bookstore," Nort said.

"No," Jake said. "Bullshit."

Mack laughed. "Sure, for five hundred bucks, I'd be happy to." He held out the palm of his hand to Nort.

"The old man doesn't give me that much money," Nort complained. "You got enough scratch on you, G-P?"

"I'm flat broke," Jake said.

"Hellfire, I'm just kidding, kid, take it, free-gratis. I know you, Mosby. You're one of Seattle's heroes. Hey, I have a couple of traffic tickets, is there anything you can do?"

"Just pay them," Jake said. "The city needs the money."

On the way back to the police station, Jake pointed to a Valero Gas Station.

"Pull in," he said. He sorted through the clothing stuffed in the Buick's back seat. He found a few things to try. He leaned in the driver's side window. "I'll be right back," he said.

He was worried about the fit, but, as flabby as his belly was now; he'd lost weight since his days in Internal Affairs and later return to Cold Cases-Homicide. The white shirt and black suit fit fine. A necktie was rolled up in the jacket pocket. He put it on and got it tied properly after a couple of tries. His white running shoes and scraggly whiskers looked out of place, but Jake shrugged.

A man can only be expected to do so much.

One of his old saps weighed down a side pocket. He hefted its weight and thought about the times he'd used it. Then he remembered the time it had been used on him and his grin turned into a grimace.

Lost in thought, Jake turned the overalls over in his hands, before stuffing them in the trash can.

Back in the car, Nort did a double take.

"Holy crap, G-P. When Maureen sees you she's going to shit boulders. You're a stylin' old dude."

"Shut up and leave me alone," Jake said.

After fighting Mount Vernon's midafternoon traffic, they parked near the police plaza. Soon, they were back in the Homicide Department.

Greenburg whistled through his teeth.

"That suit is so old, it's back in style. You look great, Jake. Get rid of those hideous shoes and stand a little closer to the razor and I'd worry about you wanting my job."

"Don't worry about that," Jake said.

"We gotta get a picture. Somebody get an iPhone."

It struck Jake as silly to use a telephone to take a picture, but he held his tongue. When the *Skagit Valley Herald* printed the picture on page A22, they'd cropped out Nort with his Insane Clown Posse t-shirt and huge cheesy grin.

The photo caption said: *Former and current homicide Lieutenants working together on an undisclosed case*

Greenburg introduced Jake to the only detectives in the office. There were two…the other officers were out in the field. Both cops were young. Petris was tall and wiry with close-cropped black hair. He claimed to be a Moroccan, but Jake took him for an Iranian. Usually Iranians claimed to be Persian and hoped American ignorance of geography would shield their origins. Regardless, he was from the Middle East. Ng was even tinier, Vietnamese, and she wore a pair of black slacks with a white, frilly blouse under a dark blazer.

"It's an honor to meet you, sir," Ng said. Petris shook Jake's hand but grunted noncommittally. Greenburg led them down a corridor and ushered them into a small room—a cubbyhole filled with banker's boxes of old files.

"You can use this as your war room," Greenburg said. "I apologize for the cramped quarters, but it's all we can offer. These files are all scheduled for shredding—I'll get someone to haul them out."

Jake looked around. "It will do fine," he said. "Leave the files. I'll look through them when I have nothing better to do."

"We're not supposed to keep these files longer than 13

years, but the shredder truck hasn't come yet."

"Leave them," Jake said, "and get the kid a temporary keycard so he can use the employee entrance."

"You sure, Jake?" Greenburg asked.

"Yeah, the kid's all right. He's part of my team. He can come and go."

Greenburg shrugged. "Okay." His cell phone buzzed. "Sorry. Duty calls," he said before leaving.

"Thanks, G-P," Nort said, beaming. To Petris, he said, "Who's your tailor, Mohammed? Now that I'm a detective, maybe I should dress spiff like you."

Petris stared at the kid coldly and growled.

Jake spent an hour repeating everything he'd told Greenburg and then asked for suggestions.

Petris grunted. "We're working nursing home murders?" he said. "I don't think so."

Ng made a wry face. "I'm sorry about your dad. I'll get back to you if anything comes to mind," she said.

When the two detectives left, Jake, exhausted, sprawled in his chair.

"You know your shit, G-P. I'm impressed."

"I'm a tired old man playing at being the man I once was. I'm not fooling anyone. I don't blame them, they're right, this is bullshit."

"Greenburg caught on right away."

"Sure, and he gave us an office. That's good, but all he really cares about is getting his mug in the newspaper."

"Do you miss the old days?"

"No," Jake said, considering. "Not one bit."

They drove home. In the bookstore breakroom, Maureen stirred a big pot of macaroni, cheese and cubed Spam. Jake lounged in the doorway until she noticed him.

"Oh," she said. She dropped the spoon on the floor. Tears collected in her eyes. She insisted Jake spin around for her to admire. "This is the Jake I once knew." She threw the steaming pot of macaroni into the utility sink. "Screw this mess. Go find some black shoes—we're going out to dinner."

"Hell, yes," Nort said. "That's more like it. We're taking Talon too."

"Let me know how that goes," Jake said.

"Bullshit, Jake. I'm putting my hair up and slapping on a face. You're coming."

"Dammit," Jake complained.

He didn't have black shoes, but found an old pair of brown oxfords in a box—in good condition, though spotted with freckles of gray paint.

"Close enough," Maureen said.

Talon was ready to escape from her family's sit-down dinner. After giving her mom and dad a peck on the cheek, she dashed out the door and ran down the walkway. Herb waved at Jake and Jake made a small acknowledging gesture. Talon wore black jeans with gashes showing black fishnet stockings beneath. With heavy, black Doc Martens boots on her feet, she ran like a lumberjack. To finish off her ensemble, she wore a pink Hello Kitty t-shirt with red jewels sewn into the eyes. It made the cute kitties look rabid. Her face was painted her typical ghostly white with the ever-present round, black circles around her eyes.

She looked twice at Jake before she could believe it was

him.

"I liked the overalls thing. I got it. It was like a minimalist repudiation of the crass materialism of Western imperialistic commercialism."

"Oh, Lord," Jake muttered. "Now I really need a drink."

"Let's go to the Chuckwagon," Jake suggested.

"The hell with that," Maureen said. "We're going somewhere nice. I feel like celebrating. I'll pay if that's a problem."

"What are we celebrating?"

"The last two days have been the best of the last twenty years and tonight, the way you look—just like the man I pined over when you walked through the police station like royalty. King Jake. I have a new life and love and I feel like I never thought I'd feel again. That's worth celebrating, isn't it?"

"Can we forget I asked such a stupid question and get to the drinking part of the evening?" Jake said.

Maureen wrapped herself around Jake's arm and cradled her head on his shoulder.

"Whatever you want, sweetie," she said.

They ended up at Max Dale's Chop House. A throwback to Mount Vernon's earlier, more rustic days, it was covered with dark cedar siding. They parked and walked in. Maureen ordered a lemondrop martini and Jake ordered a gin and tonic. The kids asked for ginger ale with twists of lime, so they'd feel sophisticated.

"Don't get too drunk, Jake, because I plan to throw myself at you—without holding anything back."

"Geez, Maureen, there are children present."

"Yeah, young people with vivid imaginations," Nort said, cringing, "and there are things we don't care to imagine."

"I think it's cute that the fossils still play 'hide the salami'," Talon said.

"Let's order appetizers, okay?" Maureen said. "Who else wants raw oysters? Taylor's from Samish Bay. They're good. Jake? A dozen?"

"Oh, Lord," Jake muttered. "Make my G and T a double," he told the waiter.

In a dark section of the parking lot, Charlie, with opera glasses held up to his eyes, watched them go into the restaurant. He resolved to add the Mosby party to the killing list.

I'll kill them all. Every last one of them.

A rumble in his stomach reminded him that he hadn't eaten for a while. He decided to go in. Graceful on his feet, he moved through the milling diners, moving directly past the Mosby table. He let his eyes slide over them, but did not lock eyes with Jake. Charlie was unrecognizable, but there was no need to be stupid.

He ordered a Chef's salad and a mineral water and pushed the bread basket away. To achieve and maintain a slender body, empty calories needed to be avoided. He looked around at the decadent corpulence of the other diners stuffing their faces.

If they were too stupid to figure out how to stay slim, then they were too stupid to live.

Jake watched the graceful man move through the crowded restaurant like a fullback skipping through defenders. Why the man caught his eye, he did not know. Handsome, he looked familiar, like a half-famous movie star. Jake didn't watch much

TV, but maybe he'd seen him on a billboard or something? The man's face teased his memory, but Jake was old and his recollection was shaky and untrustworthy.

He focused on his drink and tried to ignore Maureen slurping raw oysters from the shell.

After dinner, Nort retrieved the car and drove Talon home. The porch light was on and lights from a TV flickered behind wood-slat blinds. He walked Talon to the front door, where they stopped for a moment.

Jake and Maureen watched.

"Think he's got the nuts to go for it?" Jake asked.

"Make your move, kid," Maureen urged.

With his hands on her shoulders, Nort pulled her close for a kiss on the lips. At that instant, her mom threw open the door. Talon smiled and slipped inside.

"The kid's a mover, you gotta give him that," Maureen said.

"That's our boy," Jake said.

"Good move, kid," Jake said when Nort had settled back behind the steering wheel.

"It's no big deal...we've been kissing for a week," Nort said. "You guys should try to keep up. Are you worried about us having sex? Talon thinks her virginity is a valuable gift she's saving for her husband on her wedding night."

"What a weird idea," Jake said with a wry tone in his voice.

"She'll do some other stuff, so it's okay."

"I think we've heard enough," Maureen said.

Back in the apartment, Jake took off his black suit and hung it in the closet. After ten minutes of preparation in the tiny bathroom, Maureen appeared—dressed in a long, filmy wrap.

141

She stood in the doorway of the bathroom with light pouring around her substantial hips…rubbing glistening lubricant in the palms of her hands.

"With the oysters and my magical hands, we're going to get you good and ready, Jake. You'll ride me like a stallion."

"A stallion headed to the glue factory," Jake muttered.

She was patient with rubbing and teasing and even Jake was surprised at the result as, slowly, his body responded.

He speared between her flabby thighs and buried himself deep within her. He reveled in sensation and lost himself in the act. The heat of his swollen member built into nearly forgotten velvet friction and release.

After a minute, he rolled off of her.

"That was the best orgasm I've had in forty years, Jake," she lied.

Propped up on his pillow, he lighted an American Spirit as his heart rate settled.

"Me too," he said.

She leaned on an elbow and brushed her lacquered hair across his chest.

"Jake, I don't know exactly what you're thinking about us, but can I have your permission to be completely comfortable and happy?"

He stared at the ceiling as if something important was written there. The silence grew in width and depth. She peeked to make sure his eyes were open. He tucked a loose tress behind her ear.

"Sure, Maureen, that's fine. Go right ahead," he said before turning out the light.

Draped across him with her head on his chest, she slept.

Eventually, Jake stubbed out his cigarette and slept too.

11

Jake Mosby

JAKE, SITTING BEHIND the counter, studied a sales report. Puzzling over the numbers, he looked at the grand totals again and again and couldn't make sense of them.

The store was making money.

Not much, but some. Giving up, he set the spreadsheet printout aside and picked up a police form Maureen had printed for him. Fairhaven's Toyota had been found up-river—near Concrete—sitting on barren axles and missing all removable parts. Jake was trying to decide whether to drive up to look at the car's carcass, though he knew it would be a waste of time. It would be unusual for the Mexican gangs running the stolen car chop shops to leave any usable evidence behind. Plus, he didn't like driving up the river into Deliverance and meth lab country.

Every cliché bears an embedded grain of truth. It wasn't safe for strangers up there.

Jake looked around. Fred was alone. He didn't normally appear without his two buddies.

"Jake, can I talk to you about something?"

Jake looked up from the police report.

"It appears you already are."

Fred licked his thin lips and looked around.

"I couldn't help but notice, but recently you've been out a lot. And, when you're out, the store is closed."

Jake shrugged. "Yeah? So?"

"You'd be doing me a big favor if I could have a part-time job. I used to run a garden supply store down in Pacific, so I know my way around a till. If I could make a few tax-free under-the-table dollars for my grandkids' Christmas presents..."

"Stop right there." Jake held up a palm. "Talk to my assistant manager," he said. "He makes all of the hiring decisions."

Charlie Fairhaven

Charlie was in a great mood. He loved moving through the world without the cumbersome disguise. Dressed like a wealthy man, he liked the way people automatically deferred and catered to him. He wore a heavy gold antique Rolex watch, a gold chain around his neck and a natty, wide-lapelled charcoal suit over an open-collar shirt. His beige shoes were Italian with gold accents and leather tassels. He wore them on sockless feet.

Overall, the impression he created was of idle richness, a playboy. The effect was ruined by the beat-up Taurus, but he parked far away from the East of Eden Gentle Care Facility.

He signed the visitor's logbook. The overweight, teenaged receptionist, interested, looked at the name. Most retirement centers were too cheap to have a receptionist, but this one catered to the wealthy.

"Joke is an odd name, Mr. Mosby."

"It's Jake," Charlie said with a wide smile. His even teeth gleamed.

"Sorry, my mistake, the 'a' looks like an 'o'. I don't remember you visiting before. Mr. Coldwell is...?"

"My great-uncle. I just want to look in on him and say hello."

"Great, no problem, I wish more relatives would check in. Our guests love it."

Guests, Charlie thought. *Right.*

"I know Uncle Barry will be happy to see me," he said.

Charlie had arrived at 1:30 so he could follow the lunch cycle. He'd be ten minutes behind the medicine cart and have the maximum time before the nurse's 3:00 round. He slipped into Barry Coldwell's room and closed the door behind him.

Mr. Coldwell peered through dim eyes. He picked up a thick pair of glasses and put them on.

"Who is it?" he said.

"Do you recognize me, Mr. Coldwell? It's Charlie from the night shift."

"No, you must have the wrong room."

Charlie laughed. "You wish. Do you have any last thoughts to share before we get on with our business?"

Mr. Coldwell furrowed his brow and thought mightily.

"I don't like Tapioca pudding," he said.

"Good enough," Charlie said.

Mr. Coldwell was 93 and very weak. He didn't struggle. Once he was dead, Charlie took Coldwell's glasses, lying crookedly across his forehead, and placed them on the nightstand.

Down the hallway, in the next room, was Mrs. Goodman. Her last word was 'pedicure'.

Mrs. Allen's last word was 'halibut'.

Mr. Jensen slept through his death. He didn't say anything.

Mr. Vincent said, "Sexetary."

Charlie studied the sign on the emergency exit. It said an alarm would go off if he opened the door, but, unless company management had spent the money in the last two months to fix the system, the sign was a lie. The bet was a safe one. Charlie pushed through the door and let it settle closed as quietly as possible. He strolled through the covered smoking area, down a path that weaved through a thick hedge and walked onto the sidewalk. A block away, his Taurus waited. He looked at his gold watch. Twenty minutes to three. Plenty of time to roll away before hell unleashed in the East of Eden hallways. Before starting the car, he took the time to mark the score on a tablet.

Five.

He was filled with pride.

A great start to my geriatric genocide.

Jake Mosby

Jake was unsure exactly when it had happened, but apparently Nort had made a hiring decision. Fred roamed the aisles and nooks with a huge bundle of keys he constantly jingled. When Fred was on duty, there was no escape from the sound. He found a dusty utility apron with wide pockets and *Mosby's Used Books* emblazoned across the front. He liked wearing it and spent a lot of time in front of a mirror on Aisle 2 admiring his image and adjusting his 'FRED' nametag so it was straight.

Why he bothered with the nametag was a mystery, as the first thing he said to any customer was: "My name is Fred. Let me know if there is anything I can do to help."

After overhearing the following conversation with a customer, Nort was well-pleased.

"Thirty-nine dollars? I'm ever so sorry, sir, we've mistakenly mismarked that first edition. I feel horrible about it, but I can't sell it for such a low price. You can try the used bookstore across the street—they might have one."

"I'm not going to go elsewhere when I have the damned book I want in my hand, you old fool."

Fred reached for the book and tried to pull it from the customer's hand. "I can't let it go when we've made such an obvious error in pricing."

"I'll give you fifty bucks for it…"

"Sold," Fred said. "My name is Fred. We appreciate your business and hope you'll come see us again for all of your reading needs."

After the customer left, Fred put the fifty-dollar bill in the till. Nort walked over and shook Fred's hand.

"Well done," Nort said.

"Any man wearing a solid-gold Omega watch can afford to pay a fair price. Call me a fool; I don't care so long as I get the cash. For the store, I mean."

Nort clapped him on the shoulder. "I know what you mean, Fred," he said. "We should talk about a sales commission program. Keep up the good work."

Fred beamed. "Commission. I like the sound of that," he murmured.

Jake was on his bed reading a novel with his eyes closed when the phone bleeped and chattered. Nort made him carry a press-to-talk phone. Jake would never admit it, but it was handy.

He pressed the button.

"Kind of busy…what's up?"

"You need to come up front," Nort said.

Groaning, Jake put aside his novel and got up from the bed. He poured a cup of coffee in his mug and added sugar and cream until the flavor suited him. He wandered toward the store.

Pete, leaning on the counter talking with Nort, was waiting.

"Oh. Hi, Pete."

"We have something you need to see. My cruiser is out front. Let's roll."

Nort waved at Fred who was on aisle 2 adjusting the strings on his apron.

"Are you okay on your own for a while?" Nort shouted.

"Of course," Fred said. "You boys go have fun. Don't worry about things around here."

To ease their way through traffic, Pete used the flashing lights but not the siren.

"What's up?" Jake asked.

"We got five dead codgers and an odd name in the visitor's log book. Jake Mosby."

"That's got to be our man. Charlie Fairhaven."

"That's the thing, Jake. We have a very good description from a star-struck receptionist and it's nothing like Charlie."

Jake examined the log book. Behind the wide desk, the receptionist looked pale and shaken. Petris and Ng talked to her and jotted notes.

"There's a different-colored pen mark," Jake said.

Ng looked at the name with a jeweler's loupe.

"You're right," she said.

"He said his name was 'Jake', but it looked more like he'd written 'Joke'. I fixed it."

"What about security cameras?" Jake said. "A ritzy place like this must have a buttload of them."

"Sure, of course, but we respect our residents' privacy. There are cameras in the public areas, but not in the rooms. We looked at the security system videos. It's funny, but it's like he knows where the cameras are…where they're pointed and what they see. We have some video of his feet, his lower legs. That's it. He wears great shoes and crisply creased slacks."

"Great," Jake said. He handed over a flyer with the artist's drawing of Charlie Fairhaven.

"This is the guy we're looking for," he said. "Big guy, about 250 pounds with big, fat cheeks. Looks a bit like Glenn Beck."

"I remember Beck when he was a chubby-cheeks kid at the City Bakery, so I know what you're saying, but that's the thing, sir. I know Charlie Fairhaven. He worked our night shift a while back. The man who visited is not him. The man that signed in was slim and sexy, sir, like a Playgirl model. He looked vaguely familiar. Or better yet, I know who he reminds me of, he was like the James Bond guy. Pierce Brosnan. Handsome, dressed well. He walked like a cat. Charlie walked like an elephant."

Jake's subconscious produced an image of the graceful man

walking through Max Dale's Chop House.

"Fuck me," Jake said. "Fairhaven worked here? That explains why the cameras got nothing. If he didn't like where they were pointed, I'll bet he moved them. Double-fuck me."

"Please watch your language, sir," the receptionist said.

"Sorry. Okay, forget the old flyers and get an artist to make a new sketch. We're not looking for the old Fairhaven anymore."

"You think he has magical powers, like a shape-shifter?" Petris said. Inscrutable, Jake stared at Petris for a half-minute. Petris was cool for a few moments, then squirmed. "I'm not trying to be a smart-ass, Mr. Mosby. I'm just trying to figure out what you're thinking."

"I'm thinking Fairhaven might be a lot smarter and more dangerous than I thought."

12

Jake Mosby

JAKE WAS ALONE in the space they were assigned in the Mount Vernon Police Department building. It wasn't an office, it was a converted storage room with no windows or skylight—illuminated only by the sickly yellow glow of flickering fluorescents set in leak-stained acoustical tiles.

The ceiling was low and it was claustrophobic—the table dominating the room's center had a laminated, imitation-wood-grain top and wobbly legs. The chairs were uncomfortable fold-out types. One wall was covered with whiteboard and decorated with dry-erase ink and yellow sticky notes.

He'd sent Nort to the lunchroom to get coffee. Ng and Petris were not in yet.

He wondered if he was up to the challenge of taking down Fairhaven. Realistically, it seemed unlikely. Jake's body was failing; he was clumsy and could not move quickly. Every loose muscle complained. Every tired joint ached. His gray skin had no muscle tone and hung from his bones like old drapes.

Instead of investigating murders in the old folk's home, I should sign the paperwork and check myself in. Watch TV and let the days flow by until death stops by for a visit.

The idea of sitting in a dayroom watching westerns on TV with other obsolete relics of earlier days did not scare him; there was a comfort and release in the image. He'd worked for nearly all of his adult life.

I should be able to kick back and do nothing in my waning years. Let someone else shoulder the burden. The world belongs to the young; let them have the worry and responsibility.

He was nearly done. He could give up and wait for God's final whistle with the hard day's work over. Time to belly up to the bar and drink until the physical pain fades and, like a handful of butterflies freed in a meadow, release himself from the mental agony of thought. Embrace nothing and nothingness.

His acuity was fading. Often—like a blind man tripping over furniture in an unfamiliar room—his thoughts stumbled. He lived in a stew of memories, regrets and guilt. He should be sitting on the sandy bank of the Skagit River feeling the burn of that final slug of whiskey…sliding through the exit door of this earthly veil of shit and tears. He craved minimalistic simplicity, but got complication and responsibility instead. He held up his gnarled hands—browned by the sun and seamed with protruding, purple-veined plumbing. They shook with tremors.

Greenburg tapped on the door, and then poked his head through the doorway.

"I heard you were here."

He entered, sat down across from Jake and smoothed a folded flyer on the table. The center of flyer was dominated by the police sketch of a thin-faced man with cruel, mocking eyes.

Eyes that seemed to say…I'm smarter than you.

Jake did not like looking at the image. He agreed…Fairhaven was smarter…and younger, filled with energy and spunk…and purpose. A horrible purpose.

"This is our guy? The same guy?"

"Yeah," Jake said. "I think the fat version was a disguise."

"This guy is that clever?"

"I'm afraid so." Jake passed over a list of facilities that catered to seniors. "He worked at almost a hundred places here and in the adjoining counties."

"We can't cover them all."

"I know. We'll have to do our best and hope to get lucky."

"The Mayor is taking a personal interest…reliving his glory days as Skagit County's lead prosecuting attorney. He wants the courtroom drama and media circus because he thinks it will help his reelection campaign. I should have told him about your team." Greenburg grinned. "Your 'task force'. But, I didn't. Personally, I am equivocal. Either way, dead or alive, as long as this creep goes down, I'm happy, but it's my job to pass along the Mayor's preference. He wants the guy to stand trial and face justice. The Mayor wants to be on TV and on the front page of the *S-V Herald*."

"Okay, I'm with you," Jake said. "Courtroom drama, not a dead perp on the coroner's slab."

"Is there anything else you need?" Greenburg asked.

Jake considered.

"More guns. Confiscated ones are fine. Two snubby .38s and a Colt .45."

"Old school?"

"Yeah."

"Okay. Done—if you'll aim for Fairhaven's knees and not

his melon. Ask the admins to fill out the forms and I'll sign them. Give me an hour or so for that. And, let me know if there is anything else I can do. I don't want this creep loose on the street for another hour if we can help it." He shook his head with wonder. "The legendary Jake Mosby," he said. "I still can't get over it. Already, with just the rumor spreading that you're doing an internal investigation—a few people are nervous...excreting masonry if you will. Plus, I'm sure you'll get a visit from the union steward. Let me know if she says anything interesting. This department has never been too bad because it's tough to get away with much in a small town. A few bundles of property room cash go missing and sometimes, if the nabbed cocaine is especially good, the bricks get lighter. We'll never wipe all that out completely; all you can do is keep after it and make sure it doesn't get out of hand and run out the bad cops when you find them."

Jake sighed and ran a rough hand across his stubbly cheek. "The story never changes," he said.

As Greenburg left, he held the door for Nort who carried paper cups of coffee in a cardboard carrier.

"I brought you half a blueberry muffin," Nort said.

"You ate the top. That's the best part."

"And I'll eat the rest if you're going to bitch about it."

Ng and Petris knocked and then entered. Jake pushed across the printed list of contract labor agency employees.

"He worked at almost every place in town. He probably has access badges and he'll know the entries and exits. Try to get the places to change their codes and watch out for him. Don't take any chances with this guy...we don't know what he's capable of. Ng, any luck with filling out his history?"

"No. I don't think Fairhaven is a real name. All of the

entries in his job applications are fake. Dead ends. Apparently, there is a shortage of elder care workers and they don't check references or work history very carefully. If a guy's willing to work with seniors on the cheap, that's all that matters."

"Petris?"

"I've been looking for similar cases in other counties and states. A lot of old folks die. It's like looking for a needle—"

"I hate that cliché," Jake said while stopping Petris with an upraised palm. "Don't say it."

"Okay," Petris said. "I'm combing through death records and calling around, but I'm not finding anything useful. Most places are understandably reluctant to talk about euthanasia. I suspect they all do it to some extent."

Jake rubbed his eyes.

"I can't blame them. I don't want to die as a drooling vegetable hooked up to life support. Keep at it. Anything else?" When the team did not respond, Jake shrugged. "Okay, that's all. If you engage with this guy, err on the side of caution. Take him down."

Petris and Ng left. Nort and Jake sipped their coffee and tore pieces from the mangled muffin until a young clerk came in and dropped printed and signed forms on the table.

"What's this?" Nort asked.

"Possibly a very bad idea," Jake replied.

They walked to the elevator and took it to the third floor to visit the property room. Jake pressed a button by the door and smiled at the security camera. The door buzzed and they entered. Jake slid the paperwork across the counter.

The clerk was thick-waisted—an older man who peered myopically at the world through thick glasses.

'Webster', his badge said.

He stared at Nort with open curiosity.

"The department is hiring millennial slackers now?"

"The kid is older than he looks...working a deep undercover operation at the high school," Jake said. He tapped the paperwork. "Filling these requests quickly would suit me."

"No need to get snippy, I'm on it. Mosby...that name is familiar. I've heard of you, but I thought you were dead."

"You're almost right," Jake said.

In a few minutes, Webster reappeared and slid three weapons with short-boxes of Federal Premium ammunition across the counter. Jake signed the forms and dropped the guns and ammo into his jacket pockets.

"Thanks," he said.

"Don't mention it," Webster replied. "You remind me of someone I knew a long time ago. Ever work in Florida? Miami?"

Jake twisted his jowly face into a grimace.

"No," he said. "Never."

Jake tugged at Nort's sleeve and they left the room.

"Mom said you were in Florida for a while after you got out of the Army."

"Like most women, your mom talks too damned much."

"Is one of the guns for me?" Nort asked. "That would be fucking awesome."

"Shut the hell up," Jake responded.

Jake gathered the ragtag team in the bookstore breakroom.

"My gut tells me that Fairhaven will come after us. Carrying a gun is a risk and a big responsibility, but I want you armed."

He dropped three revolvers on the table and pushed them

over. He showed them how to flip out the cylinder and how to load and eject the cartridges.

"The revolver is as simple as a gun can be. Snub-nosed pistols are only effective up to ten yards or so, so you need to be close or don't bother. Don't pull them out unless you're prepared to use them." He glared at Nort and Talon. "These are not toys. Got it?"

"Why do you get an automatic?" Nort asked. "These little guns are nerdy."

"Because I'm a trained professional and I want more stopping power."

Maureen picked up her revolver.

"Are you sure this is necessary?"

"No, but the risk is worth the reward, I hope," Jake said. "Eject the cartridges and show me the empty chamber. Then practice aiming and pulling the trigger."

The room was filled with clicking.

"Don't point it at anyone unless you intend to kill them," he warned.

"On QVC I saw cute pink guns…designer…with satin holsters and sequins; can't I get one of those?" Talon asked.

"No. Any other stupid questions? No? Okay. Load 'em up. You're as ready as you're going to be."

"Do we get extra shells in case we run out?" Nort asked.

"No. For our purposes, six shots are enough. Most often, just showing your weapon is enough—you won't need to fire. These things are for emergencies only, as a final resort. Please tell me you get this."

Maureen nodded. "Okay, Jake. I'll trust you on this."

Talon shrugged. "I'd still rather have a pink one."

Nort grinned. "This is over-the-top way-cool."

"Lord help us. Put them away and I'll start warming stew for dinner."

"No," Nort complained, "I'm sick of your disgusting stew. I'll call out for pizza."

Charlie Fairhaven

Charlie, grunting with exertion, lifted free weights in the extended stay hotel's exercise room—until his body glistened with sweat. In a mirror, he admired his flat stomach and strong arms. He'd been fat as a boy, but no longer.

Puffing out his cheeks and acting clumsy, he stomped around the room with absurd exaggeration.

"Ha, ha, look at me. I'm fat loser-boy, Tubbychuck. Make fun of me."

Thinking back to his high school years, he was filled with rage…jocks mocked him and pretty girls ignored him. Out of the fat suit he could attract a girl—he recognized the hormonal interest painted in their eyes—but he didn't bother.

They are a waste of time.

The only time he felt good during the dismal days of his youth was when he killed cats. He worked as a volunteer for the Humane Society and, late at night when no one else was around, he held their little heads before his face and slowly strangled them instead of putting them in the carbon monoxide gas chamber. After, he tossed their bodies in the cremation box and twisted the dials. In the roiling discord of his mind, he could still hear the roaring, crackling, all-consuming flames.

He'd been smart about it and had never been caught.

Sometimes he tried to estimate how many cats he'd killed that glorious summer.

Fairhaven

Hundreds.

All these beasts were abandoned—discarded and doomed. Their cage numbers were listed on the cruel schedule...the animal version of death row...waiting to be killed.

Why waste their little lives when they could bring me pleasure? Surely the God presiding over these sad affairs would despise the waste.

For precious instants in concrete-floored back rooms the public never saw, the screaming, accusing voices in his head were stilled as the pitiful animal spirits left their thrown-away bodies. Maybe these souls were part of him, even today...feeding and nourishing him.

Then he'd scoop ashes and brittle bones out of the furnace—shovelful after shovelful—into the rear parking lot dumpster. And, precisely per procedure, he'd mark off and initial the kill sheet clipboard hanging on a nail in the corridor.

It was work everyone else hated. Though jobs for teenagers were scarce, the squeamish and sensitive did not last a week. He pretended to hate it too, but it was a job that needed to be done—there were far too many animals and far too few homes for them. As unpleasant as it was, disposing of the excess population was inevitable and unavoidable. Litter after litter, people did not neuter their cats. The cats kept breeding. Some of them ended up in his hands with their beady little eyes inches away as he released their souls from their pathetic bodies.

It shamed him, but later he would masturbate in the tiny employee restroom and flush Kleenex-captured semen down the toilet. Then, the mad chemicals in his brain would settle and he would enjoy a peaceful calm while all was right with the world for a day or two. Maybe three. Then the pressure would build. He would try to resist...to ignore and defy the rising

159

cacophony in his head. But...

He stopped pacing and raised fists to the ceiling.

"Make fun of me and die," he said through gritted teeth.

He remembered the episode that drove the point home—the first time it became crystal clear that he was different from everyone else, superior because he could make decisions and do the logical things others would not do...without the enslaving bonds of emotion...without weakness or second-guessing. His mind travelled back in time.

Heidi looked scared.

"What happened to Patches?"

Charlie remembered Patches...a yearling cat—nearly fully grown with black spots splattered on ivory-white fur. Late the previous night, Patches' limp body had gone into the furnace.

"It was on the clipboard."

"No, I told Terry I'd take her. I already paid for her shots and neutering...I have the receipt."

"You already have...how many cats?"

Tears brimmed in Heidi's eyes.

"Five, but my boyfriend said I could bring home one more. I loved that cat."

"Terry didn't tell me. It was on the list, so it got..."

Heidi pounded the heels of her hands on his chest.

"Don't you dare say it," she said. "There's something wrong with you. Something seriously wrong."

A cold fury rippled through Charlie from head to toe. He could see it clearly...wrapping his hands around her neck and ending her sadness and stupidity once and for all. No more bouts of acne on her plump cheeks. No more menstrual sullenness. No more loose tears over the latest inconsiderate boyfriend. It would barely fit, but he could stuff her body in the furnace and later…shovel *her* ashes into the dumpster.

There was no one else around. He could do it. He wanted to do it. His hands itched and overheated blood throbbed in his veins.

"No," he said. "There's something wrong with *you*. No sane person needs six cats."

He turned on his heel and walked away. The dog food was kept in a steel garbage can. They wheeled it around on a dolly. He busied himself with feeding the noisy, eager dogs.

Heidi quit and he never saw her again. But, soon after, his days at the animal shelter also came to an end—when they installed security cameras.

This increased his odds of being caught.

The pleasure of this job was not worth the risk, so, with falsified sad regret painted on his face, he turned in his resignation and collected a final paycheck.

There were security cameras hanging from the corners of the exercise room…they were everywhere else too. Banks, supermarkets, traffic intersections, everywhere. Unconsciously, Charlie watched for them and was careful when under their evil little sneaky, prying, unblinking watchful eyes.

The door opened and a young lady with streaky blonde hair tied back in a ponytail entered. She wore white earbuds, tight lycra shorts and halter top and carried a water bottle.

Her erect nipples were prominent under the taut, thin fabric.

Charlie could tell. She was naughty.

She smiled warmly at Charlie, but did not speak. After a

series of warm-up stretches—while Charlie worked at a Bowflex Revolution XP machine—she climbed on an elliptical exercise machine, plugged in her iPod, pressed a button to start a music video and began her routine. Charlie, feeling sick to his stomach at her decadence, fought the urge to wrap his hands around her skinny neck and choke her until she was dead.

He toweled off his bristly hair and, with muscles quivering from exhaustion and anger, left the exercise room.

It was time to go to work.

Eleanor Bradley

Malcolm Smith was nearly ready to leave Peaceful Meadows. He could walk several laps around the building without excessive pain. He'd packed his books and clothing.

As he walked by leaning peripherally on a cane for support, Eleanor stopped him.

"There's someone I want you to meet," she said.

"Who?"

"Follow me."

They walked to the B wing and stopped at Room 10.

"She reads. Angie West. Hip replacement, so she's not a permie. Be nice to her."

"I'm nice to everyone."

"You were a trifle sharp with me when I ordered you to get up and do another PT lap around the building back in April."

"I already apologized. I was trying to cut back on the painkillers. My temper ran away with me. I'm sorry."

Inside, a woman, with the bed cranked up so she could read, looked up. She was seventy, but still pretty—with gray hair pulled up in a French roll and tattooed eye liner. She was reading *Pride and Prejudice*.

"Am to rejoice in the inferiority of your recent circumstances?" Malcolm said.

Eleanor looked at him with disapproval. "Mr. Smith. I told you to behave yourself."

Angie laughed. "It's okay, Eleanor. He's mangling a quote from my book. 'From the moment I met you your arrogance and conceit and your selfish disdain for the feelings of others made me realize that you are the last man in the world I could ever be prevailed upon to marry'."

She turned the book over and spread it across her lap, and then extended her hand. With regal slowness, Malcolm took it and kissed it.

"Malcolm Smith," he said.

"Angie…Angela. West."

"I hope you'll excuse me," Eleanor said. "I have to get the afternoon sing-along started. People who read books can jibber-jabber all day, so I'll leave you to it."

"Would you take a seat, Mr. Smith?"

"I'd be delighted," he replied.

Quietly, Eleanor pulled the door closed behind her as she worked her walker through the doorway.

13

Jake Mosby

WITH HIS HEAD buried in his massive hands, Jake was either deep in thought or sleeping. Nort was texting on his cell phone. Ng tapped on the door. Jake lifted his head.

"Come in," he said.

"Can I show you something, sir?"

"Hell, yeah," Nort said. "We're dying of boredom in here. What do you got?"

Jake shot Nort an irritated look, but said nothing.

Ng handed over a file folder.

"I didn't go to the scene, but I caught wind of this. We had an unexplained DOA last night and the coroner spotted something."

With Nort hovering over his shoulder, Jake looked over the report and thumbed through the pictures. A girl. Young. Prior charges of prostitution, dismissed. Misdemeanor conviction: meth. Six weeks in juvenile detention. In the crime scene photographs, she looked like a discarded rag doll. Naked except for red, satiny panties.

"Are you sure you want your grandson to see this, sir?" Ng

asked.

Without looking up, Jake grunted in reply. He scanned all the pages and then closed the file.

"I hate it when our sleepy town gets a sample of big-city crime," he said. "Sad. What caught your eye?"

"In a canvass of the area, Officer Carlton talked to the assistant manager at the oil change place across the street. The manager said he saw a Toyota pull into the alley. It was night, but he'd forgotten his paycheck in his overalls. He didn't get a plate, but the car matches the description you gave us of Fairhaven's. It also matches the car carcass we found up by Concrete."

"You think this is one of Fairhaven's customers?"

"I think it's possible, sir."

"Any sign of assault?"

Ng glanced at Nort, and hesitated, but then continued.

"We're not sure about assault, but she was sexually active. Very. There was semen from two men in her panties and another two men…ingested. Also, she'd been drinking and the alcohol in her stomach was very strong. Medicinal."

"Everclear?"

"Yes," Ng said.

"Okay. Thank you. It seems reasonable…Fairhaven is a psychopath and he's branching out. I'm not surprised. I don't see any sign of struggle."

"She had bruises, but they were all at least twenty-four to forty-eight hours old."

"What did the coroner say about the cause of death?"

"Asphyxiation."

"She aspirated something?"

"No, and she wasn't smothered either. We don't have

165

spectral analysis equipment to confirm this, but it looks like she was gassed. Carbon monoxide? We don't know for sure. And, there's one more thing, sir."

"Go ahead."

"It was missed on the street, but the coroner found a fortune, you know, like from a fortune cookie? It was thumb-tacked to her lower abdomen."

"Stabbed in her belly? That's sick. Gross," Nort said.

"What did it say?" Jake said.

"I brought it."

She pulled a plastic bag from her jacket pocket. Jake rotated the bag so he could read the slip of paper in the dim light.

The next full moon brings an enchanted evening.

"I suppose you looked it up?"

"Yes, sir. The next full moon is on Sunday…five days from now."

Jake leaned back in his chair and rested his chin on his chest. Ng and Nort exchanged a glance.

Was he sleeping?

Nort shrugged.

"When he's like this, he claims to be thinking," he said.

After a silent minute had stretched out, Jake spoke.

"Anything else, Ng?"

She cleared her throat. "I heard you'll be interviewing everyone in the station."

"Everyone?"

"That's what they say. Everyone knows you used to work Internal Affairs and busted some bad cops in Seattle. I'm not sure how you'll go about it, but, if you don't mind, I'd like to get it over with so it's not hanging over my head, sir. If I might ask, please do me first."

"Goddamned Greenburg," Jake muttered.

"What was that, sir?"

"Nothing. You want to get it over with? Fine. Sit down."

"What?"

"You heard me."

Ng took a deep breath and looked at Nort before perching on the chair in front of her.

"Won't we be doing this privately?"

"Yes," Jake said. "Nort, go get a sandwich or something."

"Fuck no, G-P, not when things are getting interesting. I'm not going anywhere."

To Ng, Jake said, "See, he doesn't listen to me—there's nothing I can do." He leaned his chair forward and pulled an ivory toothpick from his inside jacket pocket. "Huh," he said. "I forgot about that."

He put the toothpick in the corner of his mouth.

"Where were you born, Ng?"

"We really should do this privately. I'm uncomfortable speaking in front of Nort."

"He's impossible to reason with and it's not worth the trouble of arguing with him. Besides, I don't give a flying fuck-all about your comfort. I said he can stay. Please answer the question."

Ng shifted in her seat.

"I forget, sir. What was the question?"

"I asked where you were born."

"Ah. I don't see the relevance, but I'll tell you. I was born in Vancouver, BC."

"I thought so. You don't have much of an accent so I didn't think you were raised overseas. I was in Da Nang, did you know that? Sixty-seven and sixty-eight. Army liaison to a Combined Action Program. Mainly it meant drinking in village bars with the farmers. When did your family get out?"

"Early in seventy-five. Not the whole family, sir. Just my mom. We never did find out what happened to her first husband. She remarried. To my dad. He's an electrical engineer and designs cell phones."

"I see. On behalf of the United States of America, I apologize to you for what we did to your country when we quit and ran in '75. Will you accept my apology?"

Ng looked confused.

"Excuse me?" she said.

"You heard me," Jake asked with a brittle tone. "Will you accept my apology?"

"Sure, of course, I guess so."

"Okay. That's it. You can go."

"Uh…"

"Unless you want to stay—we can get way down and dirty if you prefer. We can talk about your sleazy dope-dealing boyfriends, the pot you smoked in college, your short affair with a lesbo women's studies professor—the mornings when you woke up with a headache, a sour taste in your mouth and not much idea of what happened the night before. I like you and see no reason for a full gynecological examination, but we'll go all the way if you insist."

She stood.

"No, that's okay, I think," she said.

"And, please keep your eyes open. If anything else pops up that seems like it might be related to Fairhaven, don't hesitate. I appreciate you bringing the dead whore to my attention."

"Yes," Ng said. "You're welcome." She stood.

"And…"

"Yes, sir?"

"Spread the word that I ran you through the wringer. That I asked a lot of probing questions and zeroed in on serious issues…every speck and blemish in your history. Tell people I scared the hell out of you."

"That won't be hard, sir. I *am* afraid of you."

Jake grunted…a snort of sardonic laughter.

"And this 'sir' thing? 'Sir' this and 'sir' that?"

"Yes?"

"I like it. Keep it up. And, tell Petris I want to see him next."

Ng bowed her head respectfully. She could not hide a small, bemused smile.

"He'll be delighted, sir," she said.

She gathered up the scattered papers and left the room.

"You are one seriously fucked-in-the-head dude," Nort said.

"I never claimed to be anything else," Jake said.

Charlie Fairhaven

The Ford ran fine, but Charlie craved an upgrade. For years, he'd passed by the Exotic Motors pre-owned car lot and admired the shiny imports. He had money stuffed away, lots of it…and soon it would be useless to him. On impulse he pulled in. In seconds, a salesman, after an involuntary sour grimace after looking at the battered Ford, checked out Charlie's shoes and watch and manufactured a big grin.

"Good morning, sir, how can we help you?"

"First, get this crappy heap of shit out of my sight," Charlie said.

The salesman snapped his fingers and a trim Hispanic dressed in bright-blue overalls dropped the brush he was using on the spoke wheels of a Jaguar and ran over. In seconds, the Ford was driven around back.

"That's better," Charlie said. "I want to be clear about this. I don't want that Ford going to wholesale. I want it crushed and melted down as scrap right away. Get me?"

"I understand perfectly, sir. I know a guy. I can guarantee it will be recycled in twenty-four hours with no questions asked. It will cost you a few dollars for expedited service, that's all."

"No, it won't," Charlie said. "I'm looking for something reliable and nice that won't stand out too much."

"Do you have a preference, sir? Are you thinking about a high-end Japanese car? Perhaps an Infinity or Acura?"

"I'm thinking...BMW. Nothing really fancy, maybe a three-series."

"Ah, an excellent choice, sir," the salesman said. "We have a local trade-in in excellent condition. 325i. A great car that won't attract much attention. White."

Charlie smiled. "Perfect," he said.

"How will you be paying, sir?"

"Check," Charlie said.

A flicker of stormy weather flashed across the salesman's face. Just an instant, and then it was gone.

Charlie grinned. "The check is drawn on my bank." He gestured. "That one. Across the street."

"That's outstanding, sir. Shall we take a test drive?"

"That won't be necessary. Just give me a grand total and I'll write a check. If you know anything bad about this car, let

Dead. Cut open and sewed back together on a slab in a medical lab. It made me sick to my stomach. I wanted to puke up my gall bladder, but I didn't want to let Jake know how it bothered me. I don't think anything bothers him. I think he's seen too much in his life and has a dead soul. It's no wonder he's miserable all the time. There was jizz in the girl's belly...they look for shit like that when they cut her open. I don't want to think about it."

Talon lifted her head and looked into Nort's eyes.

"Then...maybe we shouldn't be in such big-assed hurry to grow up," she said.

14

Charlie Fairhaven

CHARLIE OPENED THE throttle on a straightaway and the BMW jumped. He eased into a corner and the car hugged the road as if in a lover's orgasmic embrace. He had the sunroof wide open and wasn't exactly sure where he was...on the south side of the Skagit River and headed east toward the snow-capped Cascade Mountains, that's all he knew. The river's emerald green, accented with boiling white rapids, gleamed through the brambles and blackberry vines as, overhead, the sun peeped through overhanging forest. The only other vehicles he saw were monstrous, lumbering logging trucks...going the other way.

He was doing sixty on a straight stretch when he passed the girl. Standing. The slipstream ruffled and lifted her cotton dress and mussed her hair...she pushed it out of her eyes as she swiveled her head and watched him pass.

The BMW, with wide tires, stiff suspension and four-wheel disk brakes, had an excellent anti-lock braking system. Smoothly, the car nosed down slightly and his body pressed against the firm embrace of the seatbelt system. The car seemed to anticipate his desire…rather than simply respond to his braking and acceleration.

He stopped and, while stretching his neck and looking backwards, drove the car back toward her. With her legs spread, she stood solidly and waited for him. A stray sunray illuminated her from the back and limned her slender legs.

As he got closer, he found she was older than he first thought. Maybe as old as thirty, but slim and, though a little world-weary, she was pretty enough. Her hair was auburn…glinting with henna accents in the dappled sunlight. Charlie put the transmission in 'Park' and poked his head through the sun roof.

"What a great car," she said. "It's real pretty."

"So are you," Charlie said. He looked up and down the highway, but there was no sign of anyone coming. "What are you doing out here all by yourself?"

"What makes you think I'm alone?" she said. She laughed. From a clump of brambles, a young man appeared with a revolver hanging loosely by his side. "We'll be taking your pretty car now."

Charlie had an instantaneous knot of fear in his stomach, but it was fleeting.

One second, that's all, and then he was red-hot angry…and very glad he'd stopped at Big 5 to buy a graphite-composite baseball bat. Expensive. It was a DeMarini Vexxum. On sale for a hundred and ninety-nine dollars. He reached into the back seat and pulled it out. He lunged and hit her on the side of her head with the bat's sweet spot. It made a solid sound—the side of her skull collapsed with a satisfying crunch.

The boy looked on with disbelief. He dropped the gun to catch the girl as she collapsed. This gave Charlie time for a full wind up. Though awkward and off-balance while reaching through the roof of the car, he was able to clobber the boy hard. Then they were both lying by the side of the road.

There was a turnout ahead. Charlie settled back in the seat and pulled forward to park the car. He found their beat-up motorcycle hidden behind a rusty guardrail. It was visible, but only if you were looking for it. He kicked it over and it slid down a gully toward a creek that gurgled at a culvert. He whistled while walking back to the bodies with the bat resting on his shoulder. Still no traffic.

One-by-one, he dragged the bodies into the brush and up a slight rise, and then went back for the gun. It wasn't loaded. Charlie stuffed it in his jacket pocket.

He picked a Douglas fir tree for the man and a Western hemlock for the woman. He adjusted them until they were propped upright and stood for a moment catching his breath. If they'd been alive, he'd have broken their legs and tried to extend the fun, but both were dead.

Very dead.

The effort would be wasted.

He gripped the bat and smashed their heads into bloody pulp. He lay into their ribs until jagged stubs were visible. Working up a healthy sweat in the cool shade, he broke their thighs and lower legs and was not satisfied until their bodies were shapeless masses.

Gasping for breath, he stood over the bodies.

"We'll be taking your pretty car now," he said.

This struck him as funny. He dropped the bat and leaned forward with his hands on his knees while laughing and laughing. Then he noticed splashes of blood on his cream-colored Italian wool slacks. This filled him with an unreasonable anger.

They ruined my beautiful trousers.

He kicked them over and worked on the bones of their pelvises.

When he was done, there was nothing left of them but bloody mush. His shoulders ached and his palms were blistered and raw.

He walked back to his car. The river, roaring over rounded rocks, was only thirty yards away. He spun around and launched the bloody bat...it rotated through the air and splashed into the river.

Gone.

It was gone. Charlie stared at the rippling, roiling water. It drew him in. His brain was flooded with endorphins. He felt better than great. Superior. Outstanding. Like God on a good day—filled with the warm satisfaction of a hard job well done.

A downshifting truck roused him. He jogged to the car...it still idled smoothly. The radio whispered. He put the car in 'Drive' and pulled out.

Ahead, a bridge turned north and crossed the river. With the blinker click-clicking, he waited for the logging truck to growl by—then took the turn and headed back toward town.

Near milepost 61, a boy, around eleven years old, was walking on the side of the highway with a fishing pole on his shoulder. Charlie watched him recede in the rearview mirror.

His hands were raw and his shoulders ached. He was tired.

A man can only do so much.

A few miles down the road, he looked through the sunroof at the sky. The cheerful sun peeped through a broken cloud.

Okay. I can deliver one more if you're making it easy.

He found an easy place to turn around and headed back,

but the kid was gone.

He looked into the sky through the sunroof.

Okay. Okay. I get it.

Nort and Talon

Nort was angry and Talon was crying. The painting contractor, Earl from Artistic Paints, wanted an additional thousand dollars and was threatening to pull his team off the job with the walls half-painted. The brown-skinned crew was loitering near an overflowing dumpster—smoking cigarettes. The electricians and plumbers were done. The carpet installers were scheduled for the next day. If the painting was not finished, they'd miss the opening day advertised in the newspaper and announced on every online social network they'd been able to think of.

Talon waved the contract.

"It was a fixed price for the full job."

"Kid, you don't know what you're talking about. We didn't bid on detail painting of the wainscoting and the raised moldings. That's extra."

"We already paid you an extra three thousand for painting the cornices."

"Now you'll pay another grand or get someone else to finish the job. I'm sure you can find someone in a month or two, but it won't matter because I'll register a lien and shut you down. Your daddy is a lawyer; ask him how smart that is. All for a measly thousand dollars."

"You're a creepy fuck-wad..." Nort said.

Talon tugged at the sleeve of his sweatshirt.

"Go get Jake," she whispered. "We can't handle this guy

on our own."

"He's been screwing us every step of the way. If we give him another thousand, he'll come up with something else."

"Please, Nort. Listen to me and do me this one favor. Get Jake."

Nort's shoulders slumped. "Okay," he said.

Nort walked out of the shop and across the parking lot to the bookstore. He eased by the Buick, unlocked the store's backdoor and strolled through the building. Jake leaned back in a wooden chair by the pot-bellied woodstove working on a Sudoku puzzle. Maureen, in an overstuffed recliner, read a romance novel with a genie on the cover.

Nort stood quietly until Jake grew tired of ignoring him.

"All right, kid. What is it?"

"We're getting reamed by the painting contractor."

"I told you I don't care what you do back there as long as it doesn't interfere with my peace and quiet."

"Talon asked me to come over and get you."

Jake sighed and put aside the puzzle book.

"Well, if Talon wants me…I sort of like her."

Maureen raised her book to cover her smile.

Jake waved his finger at her.

"That will be enough out of you," he said.

"I didn't say a word," she replied.

Jake stood up and stretched. "I'll get my jacket."

In the bedroom, he slipped on his jacket and smoothed the fabric. He ran his comb through his hair and slicked back gray curls. Black slacks, black shirt, black jacket. He decided to add the black necktie too.

"Fucking worthless kids," he muttered.

Back at the skateboard shop, Earl towered over Talon. Arguing, they stood with their noses six inches apart and shouted at each other.

Jake extended his hand and took note of the *Earl* embroidered on the man's painting overalls.

"Hello, Earl, it's a pleasure to meet you."

Earl studied the old man from head to toe.

"Who the fuck're you?"

"Jake Mosby. I own this place." He turned to Nort. "That's true, isn't it? I own this dump?"

Nort nodded.

"The detail work is killing me and this girl won't stop telling me how to do my job," Earl said. "These kids have been busting my ass since the job started."

"I hear that." Jake laughed. "Someone should stuff them in gunnysacks and throw them in the river."

"That's the right idea," Earl said.

"What's the bottom line here?"

"Another thousand bucks and get the girl off my back...then we'll finish the job."

"How about two hundred in off-the-books cash?"

Earl considered, and then shrugged.

"Sure," he said.

Jake pulled out his wallet and handed over two bills.

"You know what you get when you mate a warthog with a teenage girl?"

"What?" Earl said.

"Who knows? A warthog has standards and won't do it."

Earl laughed and Jake clapped him on the shoulder.

"That's a good one."

"I want to make sure I know where we are. You're going

to finish the job so we can both get on with our lives, right?"

"Yeah," Earl said. He whistled a short burst and the painting crew dropped their cigarettes and ground them out with their boots. They walked back to the building.

Jake turned to go back to the bookshop.

"Hold on, Jake," Talon said. She put her hand on Jake's arm. "I can't believe you gave him more money. He's been jerking us off from the first day."

Jake took a deep breath.

"The job will get finished and you won't have any more trouble with Earl if you play nice with him for one more day. You kids dragged me out here to solve a problem, not to make things worse. Give a little, get a little. You don't have to like it, but that's the way the world works. Okay?"

Talon raised her hands as if begging a favor from the sky. She bit her lip and closed her eyes.

"Okay, Jake." She stood on her tiptoes and kissed his bristly cheek. "Thank you."

Jake turned and walked away.

With his back turned, his face twisted into a wry smile.

Poor Nort has no idea what kind of girl this is.

There is no hope for him.

Talon

Talon was in her room updating tweets and writing on her friends' Facebook walls when there was a loud knocking at the front door. More than knocking, a pounding.

Thump-thump.

Who would not simply use the doorbell?

She jumped up and fumbled with her pistol...shoving it in

the waistband of her low-rider jeans. She arranged her sweater to cover it, but it was not secure—it felt as if it might fall out.

She ran down the stairs and beat her father to the door.

"I'll get this, Daddy," she said.

She peeked through the side window, but could not see anything. She stood up on tiptoes to peer through the peephole.

Herb switched on the outside light.

"It's the pizza guy, honey," he said. "What's with you?"

He gently pushed her aside and opened the door. It was the Dominos delivery man. They made the cash-for-pizza exchange.

"Sorry, I didn't know we were having pizza for dinner," Talon said, while pressing on the loose pistol under her sweater.

Herb put the pizzas down and looked at his daughter.

"You're acting weird," he said. "What do you have under the back of your shirt?"

"Nothing much," she replied.

He held out his hand. "Let me see."

Her shoulders slumped. After a moment, she removed the snub-nosed Smith and Wesson and showed it to him.

Shock washed over his face.

"You have a weapon? Give it to me."

She shook her head.

"You can't have it," she said.

"What? Give it to me now, young lady."

"No."

"Is it loaded?

She nodded.

His wife approached.

"What's going on?" she said.

"Your nutball daughter has a loaded pistol." To Talon he said, "Who gave this to you?"

She hung her head and stared at a corner of the room.

"Mr. Mosby," she said.

"What? That old fool gave you a loaded gun?"

"This is insane," Mrs. Meyer said. "For the last time, give it to your dad. Now."

"I'll give it to Mr. Mosby, but not to you, Daddy."

"This is insane," Mrs. Meyer said.

"I'll take care of it, honey. Get your coat, Talon."

They drove to the bookstore in silence. A few times, Herb opened his mouth as if to speak, but couldn't find the right words. They parked out front and Herb pounded on the front door until Jake appeared—tying the belt of his bathrobe.

"You fucking lunatic—you gave my daughter a loaded gun."

Jake gestured to a table in the SciFi/Fantasy section in the middle of the store. He reached around the counter and pulled out the bottle of Maker's Mark and some shot glasses, which he dropped in the middle of the table.

"Sit down, Meyer," Jake said.

"What were you thinking?"

"Sit down and I'll tell you. Let's see the pistol, Talon," Jake said.

She pulled it out—carefully pointing it at a rack of books.

"Unload it," Jake said. She looked at him with a puzzled expression. "You heard me. Unload the damned thing."

She popped out the cylinder and pressed the rod that ejected the cartridges—then pushed them into a group on the table where they stood like toy soldiers.

"Okay, now shoot the Heinlein books."

She raised the gun and pulled the trigger. It was loud in the quiet room. Herb twitched.

"What did I teach you? Shoot until the gun is empty, dammit."

She pulled the trigger five more times.

"Now load it."

Talon complied.

"Unload it again."

Dutifully, she did so.

"Shoot Heinlein."

She pulled the trigger six times.

"Good. Load it."

She did.

"Now shoot Heinlein." She looked at him. Jake raised his voice. "You heard me. Shoot Heinlein. Blast him to pieces, it will be okay."

"No," she said quietly.

They sat at the table in silence for a few long seconds.

"Give me the gun," Jake said.

Talon rotated it and offered the grip to Jake. Jake put it on the table.

"I get your point," Herb said. "It looks like she knows what she's doing. But, what are you thinking...giving a teen-aged girl a dangerous weapon? Have you lost your fucking mind?"

"I made a decision on your behalf that I did not have the right to make," Jake said. "For that, I apologize. However, I know a few things you are unaware of."

Jake stared at Herb, then got up and pulled a file from behind the checkout area. He dropped it on the table. The edges of some 8x10 photographs peeped out.

Jake nodded his head. "Go on, Herb," he said. "Have a

look."

Herb opened the folder. Inside were pictures of the two young people in the woods—their bodies shapeless, smashed and bloody.

The color drained from Herb's face. He looked through the pages, but could not hold his eyes on them.

"I thought over the risks to her," Jake continued, "and to the public, and, once I got to know Talon a little, decided she was safer armed than not armed. The newspapers haven't put all this together yet, but we have a serial killer running around...a highly dangerous madman. I gave her the safest gun I know of and showed her how to use it."

Slowly, he pushed the gun across the table to Herb who stared at it as if it were a dead lizard on a dinner plate. His shoulders slumped. He closed the folder and pushed the edges of the photos inside so they could not be seen.

Jake continued. "We live in a great, safe part of the world. Skagit County is filled with lovely mix of people—immigrants and Indians, clerks and retirees and techy types who work at Boeing. The weather is moderate—being so close to the saltwater, we don't get extremes of temperature—neither hot nor cold. We have all of the comforts of suburbia, with Walmart and Costco and the malls and Starbucks and access to the San Juan Islands and easy drives to Vancouver, BC, and Seattle. It's a fantastic place. But, the crime rate is not zero and it never will be. We have a dark side. Every place has. Even Mother Nature will try to murder you with lightning, tsunami, flood, earthquakes or if nothing else, a meteor might fly from outer space and mash your noggin. As safe as Skagit County is, we have inevitable problems with gang violence, drugs and murder. Think of that poor Navy officer who was shot in the head by those morons out on Highway 20[1]. And that head-case Zamora, the I-5 shooter who flipped out and killed six people[2]? And, let's not forget poor Lydia Varo…her murderer still has not been found[3]. It's no good to obsess on the dark side, but let's not bury our heads in the sand. There is no safe place here or anywhere else…all we can do is improve our odds a little by being ready for trouble."

Wide-eyed, as if in shock, Talon stared at Jake, while, with glacial slowness, her dad pushed the gun across the table toward her. He spread his fingers on the table and pressed

---

[1] In the early morning of July 28, 2000, twenty-three-year-old Navy Lieutenant (jg) Scott Kinkele was picked at random and killed by three joy-riding young punks: Seth Anderson, Eben Berriault and Adam Moore. While driving his Subaru, Kinkele was shot in the back of the head by a dum-dum load from a 12 gauge shotgun by Berriault. By all accounts, Kinkele was a great young man with a lot of potential while Anderson (who later committed suicide in prison) and Berriault (a convicted felon) were white-trash punks…and Moore was a young man who should have picked his friends more carefully. If you look carefully, a small memorial still lingers at the site of Kinkele's horrible murder on Highway 20 between Burlington and Anacortes.

[2] Mentally ill and drug-addled Isaac Zamora, on a "mission from God to kill evil" shot, stabbed and killed six (and wounded four) on September 2, 2008.

[3] The body of thirteen-year-old Lydia Braschler-Varo, last seen walking toward Highway 9 near Big Lake on July 2, 2001, was found near Lake Cavanaugh Road in April of 2002. The body was concealed in the woods, leading the police to believe she had been murdered. To date, the killer has not been found. The remnant of a memorial can be seen at a turn-out near milepost 2 on Lake Cavanaugh Road.

down until his forearms quivered. He closed his eyes and took a deep breath.

"Okay," Herb said, "are we going to drink or fight?"

Jake distributed the glasses…and put one in front of Talon. He gestured with the bottle and she held her fingers a quarter-inch apart.

"Oh, for Christ's sake," Herb said, "you have her drinking too? This is too damned much to bear."

Jake poured a splash into her glass, then more substantial portions into his own glass and Herb's.

Nort, wearing only a baggy pair of long surfer's shorts, came from the back of the store rubbing his eyes.

"What's all this noisy drama?" he said.

Jake gestured with the bottle.

"Have a drink?"

A grimace washed across Nort's face.

"Hell no," he said. "I'll have an RC."

Jake could not hide a smirk.

"What's that shit-eating grin about?" Nort said.

"I'm pretty sure we're out of sodas," Jake said.

Maureen

Bored, Maureen wandered through the bookstore. Fred was curled up in an easy chair singing *In the Mood* to himself and reading the June 1962 *Popular Mechanics* magazine.

He made eye-contact with her.

"One of these days, everyone will have a flying boat in their garage," he said.

Maureen rolled her eyes.

Nort strolled in from the back—eating a maple bar and

187

drinking from a box of apple juice with a straw.

"Hey, Maureen," he said.

"Where's Jake?"

"Talon is showing him the skateboard shop."

"I want to see my grandkids. Will you drive me over?"

Nort shrugged. "Okay, sure. As soon as I finish my dinner."

Nort parked the car along the street. The yard, fenced in by a trampled-down chain link fence, was filled with broken plastic toys and patches of dead grass. It was a typical Pacific Northwest winter day: mist drifted from low, gray clouds. The sun, beaten and humiliated, did not even try.

Nort stayed with the car while Maureen, after kicking a plastic dump truck off the walkway, walked to the front door.

She opened the rickety screen door and knocked.

The young man who opened the door was small and thin. Unshaven, he peered from the dark house with blind eyes like a mole.

"What do you want?" he said.

"I came to see the kids. I brought them some books."

"You're here, so you might as well come in, I guess. The kids are watching TV in the back...I'll see if they want to come out."

Maureen moved magazines off the couch and made room to perch on its edge. The cat, Poochy, lifted his head for a few seconds, then went back to sleep. Maureen's daughter, Clara, came out. The brown-eyed baby was attached to her hip like a permanent fixture. Sucking a slobbery thumb, he looked out at the world as if it was filled with hungry animals.

"Your old man got out," Maureen said.

"Yeah. The prisons are full and the state's got money

problems. They're letting the nonviolet guys out early."

"He seemed pretty 'violet' to me when he beat the crap out of that kid in Sedro." Maureen shook her head. "So, he's out. And you took him back."

"What was I supposed to do? You left. I don't have a job and I don't have no folding money in my pocketbook. The state check pays the rent and that's about it. We'd be dead except for the food stamp card and the brown lettuce and canned beans we get from the gleaners. Prison changed him. He has a little money and is looking for a job. Life doesn't deal me many choices. Besides, you shouldn't give up on people so quick."

"I gave you everything I could. Jake gave me the chance to save myself and I took it. I won't apologize."

"That bum in the overalls with the false teeth?" Clara snorted. "He seems like a real winner. You won the jackpot. Three cherries. Congurglations."

"Well, he might not look like much, but he's something. Really something. And, he cleaned up. He looks like three million bucks in his black suit and tie. It reminds me of the good days when Frank Sinatra was singing in Las Vegas and my legs looked good in nylons and high heels and your dad took me out in the T-bird convertible and beer tasted good and we parked next to a field and my skin was tight and his hands were warm and…"

"And look at us now—trapped like wiggle-bugs in a roach motel trying to get through another day so we can die tomorrow."

Maureen gritted her teeth, then felt a weight lift from her shoulders…like God had decided to forgive her for every sin, all sins, every one of them, the ones she was guilty of and the ones she wasn't.

"Jake is right. Our problem is not that we're poor. Our problem is our attitude. The world owes us nothing. We have to work—there's no way around that, but if we work and hope and plant good things in the earth, one day the sun will smile down and good things will grow, day by day."

Bill, drinking tea from an insulated plastic cup, wandered back in to the room. "Yeah, unless the world stomps us flat with a giant boot," he said.

"Sometimes, it's not the package, but the person inside that package who will save your life. I will not give in to despair. I will not. Bill, think back and remember. What was the happiest day in your life? The most golden, beautiful day of your life."

Bill sat on the couch. He sipped and then leaned back.

"I used to ride a skateboard. There was a feeling of freedom and joy when I hit a down slope and cruised." He raised his hand and made a flying gesture. "Cruising. And, when the wheels fell off, my dad let me use his tools and I fixed it. All the neighbor kids came over and we put on custom graphite wheels and painted the damned things with all kinds of patterns. Skulls, unicorns, rock band logos, everything. Karl Wilkins put Miley Cyrus on his board and we laughed at him but he paid no attention. He loved Miley more than life itself. Those were good times, man."

Maureen laughed with childlike joy.

It works. It really works.

"Are you really looking for a job? Truly?" she said.

"Yeah," Bill replied. "But, no one will hire a convicted felon. I'd do anything."

"Even for crap money? Eight bucks an hour?"

"Yeah, I'll work...I don't want to go back to the life. I don't want to go back to prison."

"Okay. I'll get you a job. Be ready to go tomorrow morning at eight and we'll come pick you up."

"What's the job?"

Maureen stood and kissed him on the forehead.

"Don't even worry about it. It will be fine."

She walked back to the car. She felt weightless, carefully placing her feet on the walkway as if the slightest bump would send her flying into space.

"What?" Nort said. "You look happier than when you went in."

"You have an employee for the skateboard shop."

"Excuse me? We can't afford to hire anyone. You're nuts."

Maureen tilted her head back and laughter poured from her body. Her eyes leaked tears and her shoulders shook.

"Right. You can't afford to hire anyone and you don't need any help anyway and things never work out good for anyone."

"I live with crazy people. I suppose I should not be surprised with whatever happens." He started the car. "Where to now? China? Afghanistan? The moon?"

With a handkerchief, Maureen wiped her face.

"Back home," she said. "I got to give Jake a blow job or something."

"Don't tell me things like that," Nort said. "That's sick. Gross."

"Drive," Maureen said.

Ken Coffman

Maureen and Jake Share an Intimate Moment

Maureen raised her head and smiled. With the back of her hand, she wiped creamy froth from her upper lip.

"That's a taste you never forget," she said. "I remember the first time. I was thirteen."

Jake leaned back and sighed with satisfaction.

"I never thought I'd do this again," Jake said. "It took a while, but it was worth it. When you suggested the idea, I admit it, I was skeptical—I thought I was way too old for this—but I'm glad I came."

With a sly, knowing smile, Maureen pulled his vein-knotted hand to her sticky lips and kissed it.

"I'm glad you came too," she said. "You earned your special reward. Shall we go at it again?"

Jake groaned.

"You gotta give me a break. Another one could kill an old man like me. There's no way I could do it."

The Big Scoop was a throwback to Mount Vernon's history: an old-fashioned ice cream parlor. A tall tulip glass decorated with two dripping straws stood empty—except for syrupy dregs—in the middle of the table. Their strawberry milkshake was completely and totally consumed.

The restaurant was busy—all the tables were full and there was a lineup of giggling preteen girls wearing brown uniforms and sashes at the ice cream counter—the friendly service was slow.

She patted his hand.

"Well, when you're ready…let me know. Ice cream is something I can never seem to get enough of." They sat back in the booth and watched the bustling crowd for a while before

Maureen spoke again. "I've been thinking," she said.

"Oh, Lord," Jake said. "That's never good."

"Stop it. I've been cooking for you and washing your filthy underwear and warming your bed. Why not take the final step? I think we should get married."

"One of the hazards of being really smart," he said, "is you can be manipulated by a logical argument." He rubbed his hands over his skull. "Look, we've both been married before. Look what horrible disasters they turned out to be."

"At our age, I doubt that we'll live long enough to create much of a catastrophe. Don't be so over-dramatic…there's no reason to make a big deal out of this. I have a ring I inherited from my aunt. A few minutes in front of a J-P and we're done. You get kinky wedding-night sex out of the deal…and a happy wife."

"I'm too old for wedding night sex…it would probably kill me. And, there's no such a thing as a 'happy wife'. That's an oxymoron."

She leaned back and crossed her arms across her chest.

"Does that mean, Jake Mosby, that you will not marry me? Never, under any circumstances?"

Jake sighed and scratched the day's growth of beard on his cheek. "No. I didn't say that."

The waitress, with dual studs poking through her lower lip, stopped by to refill their water glasses.

"We're engaged," Maureen told her. "I don't remember being happier."

The waitress looked them over.

"Congratulations, I guess," she said.

"Steaming brown shit on a vanilla cupcake," Jake said. "Here we go."

Ken Coffman

15

Charlie Fairhaven

HE LIKED READING the newspaper accounts: they were always screwed up—if not misguided or just plain wrong.

Husband and Wife found Murdered in the Woods

The subhead said: *Police refuse to rule out link to satanic cult.*

The cops hadn't let the newspaper photographer past the yellow crime scene tape wrapped around fir tree trunks, so he had photographed the trees and the tape...and the blue-light-flashing police cars parked by the road.

Charlie refolded the newspaper so he could read to the bottom of the page.

"Care for a refill?"

The Calico Cupboard was busy and smelled like fresh-baked cinnamon rolls and steamy perspiration. Outside, rain poured down.

The waitress wore a brown t-shirt.

Sweetest buns in town, it said.

Charlie produced a smile like sunlight on a summer day.

"Sure, sweetie," he said. "Hit me."

He was surprised the bodies had been found so quickly. A

logger had pulled over for a piss on the riverbank and had smelled them.

What kind of idiot wanders around in the woods in the middle of the night with a flashlight because he smells something?

The upriver community was small and there was an article about the missing kids in the *Concrete Herald*. It seemed that everyone had been looking for the missing couple.

The newspaper had a quote from the logger.

"I knew the smell. When I was a volunteer fireman, we found an old lady in her bed. She'd been dead for a couple of weeks. The smell is not something you forget very easy."

Easily. The smell is not something you forget very easily, moron.

The article did not mention the baseball bat.

"Terrible thing, that," the waitress said while looking at the newspaper over his shoulder. "That couple were no angels. They made mistakes, but they didn't deserve to die like that. Beat to death. What kind of monster would do such a wicked thing?"

"That is an excellent question, my dear," Charlie said. "Are there any more of the lemon tarts? I'm in the mood for something sweet."

Nort

Nort cursed. The sloppily milled Chinese nuts would not thread easily onto the Chinese skateboard shafts. They had 200 of the things to build and Nort was angry. After half an hour of sweating and cursing, he still had not finished assembling the first one.

He was in the back of the shop. The door was rolled open. Rain sputtered from low clouds.

195

"Go easy, kid. If you cross-thread the nuts—you'll really be fucked. They go on smooth when you get the feel for it."

Nort looked at the young man who wore a Lady Gaga t-shirt over pumped-up arms. The man was short, but ripped...his muscles bulged. His hair was cropped close to his skull and crude tats rippled up and down his arms.

"Who are you and what do you want?" Nort said.

"I'm Bill. Maureen's my mother-in-law. She said you need help and I could get a job if I came by. I brought my tools...well, the odds and ends Clara didn't hock."

"I make the hiring decisions. Maureen said you might stop by, but I didn't promise no job. You're the one that was in prison? Manslaughter?" Bill nodded. "What's prison like?"

"The food's okay, but it's real boring. There's not much to do. Read books, watch TV, work out. Try to stay out of the way of the rough crowd."

"We can't afford no help."

Bill's shoulders slumped.

"Okay," he said. "I can check at the day labor place, sometimes they have something. Go easy on the threads and they'll be alright."

Nort looked at the half-assembled skateboard and the plastic bags filled with parts stacked up in the workshop.

"Wait. What if I gave you a flat three bucks for each one you put together? Cash?"

"I'd say I'd make a lot of money 'cause once I get rolling I'll put one together in ten minutes."

"Fine. You build skateboards, I've got other things to do. We're opening on Friday and we're nowhere near ready."

Bill grinned. "You got it, boss," he said.

Thirty minutes later, Nort wandered back. He looked over the first skateboard. The graphics were cheesy—balloons and lurid yellow flowers.

"These things are ugly. Good thing they're cheap. The kids will cover them with stickers anyway." He dropped the board on the concrete and rolled it back and forth with his foot. "Seems to roll okay," he said.

He hopped on and rolled to the wall. "Hmmm. Rides sweet."

"We can sandblast them and repaint them with custom graphics."

"That sounds expensive."

Bill shrugged. "You can rent a sandblaster and paint sprayer until you scrape together the dough to buy the gear. You can get two hundred or more for a custom-designed board."

Nort rolled back and stopped with a twist of the board.

"That's good money," he said. "Hold off on building the last ten or so and we'll try it."

"Whatever you say, boss," Bill said.

Across the parking lot—parked against the boardwalk along the river—Charlie Fairhaven crouched behind the wheel of his BMW and watched the scene at the skateboard shop through field glasses. He made notes in a leather-bound notebook.

I'm going to kill you all…and enjoy every minute of doing it.

Jake Mosby

Petris knocked on the door. Jake had nodded off over a case file in a manila folder with his head cradled in his huge hands.

He started, and wiped a sliver of drool off his chin, and then off the file.

"Come in," he said. He gestured. "Have a seat." He rubbed his eyes, and then sorted through a tall stack of folders. "Ah, here you are. First off, anything new on the bodies in the woods?"

Petris shrugged. "On occasion, the girl turned tricks at the Riverside Inn. We got a john to talk off the record. Her boyfriend rousted him for a couple hundred bucks. Said he'd give pictures to the john's wife if he didn't hit the cash machine and cough up the four hundred dollar limit. The guy didn't have that much, but they let him go. Nothing special, this kind of shakedown happens all the time. It looks like they flagged someone down on the highway, but to their bad luck, they hooked a killer."

"Anything left behind? Clothing? DNA?"

"No. It rained and the bodies were tore up by a fox or something. A big mess, but no evidence. We almost lost a guy in the river, but we dragged him back. He didn't find anything, but we'll keep trying. Things are pretty rough out that way."

"Okay, just curious. Now, about you. What's your real name? It sure as hell ain't Frank."

Petris stared for a moment.

"Farzad. How is this your business?"

"I'm naturally curious. Petris is an odd name for a Farsi."

Petris clenched his teeth. "Farsi is a language, not a culture. Perhaps you mean Persian."

"Perhaps I mean Iranian. Regardless, it's still an odd name."

"My dad was French and my mother Tajik. They met at the Shemshak ski resort. The name was de Petris and I changed it. You're an American fool and subtle distinctions of race and

198

culture mean nothing to you. Again, how is this any of your business and how is it relevant to your internal investigation?"

"I'm curious. What does the rumor mill say about my 'investigation'?"

"Greenberg thinks there's a dirty cop on the force and he hired you to unearth him."

"Are you a dirty cop?" Jake said.

For a long minute, Petris did not speak. "I try to give the public a fair deal, but I had consensual sex with a witness. She became my girlfriend and we lived together for six months before we broke up. And, I did a favor for a friend of a friend and got a gift in return. A thousand dollars in cash. It didn't matter, the DAs case was crap anyway and everyone knew it."

Jake laughed. "That's an interesting strategy…the brutal, unvarnished truth. What do you think I'll do now?"

"I'm placing a bet. I don't think you give a whit about the little stuff."

"What about the watch? Rolex Submariner. That's a bit extravagant for a Detective Sergeant making what? Eighty grand a year?"

"More like sixty."

"Was that another *gift* from someone who you did a solid? Evidence disappeared? Looked the other way when something hinky went down at a crime scene? Helped someone's kid who was in the wrong place and the wrong time?"

"No. It was my dad's. He didn't die rich, but he flirted with it a few times in his life. He sold yachts when the sheiks were buying them in lots of ten in the 70's. My sister got the Maserati and I got the watch. So, where are we? Are we going to dance? Make out? Should I bend over so you can shove your dick in ass?"

"You're kind of a brittle motherfucker, aren't you? I'm surprised to see a guy like you in a small-town police department."

"Not very many white guys will work for sixty grand a year and a shitty pension. Things got tough in Tehran. My aunt signed up for a marriage service and married a wealthy potato farmer up in Edison. He brought me over. Turns out I like it here."

Jake closed the file and threw it on the middle of the table.

"Okay, we'll try this. If you were, privately and in complete confidence, to advise me on whom to look at in the department—someone who takes things too far and likes money and the high life a bit too much—who would you point a finger at?"

Petris adjusted his necktie.

"If I knew of anyone out of line…I wouldn't wait around for someone like you to magically appear. I'd gather evidence to support a case and present it directly to Greenberg or the State Attorney General."

Jake threw up his hands.

"You know what, Petris?" he said. "I'm surprised to be saying this, but I like you. In addition, I mostly believe what you're saying. I'll tell you what—you hear something I should know about, come back and see me. Otherwise, we're done. Fair enough?"

Petris stood.

"It's better than having your cum dripping out of my ass," he said. He pulled the door closed firmly—snap—when he left the room.

Fairhaven

16

Charlie Fairhaven

THE BAR WAS dimly lit, though occasionally brightened by headlights washing in from the parking lot. It was 5:00 in the afternoon and the last of the 3:30-4:30 happy hour customers had wandered home. Charlie sipped a peach Snapple the bartender had found in a refrigerator in the back. Over ice in a clean glass—Charlie had sent the first, greasy tumbler back.

He smelled the girl before he saw her. She wore a heavy fragrance, perhaps a Mariah Carey purse spray bought from the Walmart down the street. The scent was vivid and strong, but not quite enough as Charlie could also smell her musky body odor—a sour, free-range scent. The girl could use a shower and shampoo.

In the weak light, she didn't look too bad. A little rough around the edges...eyes a bit bloodshot, mascara a bit thick...with a little flap of loose skin hanging from her chin. She wore a short–brimmed hat with a red Chinese star on the front and a t-shirt carrying the iconic, chic Ché Guevara image. She dropped her canvas purse one seat away from Charlie. The bartender knew her—he poured a shot of Jack Daniels into a tall glass and topped it off with cola from the spigot-dispenser and a maraschino cherry—then slid it front of her.

Charlie tilted his head, but did not quite look at her.

"Hello there," he said.

She looked him over and apparently approved of what she saw…she slid one stool closer.

"My name is Amber," she said.

"Charlie. You live around here?"

"Just passing through. Once I get enough money, I'm headed to LA."

"What's in LA?"

"Sunshine. Hollywood. A job. My sister works at an Olive Garden and she says she can get me on. Part time for now. They make about three bucks an hour, but they don't pool tips, so I can make some money. That will leave me time to do some auditions."

"Ah, you're an actress. What have you been in? Anything I've seen?"

She sighed and drained her drink.

"I'd rather not say."

Charlie rotated away from her a little. "That was a short conversation," he said.

She sipped her drink and let out a long, tired breath.

"Naked Zombie Girls of Canada."

Charlie rotated back toward her.

"I'm unfamiliar with that film."

"Not many people have seen it, but it played a couple of years on the triple-X circuit. You can order a DVD online. I did it because they offered me ten thousand dollars in cash."

"Now that I look at you more closely, you do have an actress chin."

She smiled.

"That's my best feature. Except for my boobs, of course. Any chance you could buy a girl a drink?"

"Sure," Charlie said. He gestured to the bartender.

"You ever dated an actress?"

Charlie laughed. "No, I don't think so."

"You should try it. It can be really good."

"What kind of money are we talking about?"

"A thousand a night for full service." Charlie rotated away from her. "But, I like you, so you can get a discount. My first boyfriend was a 'Charlie'. Five hundred."

"That's a lot of money."

"How about a hundred for an hour?"

"That's more like it. Do you have a place we can go?"

"I'm staying at the hotel next door. The hundred is in advance."

"Of course," Charlie said. He fished a bill out of the front pocket of his slacks and slid it over. In an instant, it was gone. "You go on ahead and get ready."

"Room 216," she said. She finished her drink and pushed the glass across the bar, then knocked twice on the bar.

Charlie assumed that meant she'd be back later to settle the bill.

"I'll be there."

She drained her drink and slid off her stool.

"See you in a few," she said.

Charlie and the bartender watched her leave. For the instant the door was open, bright light flooded the room.

Charlie returned his attention to his Snapple.

Without lifting his head, he said, "Anything I should know before I go over there?"

Ken Coffman

"You mean: like a boyfriend? She gets rid of him. He'll be here in ten minutes asking if I can break the hundred for a Budweiser—and argue about her bar bill. She slams them down pretty good."

Charlie laughed. He slid a twenty-dollar bill across the bar. "Keep him here a couple of hours if you can," he said.

The bartender pocketed the bill.

"Anything else?" Charlie said.

The bartended stared passively for a moment.

"I'd make sure to wear a condom if I was you," he said.

Charlie grinned and his even, white teeth glowed in the colorful, mirror-reflected neon lights of the beer decorations.

"I hear that," he said.

Charlie passed the boyfriend in the parking lot. He was thin—too thin—and wore jeans, a wrinkled t-shirt and a Vancouver Grizzlies baseball hat.

Meth.

There were only a couple of cars in the parking lot. Charlie, without moving his head much, glanced left and right looking for trouble. The sun hovered over the river and fields which seemed to stretch to the edge of the world. Nothing seemed awry. Two at a time, he skipped up the stairs and tapped on the door.

When she pulled the door open, he hit her in the face with the heel of his hand and pushed her onto the bed. He wrapped his hands around her neck. She struggled, but not much. In three minutes, she was dead.

How I love the element of surprise.

Topless, she wore orange panties. He jiggled her breasts. They were firm and full and reasonably symmetrical, but

204

nothing special. She had a small tattoo of a butterfly under her left hipbone.

A butterfly tattoo.

It was so common, it irritated him. He poked it with his finger. He realized he'd been doing it for a few minutes…and stopped. Already, her skin was pale and waxy…and he'd torn open a raw, oozing spot. He was acting a little compulsive—he recognized it and it worried him. It was something he needed to watch out for.

He wanted to break her ordinary, non-actress jaw, but squelched the impulse.

I must have discipline.

The idea of framing the boyfriend amused him. Ninety-nine percent of all murders and assaults were committed by the husband or boyfriend—maybe the cops would be lazy enough to arrest the meth head and look no further.

Unlikely, but possible.

He slid the closet door aside and unwound a wire hanger. He looked around for something to twist it with and decided on a hairbrush. He twirled the hairbrush until the wire bit into her neck. He found a baggie of small white pills in the dresser drawer. He scattered them on and around the body. He crammed a handful in her mouth, pressing them in until no more would fit. He recognized this also was compulsive. She was dead…she'd turn no more tricks and wouldn't have to work for three dollars an hour at the Olive Garden. His task was complete.

I should stop messing around.

He looked over the scene and arranged her legs so the view from the door was composed in a way that pleased him. It was a perfect pose for an X-rated film actress.

Then, he left. His car was parked around the bend of the river by the auto junkyard. He walked to it—seeing no one—and then drove away.

The boyfriend was drunk. He wanted to go back to the room and take some uppers, but as long as the bartender poured free shots of Jim Beam, he would not leave.

When he did finally get up, he staggered. He put the hundred dollar bill on the counter, but the bartender waved it away. "You're covered," he said.

"Did Amber give you a hummer? Is that why I'm drinking for free?"

"No, man. Don't worry about anything like that. You guys spend a lot here; I can cut you some slack."

"Man, I'm fucking polluted," the boyfriend said. "I thought you'd cut me off."

"You're not driving anywhere, are you?"

"You know my car blew out a radiator hose."

"That's why I didn't cut you off," the bartender said.

Back at the room, the boyfriend pounded on the door.

"Amber, let me in," he said. "I'm going to be sick."

Only silence came from the room. He slumped and rested his head on the door, and then vomited an oily mess onto the walkway. He wasn't sure how long he rested like that before struggling to his knees and fishing in his pocket for the room key. He got the door open and fell into the room...flat on his face.

That's where the cops found him, ninety minutes later, after one of the other motel customers had called 9-1-1.

Fairhaven

Jake Mosby

Nort looked up when the phone rang. He listened to Jake's half of the conversation.

"What? When? Where? Okay, I'm not doing anything, send a car," Jake said.

Nort poked his arm. "No, I'll drive you," he said.

Jake tilted the phone away from his ear.

"Stop poking me." Into the headset, he said: "Don't bother with the car...we'll be there in ten minutes."

He cradled the phone.

"You should try being less annoying," he told Nort.

Nort grinned and rattled the keys.

"Where to?" he said.

In the parking lot of the motel, Jake looked up. Petris waved from the second floor and leaned over the rail.

"Maybe the kid should stay in the car?" he suggested.

"Your call," Jake said to Nort. "Could be sloppy."

"I can handle it. I wanna see," Nort said.

They walked up the stairway and skirted two officers questioning a young man seated on the stairs. The young man was teary and blubbering.

"The boyfriend is very intoxicated," Petris said, "we're not getting anything useful from him. He was passed out in the doorway when the first officer arrived on the scene."

Jake looked into the room at the nearly naked body.

"She was just like that? The boyfriend didn't move her?" Jake said.

"That's what he said. I buy it," Petris said. "He's in pretty bad shape. Jim Beam."

207

Ken Coffman

"It looks like she was posed for a photograph."

"Yeah, but a fucked-up photo. Yeah, I see what you mean. You want to talk to the boyfriend?"

"No, but I'm curious…where was he drinking?"

"Their car is broke down. The motel manager verifies that. The kid was drinking around back at the Chinese restaurant. In the bar."

"Okay," Jake said. "We'll make sure his story checks out."

The bartender looked Nort up and down…then did it again.

"The kid's with me," Jake said.

"If you say so," the bartender said hesitantly.

"You heard about the murder next door?"

"Yeah. Amber. She's been in here quite a bit the last week or so. Pulls tricks and takes them back to her room."

"What's she give you for not running her off? Ten percent?"

The bartender picked up a glass, inspected it with intensity and then polished it with a white towel. He turned around and put it on the shelf behind the bar and adjusted it until it was lined up perfectly. He did not speak.

"I withdraw the question," Jake said. "You know what I need. Who was in here?"

"There was a guy."

"Let me take a guess. He wore a baseball hat and sunglasses and you didn't get a good look at his face."

The bartended walked to the cash register and picked up a sheet of paper. He placed it on the bar and smoothed it out.

"You made a sketch." Jake scratched an annoying pimple on his chin. "Not bad."

The bartender shrugged.

"Two years of art school gotta be worth something," he

208

said.

The picture was of a man's thin face covered with sunglasses and a floppy fisherman's hat pulled low on the forehead.

Jake pulled the police artist sketch from his jacket pocket and put it on the bar next to the bartender's sketch. With his huge, knotty hands, he rotated them.

The bartender nodded.

"That's the guy," he said.

"I was afraid of that," Jake said. "Look, you and I do not have a problem, but I don't want you to talk to reporters. In fact, I would prefer it if you didn't talk to anyone but me and the other cops. What do you think?"

The bartender drew in a deep breath and let it out slowly.

"I think we're communicating very effectively."

"Make a formal statement for the cops and then keep your mouth shut."

"Got it," the bartender said.

They walked back to the car. Jake waved up at Petris to get his attention.

"Send someone over to take a statement from the bartender."

"Sure," Petris said, "I'll take care of it myself. What's going on over there?"

"Fairhaven," Jake said.

"Crap," Petris said. "You're off?"

Jake nodded and waved goodbye.

"What are we doing, G-P?" Nort said.

"Drive," Jake replied.

On the way back to the bookstore, as they approached the

Lion's Park, Jake spoke.

"Pull over."

Nort nosed the car into a parking spot and they sat for a moment looking over the edge of the berm. On the other side of the river, kids played on a sandbar. Far overhead, a kite fluttered.

"What?" Nort said.

"Shut up and let me think for a minute."

They sat in silence. A seagull flew in and began working at a McDonald's bag.

"The thing that gets me is…he's not being careful."

"He wore a hat and dark glasses." Jake turned his head and glared. Nort continued. "You mean: like he wants to get caught?"

"No. Like we're nearing the end and it doesn't matter."

Bits of the paper bag were carried off by the wind. The seagull found a prize—a golden chicken nugget—and grabbed it with its beak. Another seagull floated in and tried to take it. The lucky seagull flew away leaving the marauder squawking and angry.

"You're carrying your weapon?"

"Yeah," Nort said. He fished around in his backpack.

"I don't need to see it," Jake said. "Don't be flashing it around. Just listen, you and Talon stay alert and watch out. Whatever Fairhaven has in mind for an endgame, I'm sure we're not going to like it. If you get the chance, don't even think. Shoot him in the head."

"Boom. Light's out."

Jake sighed.

"After what we've been through, we shouldn't even dream of such a happy ending," he said. "I'm afraid buckets of blood will be shed before this is over," Jake said.

Jake and Nort were in their little room at the police station. Jake was reading old reports selected at random from old case files stored in the banker's boxes piled up along the wall. Nort was playing with his laptop…updating his Facebook page. There was a tap at the door.

Greenberg.

Jake gestured for him to enter.

"I got your message," Greenberg said. "What's up?"

"I want to interview you as part of my internal investigation," Jake said.

A cloud of confusion drifted across Greenberg's face.

"Me? Why?"

"I don't believe in leaving any stone unturned. Even the big ones. You going to claim executive privilege?"

Greenberg considered.

"I suppose that would look bad. What brought this on? Are some of the cops talking trash about me behind my back?"

Jake ignored the question. "Let's talk about Ashley. You were eight when your three-year-old sister died—Nort worked the Google machine and the news accounts don't exactly line up with the official record."

Greenberg glanced at Nort. "I don't feel comfortable talking in front of the kid."

"Pretend he doesn't exist. That's what I do."

Greenberg sighed.

"Fine. Do you believe in ghosts, Mosby?"

"I consider that answer nonresponsive, counselor," Jake said.

Greenberg fished around his mouth with his index finger

and dislodged something—which he inspected carefully before wiping it on a handkerchief extracted from the inside pocket of his silk jacket. After a deliberate folding routine, he put the handkerchief away.

"What are you thinking? That I murdered my sister? That I'm a psychopath?"

"She had a broken neck *and* water in her lungs," Jake said. "That seems odd to me for a little girl drowning in a bathtub. The MI said the cause of death was indeterminate."

Greenberg sighed and leaned forward.

"Did the report say anything about my mother's *spells*?"

"Your father was in a hot Democratic primary campaign for a spot in Congress. Vermont is a long way from Washington State. In fact, about as far away as you can get."

"My sister came to me…after she died…and told me that mother had killed her."

"Now the tale turns into a ghost story. Excellent. Then your father pulled strings and the case was closed. The cops and the press buy the story that this was a terrible accident. The campaign motors on. In fact, he got the sympathy vote from a lot of women, didn't he? You could say it put him over the top. What did you think of that? I'll bet you didn't like it one bit."

"Mother was sick. Whatever happened, it wasn't her fault. She wasn't right in the head. She was ill—running her through the legal process would not bring Ashley back. What possible relevance could this have to what is happening in my police department?"

Jake leaned back in his chair and tapped his pencil against his front teeth.

"Ever put a firecracker in a fire-ant's nest? Then, once all of the ants are agitated, throw in a field mouse with a stone tied to its tail?"

Nort, with his head hidden behind the laptop's screen, snorted.

Both Jake and Greenberg shot him annoyed looks.

"No," Greenberg said.

"Neither have I, but that's the way I like to imagine my investigational style. I like to stir things up…the way people respond tells me everything I want to know."

"Tell yourself what you want, but it seems to me that maybe you just like torturing people."

"At my age, you take your fun wherever you can find it. For the first couple of years after college, you were a beat cop in Houston. You were involved when Malcolm Whittier clubbed a Chinese diplomat's son to death. Bennie Yu."

"That case is closed."

"I was good at internal investigations. Too good, probably. And, you know why? Because I don't give a shit who I piss off, who I offend and who I have to trample to get to the bottom of things. Once I understand the details, I don't really care anymore. Unless I decide you're a hazard to the public, I don't give two farts in the wind. I don't give three raindrops in a thunderstorm. I don't—"

"I get your point."

"Right. Where were we? A Chinese diplomat's son was beat to death outside a nightclub on Long Point Drive. This could have been an international incident. Maybe nuclear missiles start flying, you know? And you know what the interview transcripts say? Nothing. Not a fucking thing. Zippo. You guys clammed up tight and there was no case. No witnesses, no video, no testimony. That seem a bit convenient to you?"

"The kid, Bennie? He beat up a girl walking home from a movie night with her friends. Broke her jaw."

"And it turns out the girl is connected somehow? It had to be something like that. Right?"

Greenberg scratched his chin and leaned back in his chair. The silence stretched. For a minute, then more.

"She was just an innocent kid."

"Yeah. Do you think I'm stupid? *Somebody's* innocent kid."

"Can we say she was connected to oil money and leave it at that? A family with a couple of billion in the bank. Okay?"

"See how easy this is? Now I have the thread and I'm happy to move on so we can talk about Portland. You spent ten years on that force and moved up in a hurry. Beat cop to running a task force. Liaison to the FBI. Big doin's. Great headlines. The Mayor's golden Jew-cop. Very impressive."

"I wrote a book."

"I see that in the notes. *Managing the Modern Police Force.* I'm impressed. You probably sold fifty copies."

"The book was embraced by police academies and sold really well. I made enough money to buy a Mercedes. S Class. I worked hard and I got ahead."

"I see. And your success had nothing to do with the whitewash job when the Mayor was caught with his pants around his ankles at a glory-hole bar in the Pearl district. With video. Sweeping something like that under the rug must have been very, very hard work. Now you're here in the thriving metropolis of Mount Vernon."

"I am going to be mayor. That's a hundred grand a year, good benefits, a great pension program and a generous expense account. And I live in a wonderful part of the world.

It doesn't seem like a big mystery to me."

"Let me ask you something."

"Okay," Greenberg said.

"Eminent domain. Suppose the city wanted to tear down a downtown bookstore to build a parking lot. Where would you stand on a question like that if it crossed your desk?"

Greenberg adjusted the lapels of his suit jacket.

"I'd have to weigh all of the pluses and minuses, but as a statement of general principle?"

"Yeah."

"I'd be against such a dictatorial abuse of a citizen's private property rights."

Jake closed the file and pushed it aside.

"Thank you for your time," Jake said.

"And that's the end of my part in the internal investigation? I'm clean and clear? No more rectal exam?"

Jake grinned. "As a statement of general principle?"

Greenberg nodded.

"Yes," Jake said.

"What about the rest of the team? Anything look out of order?"

Jake shrugged. "Not yet. Spread the word that I want to see everyone. I'll let you know if I find anything out of bounds."

Ng poked her head in the door and looked at Jake, then at Greenberg, then at Nort, and then back at Jake again.

"I can come back later if this is an inconvenient time," she said.

Jake waved for her to continue. "We were just wrapping up," he said.

"The couple up-river? Beaten to death in the woods? We think we found the murder weapon."

Jake made a 'come-on' gesture with his gnarled hand to get her to say more.

"Bat. Baseball bat. An expensive one. It was in the river. No blood or prints, but it's beat up and matches up with what the MI says could have been used on the kids. It fits."

Jake closed the file folder and heaved himself up.

"I'll take a look."

He shook hands with Greenberg who ambled down the hallway.

Jake and Ng walked through the building...weaving in and out of offices and traveling down a long corridor to the evidence room. The DeMarini Vexxum bat lay on the counter wrapped in a clear plastic bag.

"Hey, I've seen bats like that," Nort said. "At Big 5 when I was checking out their skateboards."

Ng and Jake turned to look at him, and then exchanged a glance.

"I'll go check it out," Jake said.

Ng, noncommittal, shrugged.

The Big 5 was in a strip mall across a parking lot from a Fred Meyer store. Nort led the way inside and pointed to a display of bats high on the wall.

"See what I mean? There they are."

Jake studied them. A young clerk approached. Female.

"Can I help you, sir?" she said.

"Do you have a key to this case?" Jake said.

The girl shook her head. "Only the shift manager."

"I'd like to speak with the manager."

The manager was a young man, maybe twenty-five-years old. Jake frowned.

Why is everyone so goddamned young?

"Who would spend two-hundred bucks for a baseball bat?" he said.

"It's good for an extra five yards on a line drive," the manager said. "To some, that's worth the extra cashola."

"A bat like this…how many other places around here sell them?"

The manager shrugged. "Just us, as far as I know," he said. "I sold two to the same guy. He bought one, then came back and bought another one yesterday."

"Shit," Jake mumbled. "Yesterday?"

"Yeah," the manager replied.

Jake rubbed his temples, then brought out the police artist's sketch.

"That's the guy," the manager said.

"I was afraid of that," Jake replied. "Did you get a look at the car he was driving?"

"It was white, I remember that," the manager said.

"My sidekick is Nort," Jake explained. "He's going to look at your security video tapes—"

"Everything is on hard disk these days," the manager interrupted.

"You have cameras, I can see them. So, whatever the video is stored on, Nort will look them over and make a copy of the parts that have anything to do with this guy," Jake said while pointing a bony thick finger at the artist's sketch.

"That sounds really fucking boring," Nort protested.

"Welcome to police work," Jake responded.

Ken Coffman

17

Charlie Fairhaven

IN THE DINING room of his apartment, Charlie wrote on the cream-painted kitchenette wall with a large Sharpie indelible ink pen. He didn't care; the 'Do Not Disturb' sign was on the door so the maid would not come in. The end was near.

By the time my vandalism is discovered, the adventure will be over.

He tried to imagine the angry maintenance man—futilely painting and repainting—but he could not conjure the satisfying vision.

The last three days needed to be planned out in detail.

He drew a box and divided it into three columns.

In the first column: the fifty-four residents at the Wind in the Willows hospice. Then, for the next day, in the second column: the kids at the skateboard shop.

His hands itched for the shaft of the baseball bat.

Then, on the last day, his final act of compassion: releasing more five-hundred guests at Peaceful Meadows. He didn't want to count on surviving the skateboard shop murders, so he had rented a truck, bought service overalls at a thrift store and set up the situation at Peaceful Meadows. That task was finished. It was easy; the gas cylinders were in place. The timer was set. He was done.

Now there was only waiting for the final scene at the skateboard shop. He'd break their knees and watch them crawl around in circles—crying and begging for their lives. While the boy watched, he'd beat the girl to death. Her shapeless body would be the last image imprinted on the boy's eyes. He could see it—the blood and gore and the boy's helpless, pathetic death. The death of a powerless, cowardly punk kid pleading for mercy over the crushed body of his girl.

The old man's knees collapsing as he took in the dreadful horror of the scene. Wailing and beseeching God.

He realized he was writing on the wall—one word, over and over.

Kill.

It was hard to stop, but he put the pen down and stared at the wall. He had to be careful or compulsion would derail his plans. He needed composure and careful deliberation.

He turned on the TV and paged through the cable channels. Boring. He'd seen *The Silence of the Lambs* so many times, it was boring too. He shouldn't jeopardize his grand plan, but he was fidgety. He clicked off the TV and grabbed his car keys and the baseball bat.

No plan. Just do.

While darkness fell, he drove around the streets, but didn't see anything that excited him. A young couple, with arms draped around each other, necking at a bus stop. A two-hundred-pound twelve-year-old girl with the word PINK stretched across the seat of her sweat pants getting out of a van and waddling into a convenience store. An old guy wearing a

219

straw hat hunched over a cane and waiting for a crossing signal on Riverside.

Boring.

On impulse, he stopped at a grocery store and bought bottled water, a lap blanket, a bag of apples and a turkey sandwich. He wasn't really hungry, but the germ of a plan tickled the back of his mind.

He pulled the car next to dark spot by the railroad tracks near a carpet shop. He popped the trunk latch and waited until there was no traffic, then, leaving the keys in the ignition, moved to the back of the BMW. He made sure there was an inside latch release, watched for oncoming traffic, and then settled into the trunk, making himself as comfortable as possible with the blanket. He pulled the trunk lid closed, then ate an apple and waited.

What is wrong with people?

The car screamed: Steal me!

What is taking so long?

But, the car sat for over an hour before he heard Hispanic voices. A young couple.

The female voice.

"Come away from there, Oscar."

"This is a sweet ride...and the keys are in it."

"Leave it alone...you got enough trouble already. It's probably one of those bait cars. I saw it on TV."

"It's a Beemer. Come on. These things drive real sweet. You wanna walk you walk. You wanna ride, you ride. Makes up your mind, chavala."

"You already got a warrant," she complained. But Charlie heard it—the passenger door opened and the car settled on its shock absorbers as she got in. The car started up and idled smoothly. Charlie heard the servo motors whine when the kid adjusted the mirrors and the seat.

"Ah, seat warmers. Gravy," she said. "Where we goin'?"

"For a ride," Oscar said. "No more mouth, Rena, I gotta make a call. Shut your flapper and hand me a flamestick."

The car's Bluetooth system automatically detected and connected to Oscar's cell phone as the car filled with acrid smoke.

"Whoa, that's flash. A car that talks," she said.

"Shhh, I'm talking," Oscar said.

A man's voice on the phone. "Discount Auto."

"Viktor?"

"No, this is Dmitri. What's your business?"

"I don't got time for a pretzel party, Clyde. I need a chirp with Viktor."

"*Razbavljali*," Dmitry grumbled.

Donkey's piss.

The car's exhaust rumbled as Oscar pulled the car onto Riverside.

The next man's accent was less thick and syrupy.

"Viktor here."

"Hey, Viktor, I got a sweet autorama for you. Beemer, three-series, cherry."

"A thousand."

"Ah, Viktor, don't blarg me, I was thinking three-G's."

There was a moment of silence.

"Two if it gets here in one piece," Viktor said. "Pull it around back, but not too early. Midnight."

"Roger," Oscar said before pressing the button to disconnect the call.

"Cool, that gives us time to swig some shorties; then you

can take a ride on the beef thermometer."

Beef thermometer? What language do these people speak?

Charlie covered his nose with the blanket to filter the cigarette smoke.

"I'm riding the cotton pony," she said.

"Then you'll take it in the ham flower."

"When you talk like that, I don't think you love me."

"Oh, baby, you know you're my number one hoopy frood and always will be," he said. "Let's hit the ATM so you can capital me."

"I need my money for rent."

"You heard Viktor. At midnight, we're going to be max flushed. Don't chizzle the evening when we want to get our party on."

From his cozy cocoon, Charlie listened as the car idled while Rena operated the ATM.

After she got back in, Oscar complained.

"I told you to get me a hundred, chimmy."

"I can't spare no hundred. Twenty is enough to get us to midnight."

Their next stop was at a convenience store—Charlie could hear cars pulling in and out and people with heavy accents yelling greetings to each other. The kids waited around until they found someone to go in and buy malt liquor for them.

"Give me all the change and I'll cut you back a fiver, got it?"

After a few minutes, Oscar yelled.

"Hey!"

He ran off and Charlie listened to a remote altercation of some kind. The Oscar returned with bottles clinking.

"Fucker tried to take us down," he said. He started the car. "Now we can find a quiet place to get our kinky lit up."

222

Charlie tried to imagine what they looked like. Her voice was squeaky and she was heavy—she was slow to heave herself out and the car's shock absorbers complained when she got in and out. The boy was lighter—Charlie imagined black hair, tattoos and scars.

They drove and drove, finally, after several sweeping corners, arrived.

But, where?

Charlie could hear wind whistling, but over the throbbing stereo system, he could not hear what they talked about.

He considered that a relief.

All he could hear were clothes rustling, Rena giggling and the car rhythmically swaying on its springs. Charlie thought about letting them finish, but grew impatient. He worked the latch and got out of the trunk as quietly as he could manage. The fresh, swirling air was cool on his skin. He drank it into his lungs to clear out stale air and cigarette smoke.

They were high on a rocky peak looking over the Skagit Valley. Headlights from the I-5 streamed by. Burlington and Mount Vernon city lights flickered and flashed. Overhead, lights on a cell phone antenna tower blinked. He spent a moment drinking in the view and enjoying the feel of cool air on his skin, then leaned back into the trunk to get his bat.

He peeked in the driver's window, but could not see much through the tinted windows. He rapped on the door and stood back.

After some thrashing around, Oscar came out blinking in the dim light like an owl. The kid looked nothing like Charlie imagined. He was very young for one thing, barely fifteen or so, and tiny. Thin and slight of build—dressed in a white suit with a silver necktie. Long, black hair pulled back in a ponytail.

He had a huge gap between his front teeth. Red Converse sneakers. Nothing pierced. No tattoos. A large gold cross suspended on a thin silver chain hung around his neck.

He had a huge black revolver held loosely in his right hand—which made it awkward for him while zipping up his trousers.

Charlie smiled.

"WTF?" Oscar said. "You know who you're playing with?"

"Excuse me, sir," Charlie said. "Did you see the sign? We do neighborhood patrols up here to keep kids from parking and making bastard babies."

"Sign? There ain't no sign. My family owns half of this valley. Fuck off."

Charlie wound up—put his shoulder into it—and mashed in Oscar's face. Oscar lifted six inches off the ground and sprawled backward over the hood of the car and twitched. Charlie thought about hitting him again, but the effort would be wasted.

Oscar's body had not received the full message, but he was dead. His face was creased across the middle...nearly folded in on itself. Hamburger. Something glittered in the blood. Charlie looked closer. A silver tooth.

That's disturbing.

He turned his attention to the girl. She sat as if frozen, then fumbled with pulling her bra over her substantial breasts and buttoning her blouse. Charlie picked up the revolver from where it had fallen in the crushed gravel.

"Relax, young lady," he said while settling into the driver's seat. He dropped the gun on his lap. "I'm not going to hurt you."

He started the car and put it in reverse. With a quick lurch, the car slipped from under Oscar's body. By backing and forthing, Charlie worked the car around and back on the paved road. They slowly descended down the steep road.

"I have a high level of curiosity about the Russians Oscar talked to on the phone. Once you show me where they are, I will let you go. Okay?"

Wide-eyed, Rena nodded.

"Okay," she said through chattering teeth. "But, I think they're actually Ukrainians."

"What's the difference?"

"I don't know," Rena said.

They parked on a dark stretch of road along the railroad tracks. Heaps of rusty, mangled machinery were piled around a scrap metal recycling facility. A little farther down, behind a chain link fence topped with razor wire, a gate rode on large rubber wheels. Before pulling around back, they'd first made a slow pass around front.

Valley Discount Auto.

Reliable pre-owned cars.

Your job is your credit.

Low monthly payments.

90 day warranty.

Charlie turned to Rena. She was biting her lower lip and nervously wringing her hands on her lap.

"You killed Oscar," she whispered.

"You're been here before. How do they do it?"

"I followed Oscar in my car. He pulls up the gate and honks. They let him drive in and he comes out with cash. That's all I know. You said you'd let me go."

"You want to live? Really?" She nodded. He glanced at her

breasts. Her blouse was buttoned wrong...her bra and flesh were visible in a big gap. "Give me a kiss on the cheek and thank me for your life."

She leaned over. He turned and captured her kiss on his lips.

Her plump lips were greasy with smeary gloss.

Her breath smelled like fish.

He pulled away.

His body was flooded with warm hormones. Desire. It disgusted him. He could do it...he could fill this inconsequential girl with his seed. He could imagine it—working over her fat body and pumping away like a mindless farm animal.

His penis stirred.

He hated himself for being so programmed. He hated the instinctual, automatic response of his body.

"Let's..."

"Thank you for my life," she interrupted. "I'm scared of you," she said.

He picked up the gun and squeezed the grip as hard as he could.

"Go on," he said. "Vamoose. Don't talk to the cops for a while and I'll leave you alone. Got it?"

"Thank you, sir."

She opened the door and slowly walked away. When she got to the main road, she started running.

Charlie laughed at the sight of her awkwardness—trying to run in three-inch high heels. CMFM[4] heels.

Stupid girls.

---

[4] Catch Me, Fuck Me

Fairhaven

He didn't know what was going on…he felt as if his soul was twitching inside his skin. As if, if he didn't hang onto the gun tightly, he'd lose himself…his essence, under high pressure, would spray out and fly away. He wouldn't be *here* anymore. He wouldn't be anywhere.

This is no good. It's better when I feel nothing.

He put the car in gear and pulled forward with gravel crunching under the car's tires. On the gate, there were large metal signs with lurid red printing.

Private Property

No Trespassing.

Guard Dogs on Duty

Charlie tooted on the horn. Overhead, bright lights flickered and illuminated the yard with brutal harshness. The gate opened to reveal scattered automobile carcasses and engine parts. There was barely room to pull the car in.

Carefully, Charlie eased forward.

A man dressed in greasy overalls peered into the headlights and held up an oil-black palm.

Stop.

Charlie felt an impulse to floor the accelerator and crush the man, but he held back.

The man gestured for Charlie to get out of the car.

Charlie tucked the pistol into his belt and reached into the back seat for the bat.

Charlie grinned.

This will be fun.

Massive brown dogs strained at heavy chains. Eerily, they did not bark. Their claws scratched at raw concrete.

He got out of the car and stretched his back.

Big hands reached around him and grabbed the bat and the

pistol…then shoved him forward.

"Hey," he said as a knot tied up his intestines.

He felt naked without the bat.

The man behind him poked him in the back to urge him forward. Only inches out of reach of the slavering dogs, they walked along a gravel-strewn path to a battered metal door. The man in front opened it and, with a gappy smile under a black mustache, waved Charlie through.

A man sat behind a massive wooden desk. The desk was covered with scraps of paper with gleaming engine parts as paperweights. His face had a look of mild curiosity.

"He's driving a nice car."

Charlie glanced at the man who had spoken. A cigarette hung from his lip. His face was pockmarked with acne scars.

A sudden realization flooded Charlie's body.

I want to live.

I really do.

It was a surprise…something he never realized before…an answer to a question he never thought of asking. He was scared.

The man behind the desk spoke.

"What's your business?"

Charlie considered the proper response.

"You're Viktor?"

From behind, another man came in and put a bundle of papers on the desk. Viktor looked the papers over and chuckled. His chuckle was low-pitched and deep…seismic.

"The car is yours? The title is free and clear?" Charlie nodded. "Let's start by you signing it over. Don't worry about the mileage or sales price; we'll fill that part in later. Right, Dmitri?"

Dmitri laughed. "That's right, boss," he said. "We'll fill in the details later."

Viktor lifted a sheaf of papers and found a pen. He pushed it over.

"I just bought that car," Charlie said.

He didn't see how the message was communicated, but the man to his right swung his arm sideways and—back handed—hit Charlie in the stomach. The blow was not hard, but Charlie doubled over and gasped for breath.

"That wasn't necessary," Charlie said, after a minute of wheezing. "I'll sign."

He picked up the pen. Dmitri pointed with a dirty finger. Charlie signed. Viktor reached over and picked up the car's title. After glancing at it, he dropped it into an overflowing basket.

"I'm a reasonable man," Viktor said. I don't want you to have to walk home." To Dmitri, he said, "We still got that Ford Country Squire?" Dmitri grinned and nodded. "Grab the keys, will you?"

Dmitri walked off.

"Fair warning, it gets about three miles per gallon. I suggest you fill it up at the first gas station you see. And the next one too, probably." He looked at Charlie with intensity. "That was a joke."

A pained look spread across Charlie's face as he tried to smile.

"And a good one too," Charlie said.

"I don't do business with people I don't know," Viktor said.

"I understand, sir," Charlie said.

"I'm not sure if you do," Viktor said. He glanced at the man at Charlie's side and nodded—a small, barely perceptible gesture. The man balled up a fist and hit Charlie's stomach again.

"Call ahead the next time you come for a visit," Viktor said.

Tears cascaded down Charlie's face and he barely avoided vomiting.

"Yes, sir," he said when he was able to speak again.

With a thick finger, Viktor pointed at the door.

The man took Charlie's arm and tugged him along. They walked though a rundown front office and into the car lot.

A massive white Ford station wagon with a leaky, rumbling exhaust idled roughly in front of the doorway.

Dmitri held the driver's side door open and gestured to Charlie.

"Come back and see us again real soon," he said. A man at the doorway tossed the bat over the car—Dmitri grabbed it out of the air with grace and handed it to Charlie. "Here's your bat."

Charlie leaned the bat on the passenger seat while another man dropped the chain—decorated with colorful plastic flags—blocking the main entrance at the car lot's entrance.

With gritted teeth, Charlie drove away.

The gas gauge was hugging E and the yellow low fuel warning light was flashing. He stopped at the Arco by Costco and watched the numbers on the gas pump as he filled up the tank.

$84.58

He decided to check the oil…it was a quart low. That was another four bucks. A tire was soft, so he dropped quarters in the air machine and filled it.

He wanted to thrash the monstrous car with the bat, but, even at one o'clock in the morning, there were a few people around…beating on the god-awful car would draw attention.

Fairhaven

Attention he did not want.

Yet.

The car was shameful. An embarrassment.

I could leave the keys in it for a week in the worst section of town and no one would touch it.

While fighting the steering wheel on the freeway—the car pulled hard to the right and shook hard in the front end like it was going to fly apart—he thought about the Russians.

He corrected himself.

The Ukrainians.

Goddamn it, who are these people? Where do they come from? Why are they here?

He thought about going up the highway to the gun shop and buying one of everything…with cases of ammunition. Properly prepared, he could return to the car lot and teach those people a lesson in civility.

He could visualize the carnage.

He could smell the cordite smoke in the air.

But, thinking of the stolid, impassive stubbornness etched into Viktor's broad Slavic face, Charlie decided it would not be worth the trouble.

Even with an arsenal, I'd surely get hurt.

Or be killed.

He pressed a fist into his aching belly.

Who are these people?

Jake Mosby

Jake looked around the skateboard shop. It was not busy, but there were four young punks looking at boards while one, wearing a helmet and knee and elbow pads, noisily rolled back and forth on a large curved ramp. While Jake watched, the kid lost the board and sprawled face-first across the ramp.

"I'm okay," the kid said, grinning.

Jake shook his head and continued walking through the store.

Talon was behind the register. Her spiky hair had hennaed tips and she wore pukey green eyeglasses. She looked like a cartoon.

"Hey, Jake. I don't think I've seen you in here before. Come to say hello to your money?"

"Goodbye is probably more accurate," he said. "Sell any of this shit today?"

She poked at keys on the cash register.

$111.84

"Some. We figure we have to pull in an average of one-fifty a day to break even. We grossed over five hundred on Saturday, but the margin was small because of the grand opening discount."

Jake was speechless. He looked at Talon as if he'd never seen her before. The medallion on a heavy chain around her neck looked as big as a hubcap.

Is this what the next generation of capitalist swine looks like?

"Nort around?"

She hooked a thumb over her shoulder.

"Check out back. He's supposed to be upstairs studying, but I think he's bullshitting with Bill in the shop."

Jake waved goodbye, but she'd already turned her attention to a young man buying a chrome wing nut for a quarter.

Jake pushed through the swinging doors to the workshop area. Nort sat on a stool talking to Bill, who was working on the rear wheel gears of an old bicycle.

"Hey, Jake. Bill was telling me about when he watched Eric Dressen pulling three-foot Ollies at the Glendale skate park back in the day."

"I'm sure I'd find it fascinating if I had the slightest clue what you were talking about."

"An Ollie is when you jump…"

"Stop," Jake said, with a pained look on his floppy face. "I really don't give a watery shit. Give me the car keys."

"Where are we going? I'll drive."

"You're supposed to be studying."

"I'm a week ahead, so don't worry about it." To Bill, he said, "Catch you later."

They walked out the back and around the building to where the Buick waited under the carport.

"How's Bill working out?" Jake said.

"He's cool. If it has wheels, he can fix it. If he still has anger-management issues, I haven't seen it yet. What's up?"

"Ng called. They found the BMW at a used car lot."

"Hmm," Nort said. "Good thing I found that Big 5 parking lot video, eh?"

"Yeah, I guess."

Guided by Jake, Nort drove the car across the river and immediately turned right. They drove by soccer fields and pulled into the car lot. Ng was talking to a huge man. Jake walked up them.

"Who owns this place?" Jake asked.

The giant looked Jake over, then glanced at Nort who walked up from the car.

"I do," he said.

"I don't think so," Jake replied.

"Fuck you," he said.

To Ng, Jake said, "Seems like a nice-enough guy."

He walked to the front of the office—a converted mobile home with a huge rainbow-colored awning. He went through the open space and pushed through the door at the back. Inside, Viktor sat in an office chair with his feet on the desk. In the guest chair sat a man wearing dirty overalls.

"Private," Viktor said.

Jake pointed at the man in visitor's chair.

"Take a hike, pal."

Slowly, the man rose and wandered out the back door.

Viktor took in Jake's black suit and tie.

"Another decade or so and that suit will be back in fashion."

"I'm glad to hear that," Jake said, "since I plan to be buried in it. What's your name?"

The man considered.

"Viktor Suvorov. What do you want?"

"I want to talk about the white BMW. Where'd you get it?"

"I know my accent can be a problem, so I'll speak slow. Go. Fuck. Yourself."

Nort smiled and leaned against the doorway—waiting to see how Jake would handle this.

Viktor's face had a stormy expression.

"What are you grinning about, boyo? I'll gut and filet you."

"You'd be doing me a solid," Jake said. "My grandson specializes in being an annoying twit." He chewed on a piece of dead skin on his thumb. "You probably have a bottle of vodka in your drawer."

"Maybe."

"You don't want to be reminded of your manners by an ugly American."

Fairhaven

They sat in silence until Viktor made up his mind. He reached into his desk drawer and pulled out a bottle of *Dovgan Admiralskaya* and three small water glasses.

"None for me, thank you," Nort said. "I don't drink."

Viktor poured an inch in each glass. "Drink or walk," Viktor said. He looked deeply into Jake's eyes and said, "*Za milyh dam.*"

"Yeah," Jake said, staring back. "To lovely ladies."

They tapped their glasses on the desk, and then drained them. Nort picked up his glass, looked at it for a few seconds, then tossed it back. His eyes watered, but he did not cough.

Viktor gestured with the bottle and Jake nodded. Viktor poured an inch and a half. Nort held onto his glass and got nothing. Viktor ignored him. The men sipped.

"I don't care about cars or car parts or anything else that goes on around here. All I care about is the guy that used to own that BMW." He flicked a finger at Nort. Nort handed Viktor the folder he carried around.

Viktor flipped the folder open and looked through the photographs of the crime scene. He glanced at, but did not study the broken bodies of the young couple.

"Ugly mess," Viktor said. "That's not our work."

Jake pulled Charlie's photograph from his jacket's inside pocket.

"Is this the BMW guy?"

"Yes," Viktor said. "He carried an aluminum baseball bat. I thought he was a weak horse. A coward. How do you say it? A pussy."

"They often are," Jake said. "Tell me everything you know and I'll make sure the cops don't impound the vehicle."

Viktor held out the bottle.

Jake responded by holding his thumb and index finger a half inch apart. Viktor poured a splash, then screwed the cap back on and slipped it in his desk drawer.

"Deal," Viktor said. "We were in the middle of a round of *durak* when this guy," Viktor tapped a heavy finger on Charlie's photograph, "pulled up to the back gate and honked."

Fairhaven

18

Charlie Fairhaven

THE NEXT MORNING, after a few hours of troubled sleep haunted by dreams of dogs and large men with thick accents, Charlie drove the car to an auto junkyard out by Woodinville. He climbed the stairs to the ramshackle office and dropped the key and title on the counter.

The clerk was tall and very thin...skeletal. A quarter-inch of stubble decorated his gaunt face. Shiny, golden Calvary cross earrings dangled from both ears. He looked at the title, and then walked over to look at the parking lot through a dirty window.

When he came back, he said, "There's a fifty dollar fee for taking in pig-iron relics like that."

"It runs. I drove it here. Take it for free, I don't want anything for it."

"Give me fifty dollars or drive that piece of shit somewhere else."

Charlie was angry.

Furious.

He wanted to wrap his hands around the man's skinny

neck and strangle him, but people were wandering around the junkyard carrying greasy car parts. People were strolling through the parking lot. There were too many of them.

He couldn't kill them all.

Plus, the idea of using the lumbering Ford as a getaway car filled him with revulsion. The thought of going back to Discount Auto and offing to buy back the BMW briefly crossed him mind…along with a flood of shame that flooded though his body.

No.

He'd had enough of the Ukrainians.

He carried his money in an envelope…and the envelope was a lot thinner than when he'd filled it at the bank. He pulled out a fifty dollar bill and smoothed it out on the counter.

After glancing at the envelope, the clerk spoke.

"Need a car? We have some real good, reliable ones."

"No, thanks," Charlie said. "I'll walk."

On the busy Highway 9, Charlie, buffeted by traffic and pulling up his collar against a stiff, cool breeze, walked north. He didn't have a plan, but noticed the signs for the auto auction:

Next auction: 5:00 Today.

He walked though a gate and into the office. A young man leaned against the counter and paged through an *Auto Trader* magazine. He didn't bother to look up at the sound of the jingling bells.

"Closed," he said. "Dealers get an early look at four."

"I need a car and I have cash."

The kid sighed and closed his magazine.

"You got a dealer's license? We don't sell anything to the

public. This is a *wholesale* auction."

"I have cash and I'm not walking out of here without a car, so quit arguing."

The kid glanced at his watch.

"Give me five hundred bucks in cash and we'll go out in the lot and take a look, okay?"

"Five hundred? For what?"

"For my commission. For pencil-whipping the paperwork and running it under the boss's nose."

"Do you know Viktor from Discount Auto up in Burlington?"

"Sure, his guys buy cars here all the time. Why? You know him?"

"We've done some business together."

"Big whoop. It's still five hundred. And, I said cash, didn't I? Pay or toddle off. Make up your mind."

Charlie gritted his teeth and reached for the envelope. He spread hundred-dollar bills on the counter.

"Okay," Charlie said.

The kid pulled a clipboard from a nail pounded in the wall.

"Right this way," he said.

Cars were parked nose-to-tail in the lot.

"Pick a car at the front of the line," the kid said. "I'm not moving anything for you." Charlie stopped to look at a Mercedes sedan. "Your best bet is one of the Japanese cars. That naziwagon has three hundred and fifty thousand miles on it, but it's your call. You got to have it, you got it."

Charlie walked farther up the line. The only Japanese car was a blue Toyota pickup with tinted windows and mud flaps.

"L4 engine," the kid said. "Keep oil in it and it will run

forever. You okay with a stick shift? Every week the Mexicans come in to buy these things…they don't hang around long when we get them."

"Where'd it come from?"

The kid looked disgusted. "My grandmother traded it in. She only drove it back and forth to church at Easter, that's why it has seven hundred miles on it. We dealing or what?"

"How much?"

The kid paged through the papers on the clipboard.

"Eight, no, ten grand. Cash, of course, did I already say that? You pay cash and I never see the car again, got it? No warranty stated or implied. Drive off and I don't see you again. Cool beans?"

Frustrated, Charlie kicked the truck's tire.

"Fine," he said.

The kid grinned. "I'll pull it around front."

He revved up the engine and sprayed gravel.

Dejected, Charlie walked back to the office. He counted out the money and put the stack of bills on the counter. The envelope, once filled with a thick wad of bills, was nearly empty. He thumbed through it. A couple of hundred dollars left—that was all.

Shit.

The kid counted the money, and then counted it again.

"Okay, now for the paperwork."

Charlie grabbed the keys.

"You fill out the paperwork. I don't care."

My entire life savings—gone in a couple of days. And, I'm now driving an old Toyota pickup with mud flaps. Girls were not going to be impressed with this bucket of bolts.

The beautiful BMW was gone.

Fairhaven

Charlie waited for a gap in traffic so he could make a left turn and head north.

Life fucking sucks. Everyone has a hand in my pocket and is trying to screw me.

Maybe I'm not a winner. Maybe I'm a loser.

Jake Mosby

Despite, or perhaps, encouraged by Jake's sighing and firing aggravated looks across the table, Nort chewed Corn Nuts with enthusiasm. The crunching sound was loud in the quiet room. He also slurped noisily from a can of Diet Pepsi. Jake gave up on trying to read a case file. He closed the file and pushed it into the middle of the table.

"I don't see how you could be any more annoying," Jake said.

"What are you talking about?" Nort replied around a mouthful of mashed Corn Nuts. "Who are we seeing next?

Jake looked at his notepad.

"Sergeant James Howard."

Nort leaned back in his chair and scratched his close-cropped head.

"I know that name. He's the main murder guy."

Jake looked annoyed. "He's one of the Sergeants in criminal investigations…crimes against persons."

"That's what I said."

There was a knock at the door. Without looking up, Jake said loudly, "Come in."

Sergeant Howard was a small man with very black hair; he was furry like a little bear. He peeked at the world through small glasses with wire-rim frames and wore a crisply pressed, dark blue uniform with a necktie and silver pins in the collar.

"You look like a TV cop, not a real cop," Nort said.

"Knock it off, Nort," Jake said. "You'll have to excuse him," he said to Sergeant Howard, "the kid is an idiot."

"Okay," Sergeant Howard said. "I heard about him being with you all the time and wondered about the appropriateness of it."

"*Appropriateness* is the very least of his problems," Jake said. He gestured to a chair. Sergeant Howard sat down. "I've been looking at your file, Jimmy. Do you mind if I call you Jimmy?"

"I go by James."

"Great, Jimmy. You've been doing some good work for the department. Working on alternative security correction programs for non-violent, non-predatory offenders, for example."

"If the offender is unimpulsive and non-violent, then they take up valuable corrections space and resources. In the tax-payers' interest, we have to prioritize."

"Can't jail all the fuckwads, am I right?"

Sergeant Howard shifted uncomfortably in his seat.

"We have to be accountable to the stakeholders in our community," he said. "If a perpetrator is a hazard, then the community deserves protection, otherwise we're misapplying our resources. We have a variety of tools at our disposal, including alternatives to incarceration like work release programs, electric home monitoring, work programs, drug court and mental health court."

"I have a question," Nort said. Jake looked disgusted, but did not speak. "Are you a robot?" Nort asked.

"I have a more relevant question," Jake said. "What's a multi-purpose police vehicle?"

"Armored vehicle. SWAT truck."

"Ah," Jake said. "I suppose you have bright ideas for the future of police work…"

"Yes, of course. We can take advantage of advancing technology with increased installation and networking of surveillance cameras, computerized image processing, thermal imagers, night vision scopes, intoximeters installed in private and commercial vehicles, data collected from banks and supermarkets, DNA collection and analysis—"

Jake held out a hand to stop him.

"I get it. It's a brave new world. Say no more. How'd your 'alternative to incarceration' work out with Abdul Abdullah when he ran off from work release and raped that girl in the Skagit College parking lot?"

"There will be problems with any system, but overall the programs work. Please don't throw the baby out with the bathwater."

"I don't like your progressive ideas, Jimmy, so I'm going to write my report for Greenberg and suggest you be fired immediately and sued for your last penny. I don't like cops who sexually harass the ladies, who fix tickets in exchange for sexual favors and who take advantage of scared young innocent women and make them perform nasty, disgusting blowjobs in dark alleys."

Sergeant Howard's face went white and he sputtered. "What? You're mixing me up with Sprague." His voice faded out. "Crap, I didn't mean to say that. I can't believe this. You played me."

Jake grinned. "Pardon me?" he said. "I think that will be all, Sergeant."

Sergeant Howard stood and looked down at Jake for a

moment. He opened his mouth to speak, but didn't say anything.

"Despite a bizarre affinity for electronic gadgets, you're a good man. We don't have any problems—don't worry about my report," Jake said cheerfully. "Have a great day."

Sergeant Howard adjusted the knot in his necktie and pulled at the cuffs of his shirt, and then nodded.

"They warned me you are an asshole and they were right. Good day, sir," he said.

After Sergeant Howard left, Nort chortled.

"That was good, G-P."

"I'm old. I didn't catch what he said."

"Sprague." Nort pulled an org chart from the folder he carried around and pointed to a box. "Officer Sprague, patrol division. That should be a fun conversation." He stood. "I'm going to run down the hall to the machine and get another soda. You want something?"

"No," Jake said. "I'm good."

19

Charlie Fairhaven

THE WIND IN the Willows Retirement Center. He'd been assigned there several times and he knew the layout and he knew the clients—most were bed-ridden and immobile, but they always had a few terminal stage cancer victims who, though they only had a month or so left on earth, were still in reasonable health. If they took opiates for pain, they seemed almost normal.

I'll have to kill them first. Quickly.

Then I can take my time with the bed-ridden remainder.

He drew the L-shaped layout on the wall of his apartment and, after studying the roster, marked with a red pen the rooms he'd visit first. The night staff was a desk clerk, a security guard and the roving nurse practitioner—the job Charlie generally did.

He would park down the street under some trees, take the path that skirted the security cameras in the parking lot and led to the back door, and grab the N-P when he came out of the back door for a smoke.

Filthy habit.

Strangle him. Then he'd hide in the utility closet and grab the security guard after he passed...strangle him too.

The girl at the desk would be watching recorded daytime dramas. He'd walk right up, whip out the bat and kill her. One blow. If that was not enough, she would be stunned, so he could come back later and finish her off.

Time would be of the essence.

He'd unplug all of the security equipment to disable the evil little prying security camera eyes that were everywhere.

Then, take care of the ones who were mobile...

Room 7 for Bob Chapman. Pancreatic cancer. Then Room 18 for Roger Wales. Prostrate cancer. Then Patricia Anderton, wheezing on an oxygen bottle. Lung cancer. Then start with Room 1 and work his way around the building.

He retraced the path with the pen. Car, back door, utility closet. The wall was sodden with ink. The pen tore through into the underlying drywall, but he couldn't stop. Car, back door, utility closet.

The wall was a horrible mess. He couldn't stop.

The doorbell rang. He dropped the pen and froze. The bell sounded again.

He peeked through the peephole. It was an older man with a long, gray beard who wore a green hat adorned with colorful pins.

VFW.

"I know you're home, I can hear you," the man said.

Charlie opened the door against the chain.

"I bought a poppy at the mall," he said.

"Never can have too many Buddy Poppies," the man said. "Even a quarter will help, brother."

"I'm poor. Go away."

Fairhaven

"You can spare a quarter." The man began to sing—his voice was incongruously deep and sonorous.

In Flanders Fields the poppies blow,
Between the crosses, row on row... [5]

Charlie glanced at the bat leaning behind the door.
"Okay." He grinned. "Let me get the chain." He closed the door and released the security chain, then opened the door again. "Come in and I'll see what I can find."

"No, sir, we never enter a house. Against our rules. I'll wait out here. If you have a dollar...that would be better than a quarter."

---

[5] **In Flander's Field**
by John McCrae
In Flanders Fields the poppies blow,
Between the crosses, row on row,
That mark our place; and in the sky,
The larks, still bravely singing, fly,
Scarce heard amid the guns below.
We are the dead.
Short days ago,
We lived, felt dawn, saw sunset glow,
Loved and were loved and now we lie,
In Flanders Fields.
Take up our quarrel with the foe
To you, from failing hands, we throw,
The torch, be yours to hold it high.
If ye break faith with us, who die,
We shall not sleep, though poppies grow,
In Flanders Fields.

Ken Coffman

This would be a perfect time for you to die.

I need this.

Come in.

Charlie grinned. "That's perfectly understandable, sir. Let me see what I have. Are you sure you won't come in? We can bend the rules. Have a cold drink? I'm sure going from door to door is thirsty work."

The man reached around his back and proffered a battered canteen.

"I carry my canteen everywhere I go. Look at this crease. Cong bullet, Khe Sanh, 1968. It saved my ass. Get it? It was on my hip, you see. Are you sure you can't spare five dollars to support disabled veteran's programs?"

Charlie ground his teeth together. He reached for his wallet, then changed his mind and fished around in his front pocket. He sorted through change and found a quarter—which he offered.

The man looked at the quarter, then at Charlie. A wide smile drifted slowly across his face.

"God bless you, sir. That's very kind of you." He took the quarter and handed over a poppy, then stood up straight and snapped off a salute. "Have a great day."

Charlie stood and watched the man move to the next doorway. His hands itched to pick up the bat, but he closed the door instead.

Killing someone, anyone, would make him feel better, but he had a sour taste in his mouth from his last ventures. The bitter taste of humiliation.

The Ukrainians. The man at the auto junkyard. The kid at the auto auction.

Why are they still breathing?

248

He turned to the wall. It was a ruination of indelible ink scrawls and gouges, but he could still see the plan.

Wind in the Willows.

The kids at the skateboard shop.

Peaceful Meadows.

The old man would be powerless as he watched the legal circus show from the courtroom.

He sat down and turned on the TV. Then turned it off.

He needed to calm down…stick to the plan. He needed to stay home and play it cool until the deep, dark dead of the night. Outside, the wind drove the rain nearly horizontal. It was cold and wet…a perfect time to stay indoors…to rest and get ready.

He grabbed his coat and hat…and the keys to his truck.

Jake Mosby

Jake walked out the back door of the bookstore and marched west across the parking lot to the boardwalk by the river. Talon, standing in the front doorway of the skateboard shop, waved. Half-heartedly, he waved back. After reaching the river, he leaned against the railing and watched the deep green water flow past. A log drifted by with a seagull perched on it.

Maureen came up from behind him and put a hand on his shoulder.

"What's wrong, Jake" she said. "Are you depressed?"

"I don't know what the hell I'm doing," he said. They stood and watched the river for a few minutes. "After Roger Thompson shot me, I was here. Did you know that? I spent two months in the hospital up the hill and some afternoons I'd walk down here. One day—I remember this very vividly—I stood right over there," he gestured down the river, "and it was the first day in months when I was not in pain. After all the shit I'd been through…the rehab, the muscles and tendons finally mending, the reporters, the girl's grieving parents, the investigation and the bullet fragments still in my body and the doctors putting me back together…after all of that…it was a perfect, stunning day. The air was crisp and warm and clean. Across the river, kids laughed and chased each other around the playground. The sun poured through the drifting clouds and the world looked like a perfect picture postcard or an amazing, vibrant watercolor painted by a master. And I remember thinking…what if the reason for all of the pain and bullshit and despair was so that when the universe aligned perfectly and we got brief glimpse of heaven on earth…I mean, what if all the horror and nonsense thrown at us in life had only one purpose…so when we caught a sideways, reflected, obscured peek at paradise, we'd take it in. So it wouldn't slide right by—taken for granted and unnoticed. What if disease and war and God's random acts of cruelty exist only to make sure we notice when the harmony of the cosmos is unveiled for a brief instant."

"That's kind of heavy for me, Jake. I don't know anything about any of it."

"I heard something behind me and when I turned, a seagull had dropped a huge gleaming oyster of steaming shit on the shiny hood of a beautiful blue, metal flake Corvette. It was like God saying…you had your look…and that's all you get. Get back in the shit."

Nervously, Maureen looked up into the sky.

"Are there a lot of seagulls around here? I don't see any. You want to see a lot of seagulls? Go to San Francisco…the

Fairhaven

Fisherman's Wharf. They're all over the place down there."

"As I get older, it's not a matter of knowing what I'm doing or getting things right…it seems to me that success is a matter of fooling people for just a little while longer while my body decays and my mind packs up and leaves town. A day of triumph is another day of concealing my dysfunction…giving a final, last-gasp illusion of competence before it's obvious to the most casual observer that there's nothing left of the man I used to be. That I'm worn out, used up, and very nearly done. But I can, perhaps, deceive people one more day and that's as good as it gets."

"So? You think you're the only one in that sinking boat? Forget about it. Look at me. Without flab, there wouldn't be anything left of me. And my brain never worked like yours, even when I was young. That's what we talked about at the station all these years ago. How smart you were. Crazy-smart. Rocket-science smart. So, forget about it. Besides, I don't care how dark the world looks, I'm not letting you jump in the river until *after* you marry me." she said.

"I don't want to just simply take up space on the earth. I should get out of the way and let the young have *their* turn to fuck up things."

"I kind of liked it when you were taking up some of the space between my legs."

Jake frowned at the image. A short, swarthy man with a huge belly strolled down the boardwalk. His enormous, round head was covered with deep pits. His skin looked like football cleats had been working it.

"Hey, bro. Can you spare a few bucks for a sandwich?"

Jake scanned the man from head to toe.

"I'll tell you what…," Jake said, "you tell me the secret of life and I'll give you a hundred bucks."

The man grinned. There was a huge gap where his front teeth had once been.

"Give me the money up front," the man said.

Jake laughed. "Okay, I'm game."

He fished his wallet out of his back pocket and thumbed through bills. He had a hundred dollar bill. He handed it over.

The man looked at it, grinned and began walking away.

"Wait a minute," Jake said. "What about the secret of life?"

The man, now ten feet away, turned.

"That was it. Always try to get the money up front."

Jake thought for second, then laughed.

"Shit, why not?" he said. "Sometimes I think life is like a long joke by a drunken, third-rate comedian in some backwoods dive. You know what I'm talking about…there is a big buildup with a farmer's daughter, a sheep, a politician, a preacher, a Jew, a spook and three Mexicans and you get to the end and the comedian bungles the punch line. You're sitting there saying 'What? That's it? This whole journey and all the crap we went through and that's all there is?' We walked through swamps and jungle and across the desert and what's our final reward? A jellybean? A nickel and a pat on the head? A fortune from a cookie that says 'Sorry, fortune broken, come back later…'"

"Jake, I know you're really smart, but brains don't do anyone any good if all they do is tie you up in knots. Come back in. I'll make you some soup."

Jake chewed on a thumbnail.

"Do we have any Waverly crackers? Those things are really good with soup."

"Yeah. A whole box. Unopened."

Fairhaven

Jake stood up straight and stretched his back. He rubbed his eyes and looked down the river for an instant. A fish, silvery in the late afternoon light, jumped and reflected the blinding sun for a tiny fraction of a second. Then, it was gone.

In the blink of an eye. Gone…as if it had never existed.

"Okay," Jake said. He held out his hand and she grabbed it…and squeezed hard.

"Let's go."

Charlie Fairhaven

There were lots of people at Walmart who would be better off dead. Hundreds. Thousands.

Maybe all of them.

Charlie parked the old Toyota at the end of the parking lot of the Walmart Supercenter and watched the people stream in and out. Occasionally, a pretentious Mercedes SUV or a Lexus sedan would pull in, but mainly the customers were poor and drove crappy cars—dirty Hyundais, old Dodge Caravans with mismatched junkyard fenders and battered Ford Taurus sedans with exhaust systems held together with hanger wire and duct tape. They were people with lives held together with hanger wire and duct tape.

It would be a blessing to release these people from their bondage…from the sad chains of poverty, stupidity and despair.

On a grassy median between light poles, a young woman in her early twenties watched as her mongrel strained and worked to produce a heap of brown shit. The girl had a plastic bag on her hand, but, after looking around to see who was watching—no one—pulled the dog's leash and left the

253

steaming pile.

Charlie, with the baseball bat cradled on his lap, grinned.

You would be perfect.

He could see it.

Her blood.

He could feel it.

The solid, satisfying impact when the bat hit her flesh.

She opened the back hatch of the camper on the back of a Silverado pickup and the dog jumped in. She walked around to the passenger side and got in. As the pickup backed up, Charlie made eye-contact with the driver—he wore a ponytail and had tattoos crawling up his neck. With a blank expression and a dead look in his eyes, the driver spit out the remains of a slobbery toothpick.

Charlie smiled and winked.

A kindred spirit.

But, my eyes are not dead like that.

I bring people the gift of peace. I'm glad God didn't create me as a cold-hearted killer like you.

He felt a wave of sadness for the girl. This man would kill her, Charlie knew it…it was as certain as anything he knew.

The driver gunned the engine as he merged onto Freeway Drive and the truck fishtailed as the tires slipped on wet pavement.

Charlie laughed.

You go ahead, buddy. Have your fun.

He got out of the pickup and walked toward the store.

Inside, the building was cavernous. Over 200,000 square feet of clothing, electronics and food.

And people…

Everywhere.

He walked the aisles and studied the customers. A lot of them were almost normal—with nice clothes and well-behaved kids bearing clean faces. But there were others pushing infants in strollers with faces plugged with baby bottles filled with apple juice. Others had children screaming about plastic bags filled with Shrek figurines and candy.

"Can I have this one, mommy?"

"Buy this for me, papa."

Can I, will you, I wanna, you never, argh, spit, spew, Bobby said, groan, you're a bugger, Angela peed her pants, grunt, complain, beg, stop it, come here right now or I'm gonna.

"We can't get that right now, Tommy. Next payday."

Charlie kneeled to look into the face of the little boy.

"Is your name Tommy?"

The boy was about three and wore embroidered overalls with an absurd, grinning wombat on the front. He still wore a diaper and the seat of his pants were puffed out as if filled by a balloon. He had stuffed his thumb and index finger into his mouth—a trail of drool worked down his face. Sad eyes floated above chubby red cheeks. Longish curly blond hair framed his face.

He nodded and unplugged his mouth.

"Tommy," he said.

His mother, rail-thin and wearing a long peasant's skirt that appeared to be made of tiered pieces of snakeskin, frowned at Charlie. She touched Tommy's shoulder.

"Let's go," she said.

Charlie stood and waved goodbye.

"Excuse me, sir. Can I help you find something?"

Charlie turned. The middle-aged woman wore the blue Walmart smock...as did the man behind her...a huge, overweight man with a wide smile on his face.

Verene read the woman's nametag.

"Oh, no," Charlie said. He smiled. "I'm fine."

"Well, that's the thing, sir. It's the cameras and the computer system. You see, you've been wandering around the store for ninety minutes and haven't collected anything to buy. The cameras are programmed to detect shoplifters..."

"Go ahead. Search me," Charlie said.

"You didn't allow me to finish, sir. The computers also detect stalking activity. What you've been doing tripped the computer program—identifying you as a potential stalker."

"I haven't done anything illegal."

"Exactly so, sir. Still, we have a database we share with the police. They have your picture and a report of your suspicious activity."

"I'm just shopping. I'm not doing anything suspicious. Leave me alone."

She gestured at the display rack they stood by.

Hipster satin panties.

All sizes.

$6.77.

"Shopping for a wife or girlfriend, sir? We know from market research that most women prefer to pick out their underwear on their own. I would like to invite you to exit the store, sir."

Another blue-smocked man walked up. He too was a very big man. Ponytail. Diamond stud in his ear. He looked like he'd enjoy a fight to liven up a boring day. Charlie licked his lips. He held out his hands in supplication.

"Okay, fine, I'll take my business somewhere else."

"I want you to be aware, sir...the cameras, with facial

recognition, will track you every time you come in. At this time, we're not asking the courts for a restraining order to prevent you from coming in again, but…" she pointed upward, "we're watching. For the protection of our customers, we're always watching. Do you understand?"

Goddamned cameras. Everywhere.

He was glad he was almost done. In the future, things would get much harder for serial killers.

He turned and walked out. In a loose line, the Walmart staffers followed him. It seemed as if every eye in the store was on him. He kept his anger stuffed down deep and wore a stiff, insincere smile. Overhead, the smoke-tinted plastic covers over the security cameras gleamed.

At the front door, the Walmart staffers stopped and watched him leave.

"Have a great day, sir," Verene called out cheerfully from behind him.

Charlie was almost to his car when a woman spoke to him.

"They aren't very nice, are they?"

Charlie turned. The woman looked like a poster child for the effects of methamphetamines. After, not before. She had a blood-stained bandage on her forehead and her hair was stringy and greasy.

"Excuse me?" Charlie said.

"I accidentally put a tube of lipstick in my purse and forgot to pay for it. They treated me that way too. Cold. Rude."

Charlie gestured at the plastic bags she carried.

"But you come back," he said.

She shrugged. "The prices are the cheapest in town. I don't have much in the way of money to spend, so I have to come here. Where else would I go? Well…take care."

She walked toward her car. A massive Durango with a bumper sticker.

Saint Barack Obama's smiling face and caption:

Do you miss me yet?

Skinny. Her jeans were too large. Even when she bent over to arrange her bags in the back of the Durango, the loose fabric at the seat of her pants rippled in the brisk wind.

"Wait," Charlie said. "You seem like a great person. Tea party, right? Can I buy you lunch?"

She stopped and turned. And grinned.

Big teeth in a horsey face. Flat chest. Angry boils on her cheeks.

Loser.

"Okay," she said. "Sounds good. Follow me home and I'll put the hamburger in the freezer. Then we can grab a burger or something."

Her name was Gwen and she was heavier than she looked, so he had trouble lifting her...to stuff her cooling, scrawny, naked body in a dumpster behind a wood products factory by the Bayview Airport. He cleaned blood off the bat with her cotton shirt, then tossed the shirt in after her.

His Toyota was still running. With calmness and serenity, he got in and drove away.

20

Jake Mosby

NORT AND JAKE sat in their crowded little room in the heart of the Mount Vernon police department building. Nort threw pencils and tried to get them to stick in a photo of Sarah Palin he had clipped out of *USA Today* and taped on the wall as a paper target.

"I'm bored," he said.

"Being bored isn't the worst thing in the world," Jake said. "There were times in my life when I would have given a pound of gold for a half-ounce of boredom. Try looking down the barrel of a twelve-gauge in the hands of a cracked-out felon with nothing to lose. You'll take boredom every time."

"Whatever," Nort said. "What's our plan for rolling Sprague? He's the last guy on the interview list."

Jake grinned.

"I'm letting you run with it. You interview him."

"What? I'm a kid," Nort said. "I don't know what to do."

"You think I learned how to lean on people by getting a college degree from the University of Asshole? I got in the ring and got the crap beat out of me until I figured things out."

Nort opened his mouth to respond, but was interrupted by a knock at the door. Jake sat and looked at Nort expectantly before unfurling the *USA Today* and leaning back in his chair. He threw his feet onto the table.

"Uh," Nort said. "Come in, I guess."

Officer Sprague was a medium man. Medium height, medium weight with medium brown hair.

"Am I early?" he said.

Jake, hiding behind the newspaper, said nothing.

"Uh, no." Nort said. He looked intently at the newspaper as if trying to see through it. "Fucker," he whispered. To Sprague, he said, "Have a seat."

He opened the file and spread it out on the table. Sprague cocked his head.

"What's this?" he said.

"I'm running the interview."

"I know about you. You're a high school dropout. I'm not talking to you."

He put his hand on the door knob.

"I'm doing home study," Nort said. "I'm taking the high school equivalency test—and I'm going to pass it too."

Jake noisily folded the newspaper and moved the telephone in front of him. With skeletal fingers, he stabbed at the buttons.

"How do you work this goddamned thing to get Greenberg on the line?"

Nort pushed Jake's hand away. "Stop it. Hang up and try again. Just press 1-0-0-0."

"Damned electronic crap never works right," Jake said. He bashed the numbers. "Greenberg? Sprague is being uncooperative." He listened for a moment and then handed the receiver to Sprague. "He wants to talk to you."

Sprague reached out hesitantly and took the receiver and held it to his ear.

"Yes, sir?"

Greenburg's voice was loud—Sprague grimaced and held the receiver away from his ear.

"Yes, sir. I will, sir," he said, "but I'll file a complaint with the union. You haven't heard the end of this."

Greenberg hollered some more.

"Yes, sir. I understand, sir."

Sprague handed the receiver back to Jake. "Shall we get this nonsense over with?" he said.

Jake cradled the receiver and unfolded the newspaper again. While Sprague pulled out a chair and sat down on its edge, Nort ran a finger down the entries on Sprague's personnel file.

"Seems to me," Nort said, his voice cracking, "that being a cop might be a lot of good times, you know? I don't know myself, exactly, directly, but I hear chicks dig a man in a uniform with a badge? Is that the way it works? Foxes ask you to show them your Glock and they can't help themselves, they drop their dripping panties."

"The police officer's union steward is a very good friend of mine. This interview is inappropriate and insulting. I don't have to talk to you, kid. Just cross me off your list and we'll get on with our respective days."

The *USA Today* rustled as if Jake was laughing behind it.

"I guess what I'm trying to say, sir, is that a good-looking man like you probably has to chase the pussy away with a nightstick, am I right?"

Sprague leaned back in his chair and unbuttoned a shirt

261

pocket. He pulled out a toothpick and started working on his teeth.

"You're out of your league, kid," he said. "Write up a glowing, happy-face report and we'll both walk away as friends. You don't know who you're messing with."

Nort looked at Sprague for a long moment.

"I know this because my English teacher went over it yesterday: I believe you mean 'whom'. Not 'who'. I think."

Jake, hiding behind the paper, was not helping. Nort sighed and flipped a page on Sprague's file.

"You got a couple of complaints," he continued. "Tell me about...Melody James."

"I was cleared on all of them. The cases were dismissed. The files are sealed. We have nothing to talk about."

"Ah," Nort said. "See, that's what I wanted to natter about a little bit." He gestured at the banker's boxes stacked against the wall. "We *have* the old files. They haven't been shredded yet. And, I stumbled across some interesting stuff. Take Melody as an example. She said you raped her and had a go at her daughter too."

"She was on crack. Marijuana. Drunk out of her skull. The judge didn't believe her. The case was dismissed."

"But somebody had her up the booty exit. I don't understand everything the doctor's report says, but it looks clear enough. Somebody ran it up the old backdoor fire escape and the daughter too. Fourteen? You like the young'uns?"

"Melody James is a goddamned liar. The case was dismissed."

"Okay, what about Chelsea Whitacre? Someone messed her up pretty good. A week in the hospital?"

"It wasn't me. I had an alibi."

"Yeah. You were at a bar with several other cops. Retirement party?"

"All night. I slept on the couch. Remember the union boss I mentioned? His house."

"That looks solid. I can see why the judge tossed the case."

"I've been cleared on everything," Sprague said. "So…"

"So?"

"So…go fuck yourself."

"Yes, of course," Nort said. "But the thing is, you're not telling the whole truth when you say you've been cleared on everything, are you? Let's talk about Gloria. She seemed like a nice girl."

"That case is sealed."

"Ah, so it is." Nort waved some photocopied papers. "But, I have a copy of the preliminary report—her statement and the witness interviews."

Sprague spit out his toothpick and leaned his chair forward.

"Give me those papers. How did you get them? You're not supposed to have them."

"In a coma how long? Three months? And, you're in the clear if she dies, am I right? Smooth sailing? But if she comes out of it, she might have an interesting tale to tell, don't you think?"

"Give me those papers," Sprague said. He reached across the table and grabbed them. He crumpled them.

"Go ahead, those are just print-outs. I have the originals on my laptop."

"You got a mouth on you, fuck-bird. A mouth that'll lead you into a world of trouble if you don't learn to keep it shut. I heard about your mind-fuck games and I'm not impressed. This interview is done."

Sprague stood up. He looked at Jake's newspaper for a moment, then turned and left the room.

Jake refolded the newspaper, then rolled it up and threw it in the garbage can. With a sour expression, Nort took it out and put it in the recycle bin.

"I don't like that guy," Nort said. "He should fall down a well or something. What are we going to do about him?"

Jake shrugged. "Nothing," he said.

"Nothing?"

"You heard me. He's a political animal and has connections. There's a good chance he'll be even more careful now…maybe he'll slide through the whole rest of his life without tripping up again."

"He'll hurt other women."

"Maybe," Jake said. "Maybe not. How is that our problem? We can't be responsible for every worthless piece of shit walking on the face of the earth."

Nort studied the look in Jake's watery brown eyes.

"I'm not buying that from you," he said. "Not for a second."

Jake sighed.

"No, I'm serious. There are some problems we can't solve; that's just the way it is. We're not superheroes and we're not all-powerful angels of God's vengeance. God's got all the lightning bolts and burning bushes and shit. Let him work it out."

"No," Nort said.

Jake leaned forward and placed his gnarled hands on the table.

"I've seen this a hundred times. Sprague is tough and careful. Chances are he'll bury his crimes and slide through his life and end up happy, with a fat wife and a pension and a dog who thinks his master is the king of the western world. We should solve the problems in front of us and let the rest of them roll off...like greasy shit out of a duck's ass. Believe me, we'll have plenty of problems to solve. They crop up naturally. There's no percentage in seeking them out."

"No. I don't think you really believe that."

A grim smile worked its way across Jake's face.

"Okay, kid, I'll tell you. There's a rhythm and balance in the world. I can't think of a better word, so let's call it karma. Too damned slow—takes its sweet time, but it always seems to work. Why, I don't know. One day, Sprague will come up against some rough package the universal delivery service drops at his front door. Then, the hammer of God will come down on his head. He'll fuck up and leave some evidence at a crime scene, or some chicky will stab him in the back with an ice pick or we'll come across him again out in the world and we'll reach out...and...touch him. At the right time, it will be easy and we won't get caught. There won't be any extraordinary risk for us. That's the way it works out. Okay?"

Nort studied Jake's craggy, jowly face.

"I hope I never get as old and stupid as you are," he said.

"Give me your word. You won't follow Sprague around and mess with him. You won't go against Fairhaven on your own. I'm telling you, if you go into a dark alley with either of those guys—only one will walk out and it won't be you. I want to hear you say it."

"Yes, I agree. We'll let the magic karma come out of a genie bottle and deal with the bad guys. We'll be lazy and dodge our responsibilities when things get tough. We'll turn our backs and let more innocent people get hurt. We'll have a drink and a smoke while shitheads out in the world get away with murder. Literally. Murder."

Jake scratched a stubbly cheek and grinned.

"I think you're finally catching on," he said.

Charlie Fairhaven

He whisked his finger across the iPod's touchscreen—looking for something to listen to while waiting for one o'clock in the morning.

Miley Cyrus. *The Climb*. He liked that.

Ain't about what's waiting on the other side.

He adjusted the volume and worked the earbuds deeper into his ears.

Give me a half hour in a room alone with you, Miley.

I'll show you what's waiting on the other side.

He was parked under a willow tree on a dark section of street. The neighborhood was a working one—only a few lights glowed in the old houses. The Wind in the Willows was a block away. He could get to the back door by walking down an alley and pushing through a straggly section of hedge. Maybe it was the only one like this in the world, but there were no barking dogs in the backyards along this alley.

While driving around—scouting in his Toyota—he'd laughed when he found the willow tree. He didn't think there were any around.

I suppose Wind in the Half-dead Willow Tree a Block Away Retirement Center would be a cumbersome name for business cards.

A police car drove by slowly. Charlie covered the glowing iPod screen and didn't move. The cop didn't notice him. His lights disappeared around a corner and Charlie was alone again.

1:00

The dead of the night.

He got out of the truck and quietly shut the door. Nothing stirred except a cat crossing the road which stopped for an instant to look at him before disappearing under a bush.

Alley. Hedge. Path.

He didn't know how to feel. This was it...the beginning of the endgame. In three days the world would know his name and his life would move to the next phase. Like a beautiful butterfly, he would emerge into the golden sunlight. He could see it all: the splashy graphics on TV news shows, the angry block headlines on the newspapers...the stream of lawyers in natty suits and interviews with tabloid reporters.

He realized he was drifting while standing on the path near a stand of dripping firs. The misty air was cold.

I have to focus.

Per the plan, after a few minutes of waiting, the nurse-practitioner—Bob—came through the back door to light a cigarette. Under a flickery yellow overhead light, he stood on a gravel patch strewn with discarded cigarette butts. He poured smoke into the sky before sitting at a picnic table to thumb through a yellow *Little Nickel* newspaper. For an instant, Charlie looked over Bob's shoulder to see what he was studying.

Apparently he was in the market for a new boat.

I don't think so.

Charlie had met Bob a few times. Bob fished in the Skagit River every spare moment. He had a secret place way up-river and he didn't care about permits or seasons. His freezer was full, but he fished anyway. Though Bob was tall and husky, his back was curved and he always seemed to be bent over— slumped and appearing to search the hallway floors for lost

267

change.

He was a loser...unmarried. All he did was work in a nursing home and fish...and shop for river boats. He deserved to die.

Charlie had prepared a length of eighth-inch nylon cord with loops for his hands at each end. He slipped it over the Bob's head and pulled it tight. It dug into the man's thick neck. Bob's fingers tore at the cord, but he did not struggle much before toppling into the gravel. His cigarette smoldered. With the toe of his shoe, Charlie extinguished it.

Smoking.

A filthy, disgusting habit.

He dragged Bob's heavy body across the gravel and rolled him against the building's brick wall.

Hard work.

With his hands on his knees he leaned over and caught his breath. Pace. It wouldn't do to exhaust himself too soon...there was too much to do.

The back door was propped open. He peeked. No one stirred. Charlie slipped in and, on tip-toes, raced into the corridor and entered the utility closet. At 1:30, the night shift security guard would make a round. Ten minutes. He settled in to wait.

He woke with a start.

What time is it?

It was hard to read the small, glowing hands of his Bulova watch.

3:30.

Falling asleep was not part of his plan.

Footsteps.

Fairhaven

Charlie opened the door a crack and peeked out. The security guard, wearing a lurid, shiny red set of massive headphones and matching shiny-red Nike running shoes, seemed to be practicing some sort of jitterbug dance step. Shuffle, kick left. Shuffle, kick right. He muttered the staccato words to a song.

You don't ever need a horse or saddle
I'mma give you this dick to ride.[6]

Charlie's mind was foggy.
What was the plan?
Was he supposed to kill the security guard with the aluminum bat or strangle him with the garrote?
I need to stick with the plan.
Is there still time?
Where did two hours go?
His thoughts flittered.
Where does the time go?
When he worked for the Humane Society, a girl gave him a copy of Proust's *Remembrance of Things Past*.
He tried to remember. *Swann's Way*. Was that it?
What did Swanns have to do with anything? Or ducks? Or geese?

I would ask myself what o'clock it could be...

Charlie was scared. He didn't know what was happening in his

---

[6] Ludacris, *Sex Room*, by Christopher Bria Bridges, K. Johnson, Trey Neverson, T. Scales, T. Taylor

mind. Another fifteen minutes evaporated like ice. From a high school science class, he remembered the word: sublimation.

When ice went directly to vapor without becoming fluid first.

Can time sublimate?

This question seemed important and worthy of a few hours of thought, but he didn't have the time. He was afraid of getting stuck. His mind might freeze.

Did anyone notice Bob is missing?

To hell with the plan.

It would be quieter to strangle the guard. Leaving the utility closet, he set out down the hallway to find the man. He hadn't gone far. Around a corner, he jitterbugged and fed quarters into a soda machine. A Mountain Dew dropped down the noisy chute as Charlie threw the nylon rope around the man's neck.

The security guard was not as stupid as Bob.

Did he have military training?

The guard threw his body backwards and slammed Charlie into a fire extinguisher mounted on the wall. It hurt. They fell to the floor and Charlie, with panic filling his body, pulled on the rope. Harder. After a minute the wriggling stopped. After two more minutes the guard was dead.

Charlie released the rope and leaned against the wall. His back felt kinked. Twisted. Painful. Getting his back broken by a fire extinguisher was not part of the plan.

It made him very angry. He pulled the bat from under his long coat and was raising it when he realized he was being watched. Not just by the security cameras, but by a tiny woman in a wheelchair. Her eyes were wide and her mouth

Fairhaven

worked soundlessly. Quadraplegic.

She controlled her electric wheelchair with a joystick she could manipulate with her chin, but it did not move backwards very quickly, so Charlie easily caught up with her.

He remembered her name. Mrs. Ball. She did not sleep much. It wouldn't take much to fracture her fragile skull. He tapped her head a couple of times. Gently. He was right. Her bones crumbled like soda crackers and her mouth stopped working. The wheelchair, with servos whining, drifted to a stop.

While standing over her body, he tried to remember the plan.

With concentration, he remembered.

Receptionist.

The mobile residents.

Then the immobile residents.

To be sure, he hit Mrs. Ball once more. Hard.

There was no doubt.

She was surely dead.

A half hour later, Charlie retraced his steps on the path through the hedge and along the alley. A few more lights were on as workers prepared for their early shifts. He was exhausted.

In his truck, he sat with his head on the steering wheel. His arms were leaden and his muscles were rubbery. The palms of his hands were raw. The aluminum bat was cradled on his lap—dimpled, dented and flecked with blood and wisps of gray hair.

He worked the window handle and tossed the bat. It landed in a sad patch of bedraggled lawn by a toy stroller. The abandoned stroller was missing a wheel.

Ken Coffman

Images from the retirement home flicked through his mind. Mr. Childress wanted to know if there would be raisins for his morning oatmeal.

That was not what bothered Charlie.

Childress's granddaughter was not supposed to be there. She was not supposed to be sleeping under a pile of blankets in the guest chair. She was not supposed to be rubbing sleep from her eyes and asking about what was going on with her straw-colored hair all a'tangle.

"What are you doing?" Mr. Childress said.

His dry, faint voice was filled with horror.

That's a really, really stupid question.

Charlie turned. Dumb people were aggravating.

"Isn't it abundantly obvious? I'm killing your granddaughter who should not be here. When I'm done with her, I will kill you, too. That's the plan. We have to stick to the plan. It's your fault—family is supposed to be out at ten o'clock. She is not supposed to be here."

Mr. Childress sat on the edge of the bed pulling at the tubes in his arm and fumbling for the red nurse's call button, but he fell back across the bed with Charlie's first blow. After an overhead, full-strength blow, Mr. Childress stopped moving.

When he left the room, Charlie tried not to look at the little girl wrapped in a quilt.

Her head was lopsided—misshapen.

She's not supposed to be here.

He counted. He was almost done; there were only six more doors to go.

Beyond the sheltering protection of the willow tree, rain, in huge, oversized drops, splashed on the street. For an instant, Charlie did not know where he was. His thoughts were fractured and incoherent.

A milk delivery truck, painted black-and-white like a cow, rumbled by and stopped down the street. The driver, wearing white pants and a white shirt, ran out to leave milk on a doorstep. Dangling willow leaves stirred with the wind.

It occurred to Charlie that what he was doing was wrong.

Not only wrong, but evil.

He looked at the raw meat of his palms. One of the blisters had popped and really hurt.

It was too late for second thoughts.

He could hear his mother's voice.

What's done is done, Charlie, there's no use in crying over spilt milk. Eat your sweet potatoes. Don't play with matches. What did you expect to happen when you put your hand in the toaster? Has anyone seen Tiger? Eat it anyway. I told you a million times: stay out of mommy's closet. Tough titty. What goes around comes around. Do you need to make a pee-pee? Do you want to spend your life shitting yourself in a nuthouse? What did you do with my lipstick? Because I said so, that's why. Don't suck your thumb. You'll go blind if you play with yourself. Where are your pants? Daddy is going to whip you to within an inch of your life with the belt when he gets home from work. I'll give you something to cry about.

She'd been gone for years, but her screechy voice lived on, immortal. And, he could hear the way she giggled when she'd been drinking. And the sound of breaking glass. And the sound of a noisy muffler when his dad's car pulled into the driveway.

Spewing diesel smoke, the milk truck pulled away from the curb and disappeared around a corner.

Charlie started the Toyota and followed.

21

Jake Mosby

JAKE AND NORT walked down the hallway toward Greenberg's office. With intense concentration, Maureen peered into a computer screen and muttered to herself. Her puffed-out hair was topped with a red, clip-on ribbon. When Jake made eye-contact with the other ladies in the office, he held his finger to his lips to silence them.

He crept up behind her and kissed her neck.

She jumped.

"Jake."

She turned her head and gave him a sloppy, passionate kiss.

"That's disgusting," Nort said.

"Did you come to buy me lunch? It's early, but I could slip away for a doughnut, I suppose."

She opened her desk drawer and pulled out her purse.

"No," Jake said. "We're going to chat a minute with Greenberg, then head back to the bookstore."

"Okay," Maureen said. She shoved her handbag back in the drawer. "Don't worry about me; I can get a doughnut when the roach coach comes by."

Jake grinned and kissed her forehead.

"Good. Get me one, too."

He walked across the room and tapped on Greenberg's window. Greenberg was on the phone. He held up an index finger to buy a minute.

After a few seconds, Greenberg cradled the phone and waved them in.

"Sit, sit," he said. Clearly distracted, he rubbed his temples. "What's up?"

"I want to give you a final report on my internal investigation," Jake said.

"It might be better to do this later. I'm expecting another call. The shit is about to fling."

"It will just take a minute. Bottom line? The department is reasonably clean. I approve."

"I don't like Sprague. He's a prick," Nort said.

"That's not news to anyone. The question is, is he a hazard to the department?"

"No," Jake said.

At the same time, Nort said, "Yes."

In turn, Greenberg looked at them. "Okay," he said. The phone rang. "I have to take this."

Jake chewed a hangnail on his thumb.

"Don't mind us," he said.

Greenberg frowned and glanced at Nort.

"I don't give a shit about you, Jake, but the kid might not want to be in the middle of this."

"I can handle it," Nort said.

Greenberg hesitated, and then picked up the phone.

"As you wish, kid," he said. Into the phone he said, "Greenberg." He listened for a few seconds, and then said, "I'll be there in five minutes." To Jake, he said, "Do you know the Wind in the Willows old folks home?"

Jake nodded.

"That's where I'm going," Greenberg said. He looked at Nort. "It's bad. Really bad."

Outside, Charlie was in his truck in the far back corner of the planning department parking lot. He watched police cars tear out of the parking lot, but he didn't care about them. He watched Jake's Buick. When Jake and Nort came out, got in the car and drove off, Charlie nodded. It was time for the next part of his plan.

The Wind in the Willows parking lot was filled with police cars, emergency medical vehicles and fire trucks. As Jake and Nort looked on, three black plastic body bags were maneuvered into the coroner's van.

"It might be better if you stay with the car. So you can move it for the emergency vehicles or something."

Nort studied Jake's weathered face.

"Yeah," Nort said. "You're right. That might be best."

Jake hauled himself out of the car and walked down the street and into the parking lot. He moved slowly—as if carrying a heavy load on his back. Nort sat and watched for a few minutes, then reached for his cell phone. He put the phone back in its holster, then re-started the car, and drove off.

Charlie and Talon

The huge parking lot followed the river and the boardwalk for almost a mile. Party Central was a few hundred yards from the end, not quite as far as The Moose Lodge. Charlie found a parking place and sat to watch the river for a few minutes. The last bat was wedged behind the seat. He worked it out and tore off the plastic. It was shiny and pristine. He smelled it. It even smelled new.

Nice.

The river boiled. Far down the boardwalk, men sat on a bench drinking from giant aluminum cans of beer. He could hear them laughing. It was the middle of the day and they should be working, but they were not part of today's plan. They were safe.

He got out of the truck and walked toward Party Central. A group of kids were skateboarding down a short embankment and trying to jump a five-gallon bucket. They were not very graceful, but were generally able to stay on their boards. They were not part of his plan, so they were safe.

A thirteen-year-old wearing a backwards cap over a shaved head and red handkerchief spoke.

"Hey pard, got a smoke?"

Charlie ignored him and walked to the front door of the skateboard shop. An electronic chime made a ding-ding as he walked in. Talon was behind the counter. She looked up and waved.

"Come in and look around. We have Jinjiang Aierda shoes on sale."

She was the plan and she was not safe.

Skateboards were stacked up in a fan-like array. With the bat, Charlie tapped one of the boards and the display crashed to the floor.

Talon came out from behind the counter and approached.

"Hey, that's okay, I'll get those," she said. "I told Nort not

277

to stack them like that. You weren't hurt, I hope. We just bought the bare minimum liability insurance."

Charlie took a stance and rested the bat on his shoulder. When she was close enough, he was going to hit her. She stopped and stared at his face.

"Shit," she said.

She patted her pockets, and then glanced to the back of the store before turning and running. Her jacket hung on a hook just outside the rear door. She grabbed it, but Charlie was right behind her and he grabbed the jacket out of her hands.

"What are you after?" he said. He shook the jacket. One of the pockets was weighed down with something heavy. He worked the zipper and worked the revolver out. "You can't shoot me. That's not part of the plan."

He pointed the gun at her left knee.

She held out her hand. It held the bullets bunched up in her palm.

"My dad asked me to unload it."

Charlie pulled the trigger. Click. And again. Nothing.

He was angry. He threw the gun aside and lifted the bat. She walked backwards down the aisle and grabbed a board with a pirate's grinning skull painted on it.

"Bill!" she shouted. "I could use a hand out here."

Charlie lunged forward and swung the bat. She deflected it with the board.

Bill poked his head through the doorway. He looked down at the pistol lying at his feet, then at Talon.

"What's going on?" he said.

"This fucker is trying to kill me," she said.

With an underhand toss, she scattered the bullets in Bill's direction.

Fairhaven

"I'm convicted," he said. "I can't handle weapons."

"Oh, for fuck's sake, Bill. Kill this piece of shit before he kills me first."

With shaking hands, Bill fumbled with the bullets and the gun.

While Charlie watched, Bill tried to figure out how to open the cylinder and load the revolver. Talon slapped him with the board. Charlie staggered back and raised his bat.

"How do you open this damned thing?" Bill said.

"Push the release toward the end of the barrel."

Charlie glanced at Talon and then started toward Bill, but Bill had figured out the release and was sliding bullets into the cylinder. Seeing this, Charlie turned around and ran at full speed to the front door. Rather than open it, he smashed the glass with the bat and jumped through.

"Stop," Bill yelled.

But, Charlie ran faster. He jumped into the pickup and while Bill and Talon watched, roared away.

Bill nudged Talon and she took the gun.

"I don't want to be caught with this stupid thing," he said.

"Thanks, Bill."

"I didn't do anything."

"You did enough," Talon said.

As they watched, Nort pulled up in the Buick. He jumped out and walked up to them. He took in the smashed glass.

"What a mess," he said. "Are you okay?"

"Yeah, we're good," Talon said. She wrapped her arms around him and squeezed him tight.

"Fairhaven?"

"Yeah," Talon said.

"I had a feeling he might turn up. There is a big muddle up

at the retirement home."

"How bad?"

"I don't know, but bad. Lots of bodies. I'll help clean up this mess."

"Do you need to go get Jake?"

"He can find his own way home. I'm not leaving you alone."

"That's sweet," Talon said. "You go get the push broom and I'll call the glass company."

Charlie Fairhaven

Charlie watched his rearview mirror, but no one seemed to be following. He passed a police car on the Memorial Highway, but the cop did not take any notice of him. Without a destination in mind, he turned off the highway and drove mindlessly along the dike while low clouds spit rain onto brown fields. He found himself passing by the Bayview Airport. He turned into the parking lot of an abandoned factory, drove around back and parked by a loading dock. The sign directly in front of his face said NO PARKING.

Yeah.

His plan was good, but the girl had a gun.

A gun.

That's not the way things should be.

Teenaged girls with guns. It wasn't right.

Who gives guns to teenaged girls?

She should be dead, but she wasn't.

He twiddled with the AM radio tuning and found the local oldies station.

Smokin' Kevan introduced Stevie Wonder.

Fairhaven

My Cherie Amour.

The biggest news story in decades, perhaps ever, in Skagit County and the radio was playing *My Cherie Amour.* Charlie found himself tapping his index finger on the steering wheel with the beat and forced himself to stop.

Maybe someday you'll share your little distant cloud.

The girl with the funny hair in the skateboard shop…he'd like to send her to a distant little cloud. The song wrapped up with la-la-las and the station switched to news.

Forty-five murdered.

Have I lost count?

It should be fifty-seven including the little girl who was not supposed to be there.

Could it really be forty-five or were they messing with him?

He didn't know how to feel. Some of his plan had worked, but some hadn't. Was there some way to collect the girl, or should he give up? He was going to kill hundreds more, everything was already in place.

Is that enough?

He jumped at a tap on the truck window and looked. A blue jacket and badge. For an instant, he was terrified. A cop.

But, it wasn't a cop. It was a rent-a-cop. A security guard.

Probably a drooling moron with a loser life.

Charlie knew what to do with people like this.

He pasted a grin on his face and motioned for the guard to back up so he could get out of the truck.

The man wore a nametag: Brad.

Brad moved back a few paces and stood with his legs spread as if he was posing for a movie poster.

"Good afternoon, sir," Brad said.

281

"So it is," Charlie said. "So it is."

"Might I ask what your business is here, sir? The building has been empty for a couple of years. Unless you're meeting a realty agent with the idea of leasing the building..."

"Right. Exactly." Charlie remembered signs from around town. The same sign at the front of this building. Windermere. Cary Conklin. Commercial Real Estate. "I'm waiting for Cary...he seems to be running a little late."

Brad relaxed. He laughed.

"The way the market is, in the toilet and all, you'd think Cary would be here on time. Hell, early. Eager. With bells on. Lots of properties for lease, but not so many buyers, you know? Sorry, sir, but it's my job to keep track of things in this area. If you can believe it, I used to work here. At this company. Mechanical engineer. You should have seen this place, they had big ideas. Cyrobo—they made industrial robots, big ones, but the money came from investments in a couple of dot-com ventures. Remember what happened in 2000? Billionaires became bums, overnight. Easy come, easy go, am I right? Too bad, I'll probably never make money like that again. I should move somewhere where mechanical engineers are in demand, but I like it up here. Backpacking in the Cascades, that's what I like, and it doesn't take much money once the gear is paid for. My girlfriend does alright with a couple of espresso stands. We get by. All the robotic equipment was packed up and shipped to China. They're probably using the precision molding machines to make plastic spatulas for Walmart or something. What a world, eh?"

"Did you hear about the retirement home?"

"Yeah, it's all over the news. They say thirty-something people were killed."

"Thirty-something?" Charlie said. "I heard it was more than that. A lot more."

"Whatever the number is, it's horrible, right? Who would hurt those poor people? Isn't it bad enough they're at the end of their lives and stuck in a rest home killing time until they pass on? I don't understand it. Sometimes the world is filled with such sorrow. My pastor explains—God's will and all that—he gives us freedom to choose evil deeds and tests our will, but it doesn't make any sense to me."

Charlie looked around the parking lot for something he could use to shut the guard up. A concrete block or a metal pole—anything. Weeds grew in the seams of the concrete, but otherwise, the parking lot was barren. No junk was lying around.

"Yeah. Look, I'm okay here. I know you have other places to be. So, have a great day. I'm sure Cary will be here soon. All right. Great to meet you."

Charlie held out his hand for a shake.

"No, sorry, I don't do the handshake thing. Nothing personal. Germs. It's a disease vector, y'know? Have a good one. I hope the lease works out. It would be great to get more high tech or manufacturing going in this county. There is grant money and property tax programs to help you get going, if that helps. I suppose Cary can tell you all about that stuff. And, you need a mechanical engineer? Look me up. By the way, what business are you in? I'm just curious."

"I can't discuss that."

"Ah, it's secret, that's cool, you probably work for a Taiwanese or Indian company, I know the drill. Non-disclosure agreements. Of course. I don't mean to pry. Well, you're right. I have a schedule to keep, so I should roll. Take

283

care."

Brad walked back to his Crown Victoria. As soon as Brad was out of sight, Charlie walked to the edge of the parking lot and looked for a weapon. He wanted to be ready in case someone else came by. In a patch of weeds, he found a three-foot length of rusty rebar with a hook at the end.

This will shut up a loudmouth.

Thirty-three dead. That was a slap in the face.

An insult.

What are the cops up to? Do they expect me to call to correct the record?

It was irritating.

Wait until they see my plan unfold at Peaceful Meadows.

Charlie looked around. The parking lot was a perfect place to hang out for a while…except for the mouthy security guard.

Who would inevitably be back.

Charlie sighed. He got in the truck and drove away.

He needed to find a place to hang out until the dead of night.

Dead of night.

He liked the sound of that.

He found a motel by the freeway and checked in. After pulling the curtains tight, he took off his clothes and fell into a deep sleep.

22

Jake Mosby

A SQUAD CAR pulled up in front of Party Central. Jake got out. Leaning over, he exchanged a few words with the driver before turning around. The car pulled away. Talon and Nort, with their arms around each other's waists, watched a technician install plate glass to repair their front door. Slowly and laboriously, Jake walked up behind them. He stood for a minute and watched the kids.

"He was here?" Jake said.

"Yeah," Nort replied over his shoulder. "Talon and Bill ran him off. We're okay, thanks for asking. What's the score at the retirement home?"

"Fifty-seven dead including a little girl who was spending the night with her grandfather. It's a big fucking, ugly mess. An MSNBC crew flew in. Helicopter. We're going to be as famous as Auschwitz."

"What's an Auschwitz?" Nort turned around. Jake's face was grey and it looked like he'd aged ten years.

"Holy crap, G-P, you look like yesterday's shit. Are you alright?"

285

Jake waved his hand dismissively.

"Yeah, don't worry about me. Tell me what happened here."

Taking turns, the kids filled Jake in. When they were done, Jake said, "I should have been here. I need to sit down."

"The gun you gave Talon saved her life."

Jake walked to a bench outside the store and fell onto it.

"I wish I'd had the courage to shoot that rat," Talon said, "but I screwed it up. I'm sorry."

"We all feel as if we're paralyzed in the unrelenting gaze of God," Jake muttered.

"Uh, what?" Talon said.

"It's best to ignore him when he's quoting from *The Gift of Death*," Nort said. "It means he's low and feeling sorry for himself."

Herb pulled up front in his Mercedes.

"Great," Talon said. "It's my dad. That will help."

Herb stood in front of Jake and pointed his index finger.

"You——," he said.

"Stuff a sock in it, dad. If it wasn't for him you'd be buying flowers for my funeral."

"Get in the car."

Talon spoke to Nort. "It will take a while to settle him down, but I'll be back."

They exchanged a brief kiss.

"You——," Herb said.

"I thought you wanted to go home," Talon said. "Make up your mind."

"I'm going to kick your ass," Herb said to Jake.

"Get in line," Jake said, "and you'll get your turn."

Nort waved as Herb's car disappeared. He sat beside Jake.

Fairhaven

"Really, Jake, you look like death's pimply ass. Are you sure you're okay? Maybe you should go to the doctor."

"I hate doctors."

"I know, and insurance salesmen, tax collectors and TV preachers."

"Don't forget worthless, hopeless slacker teenaged punks who think they know everything when, in reality, they don't know anything."

"Right. How could I forget the most important group? Do you think Fairhaven is done? Maybe he'll run. Hit the road and get as far away from here as possible."

"No. No, I don't think he'll be done until he's dead or in a cage."

"What are we going to do?"

Jake sighed.

"I have no idea. Sleep with one eye open. Keep a weapon close at hand. Try to get lucky."

Charlie Fairhaven

He didn't know why, but he tore the motel's cheap flat screen TV apart. The back came off easily. He removed the connectors, the mounting screws and the circuit boards. The boards were covered with strange-looking parts and thin parallel lines on green boards.

"Someone had to know how to hook all of this stuff together. Otherwise it wouldn't work, right?"

He realized he was talking to himself. It was scary. Generally, there was an active, continuous conversation going on in his head, but never spoken out loud. His voice echoed in the cheap room.

Ken Coffman

He was bored, but now he couldn't watch TV either, so he was missing the late night coverage of the mass murder in Skagit County. Most people had no idea there was anything between Seattle and Vancouver, BC. But, now they did. From all of the news reports he heard, the body count was all over the place, but never exactly correct. More than fifty. Forty. Forty-five.

He looked at the room's clock radio again. Midnight. Three hours to go before his visit to Peaceful Meadows. He considered taking the clock radio apart too, but when he realized he was thinking about it, pushed the idea to the back corner of his mind.

I should find someone to kill just for something to do.

No. I should not do anything that will derail my grand plan...the spectacular act of murder that will put my name in the history books forever.

What do people do when there is nothing to do?

He picked up the free copy of *USA Today*, but he'd already read it. Twice. He put it back down.

Three hours—then he would jump in his truck and drive to Peaceful Meadows. There wasn't much to do, just a couple of last-minute details to attend to...chores...then he was done.

He unplugged the clock radio and started taking it apart.

23

Jake and Nort

THE CEILING NEVER changed. Occasionally it was bathed with reflected headlights from a car driving by on First Street, then the ridges and folds of the old plaster cast long shadows, but the peaks and valleys stayed the same. Beside him, Maureen snored. Not loudly. He didn't mind. She was not the reason he could not sleep. His mind worked at the events of the day. A TV reporter, a famous blonde from Fox News, had tracked him down at the store and would not leave.

She bought three Stephanie Meyer hardbacks on her black American Express card, so Jake agreed to answer one question. He didn't pay any attention to the question. In the bright lights, he held up the bartender's sketch and told her audience not to become dead heroes.

"If you see this motherfucker, call the cops. Let them deal with him. He's fucking dangerous."

On the six o'clock news, they bleeped his bad language and ran the clip on a four-times-per-hour rotation.

After that, the phone would not stop ringing, so he unplugged it. Fred worked the cash register and they made a lot of money. Over three thousand dollars. At closing time, the customers did not want to leave, but Jake chased them out with a broom.

Midnight. His body was tired, but his mind raced. He decided to get up. He took a beer from the refrigerator and sat at the kitchenette table.

Nort, rubbing his eyes, joined him.

"I can't sleep," Nort said.

"You are a master at restating the obvious," Jake replied.

Nort poured a glass of cranberry juice.

"Are you sure you're okay?"

"I'm old and tired. So, no, I'm not okay, but I'm as good as I'm going to get."

"That's a cheery thought. I feel like we should be doing something."

Jake studied Nort's pimply face.

"Yeah," he said. "Let me shake a few drops out of the big lizard, then we'll go for a drive."

Nort scowled.

"Too much information," he said.

They drove up the hill. Most of the old folk's homes surrounded the hospital on Mount Vernon's east hill. They passed the Mount Vernon Cemetery on Fir Street.

"I suppose this is the ultimate old folk's home," Nort said.

"Shut the hell up," Jake replied.

"What are we looking for?"

"I don't know. Something out of the ordinary, I guess. Let your eyes drift over the scenery and your subconscious will flag things that are out of place. That's how the cops do it."

"Kind of hard when I'm supposed to be driving."

Fairhaven

"I might be able to think more if you shut up."
"You're the boss," Nort said.
They drove for an hour, then bought gas. Nort bought a sleeve of little doughnuts and a pint of milk.
"I think I could sleep now," Nort said around a mouthful of doughnut.
"Give me one of those," Jake said. He extracted one and nibbled off a bite. "Let's give it another half-hour. Go by Alpine Vista again."
They pulled onto Section Street.

Charlie Fairhaven

Peaceful Meadows was a large facility with a ten-person overnight staff. He would not be able to use the same strategy that he used at the Wind in the Willows.
If you want to kill a lot of people, you have to be creative. You have to use your head. You must have a plan.
Around the back, by the dumpsters, were a chain link fence and a gate. Charlie had a key to the gate's padlock. It was quiet. Beyond the heat pumps was a large shed where the central junctions of the massive HVAC system for all three wings came together. He had a key for that padlock too.
Inside, the CO_2 bottles were already in place. The shed was huge. All he had to do was turn on the ventilation fans and open the valves on the gas cylinders, and then walk to the ends of each of the three wings and open a window on each so the gas could fill the building. Easy. He was done in ten minutes.
But, Eleanor Bradley was a tenant and she deserved special attention. Dying of asphyxiation in her sleep was not what she deserved. There was no time to waste, but there was time

291

enough.

Behind a wild thicket of rhododendrons, the staff had propped open a door so they could sneak out for a smoke. Inside, her room was down a short stretch of hallway. He avoided the eyes of the security cameras and slipped into her room. He put his mouth right next to her ear.

"Hello, Mrs. Bradley," he whispered.

Her eyes popped open.

"You," she said.

"Yes, me," he said. "Are you surprised to see me?"

She reached for the nurse's call button, but Charlie moved it out of her reach.

"No you don't, dear," he said. "I just stopped by to thank you for the hat."

"You killed those people."

Charlie laughed. "Yes. What's the official number?"

"I don't know. A lot. Forty?"

He clenched his teeth and tried to grin.

"More than that. Fifty-seven."

"You're a horrible monster. Those people didn't deserve to be beaten to death. And the little girl—"

"She was not supposed to be there," Charlie hissed. "It was against the rules. Those old folks were sitting around waiting for death to take them and I helped the process move quicker, that's all. They should be thankful. Their deaths had meaning. They became part of something very special. Mount Vernon will be famous around the world forever." He cocked his head and sniffed the air. It had a metallic, slightly citrus taste to it. "Now I grant you the same gift. Sorry, but there's no more time for debate."

He put his hand over her nose and mouth and looked into

Fairhaven

her eyes. "Don't struggle, dear. It won't hurt. Just let go."

She blinked and fumbled with the quilt at her side.

"We all end up in the same place and I'll see you there," he said.

He felt a sharp, warm piercing in his side. He removed his hand from her face and stood up straight.

"What have you done?" he asked. He lifted his hand. In the dim light, there was a vivid splotch of blood. "What did you do?"

Eleanor gasped and filled her lungs with air.

"We *do not* end up in the same place," she said.

"You bitch, what did you do? This is not right."

He staggered backwards.

She raised the homemade shiv…the long nail with a duct tape handle.

"Come back and I'll do it again," she said.

Holding his belly, Charlie pushed through the door and staggered into the hallway.

"This is not right," he said.

Jake and Nort

They drove by Peaceful Meadows. Everything was quiet. In the hazy night, a police car slipped by. Jake waved and the cop raised a finger in reply.

"Pull in the parking lot. The back," Jake suggested. "I think I'm going to throw up."

"Don't do it in the car," Nort said. He parked. "The rear gate is open. I'm going to check it out."

Jake opened the car door and fell out on his knees. He vomited. He felt pressure in his chest and could not catch his breath.

"Oh, fuck, this is it," he said.

He crawled a few feet, and then flopped over on his back. Mist glowed in the overhead light. Nort got on his knees and hovered over Jake.

"This is no time to screw around. Fairhaven's truck is out back, on the other side of the fence. The lock to the shed is open and there are big metal tanks spraying out vapor. Everything is covered with ice. What do I do?"

Jake could not catch his breath, but he spoke.

"I'm sorry, G-P, I didn't catch what you said."

Jake repeated himself.

"Find a shovel or something and smash out all the fucking windows."

Nort was about halfway done smashing windows when the cop, with blue lights flashing on top of her cruiser, pulled into the parking lot. She pulled her gun.

"Stop. Come out with your hands where I can see them," she said.

"Damn it, Ng, it's me. Nort. Help me break out the windows, then call an ambulance. I think Jake is dying in the back parking lot."

24

Charlie Fairhaven

HE DIDN'T KNOW where he was. At the edge of the valley, he'd driven up a steep incline and kept going after the paved road turned into gravel. Down a long stretch of rutted roadway, he'd pulled off and driven through scattered bushes along a hillside.

The hole in his belly was not very big and had stopped bleeding after a half hour, but things in his abdomen were not right. From deep inside, the pain was like a living thing.

What am I going to do? I can't stroll into a hospital. What would I say? That I accidently poked myself with a screwdriver?

He realized he could do exactly that. Who cared that they'd be looking for him? He hadn't thought he'd get away with this crime…he was ready to face the courts and have his face all over the TV. What was he thinking? They had to give him good medical care. He wouldn't even have to pay for it.

What was I thinking?

He restarted the truck and began backing up, but the front tire caught a rock outcropping and he was stuck. He rocked the truck and tried to pull forward.

Nothing.
He was stuck. He was going nowhere.
Another thing that's not part of my plan.
Great.

Nort Spenser

The room was crowded. Nort squeezed in and put his arm across Talon's shoulder.

"Is the old coot going to make it?" he said.

Maureen, with tears streaming down her cheeks, looked up.

"Doctor Valenchenko says he has a chance. That's all he'll say. They've been working on him for an hour. The doctor seems to be very smart."

"Maureen, I know this is a bad time, but I need your help."

"I'm not leaving his side."

"You have to. I don't know how long my iPhone battery will last."

"What?"

"I'll explain in the car," Nort said.

They drove down the hill toward the police department.

"You can track a phone right? I read something about it in *Wired*. They can figure out where a phone is from the cell towers or something."

"Yeah. It isn't very accurate and you have to get a warrant, but they can do it."

"I saw Fairhaven's truck and I didn't know what else to do, so I threw my iPhone behind his seat. You're going to have to call in some favors or something. We don't have time to mess around with a warrant."

"That's impossible. It can't be done."

Nort looked at her.

"It *can* be done," he said. "It has to."

At her desk, Maureen put on her headset and dialed the Frontier Communications hotline.

"This is Maureen Olsen with the Mount Vernon police department," she said. "This is a police emergency. Can I speak to your supervisor, please?"

It took a few minutes, but Maureen did it. She handed Nort a scrap of paper with GPS coordinates scrawled on it.

"There wasn't much signal, but they think they got it," she said.

Nort kissed her cheek.

"Thank you," he said. "I'll drive you back to the hospital."

"You know what to do now?"

"Yeah. Google Maps."

Maureen shrugged.

"Okay," she said.

Google Maps showed the truck's location on the west side of the Cultus Mountains in an area crisscrossed with logging roads. Due to the remote location, he couldn't get a very detailed satellite photograph, but he had a general idea of the rough terrain.

Now what?

Nort pulled up to the sliding gate at the rear of Discount Auto. He thought about honking, but decided to wait for a few minutes and see what happened. He tapped his fingers to the beat of the mix disk Talon had made for him. Red Hot Chili Peppers. *Dani California.*

Down in the badlands, she was savin' the best for last...

Slowly, the gate retracted and Nort drove in. The gate closed behind him, which made him nervous. He got out of the car and stood by the driver's door. After another minute, Dmitri came through the metal door at the back of the building and gestured for him to come in.

Inside, Viktor sat behind his desk and studied Nort as if he'd never seen him before. He pointed at the guest chair and Nort sat down.

"This is unexpected," Viktor said. "I assume there is something you want." Nort nodded. "Okay. I'm listening. You have two minutes."

"Charlie Fairhaven," Nort said casually while examining his thumbnail.

After a moment, Viktor spoke.

"The guy who killed all those people in the nursing home?"

"Yeah," Nort said.

"What about him?"

"I swore to Jake that I would not go after him alone. Jake's in Intensive Care. So, I came here to ask you...for a favor."

Viktor opened his desk drawer and pulled out his vodka. He poured an ounce into a glass and looked at it for a few long seconds before tossing it back.

"Go on," Viktor said.

Nort pulled the GPS coordinates from his jacket pocket, leaned over, and put them on the desk.

"I think this is where Fairhaven is."

Fairhaven

Viktor studied the paper. He nodded to Dmitri.
"Okay," he said. "Go."

They walked through the front office and into the reception area. Dmitri looked through keys hanging on a pegboard and selected a set. Outside, a lemon-yellow Hummer H2 was angled up in the air on a ramp.

"This one?" Nort asked. Dmitri climbed up the ramp and opened the driver's door. "Can I drive?"

"*Nyet*," Dmitri said.

He slammed the door, started the engine and worked the massive vehicle down the ramp. The engine rumbled like an extraterrestrial locomotive. Nort climbed in. Dmitri gestured and Nort handed over the slip of paper. Dmitri tapped the touch screen of the built-in GPS and loaded in the coordinates.

"It says one hour," Dmitri said.

Nort settled into the seat and fastened his seatbelt.

"Let's do it," he said.

They traveled up Highway 20 and turned off by the river on Highway 9. At Clear Lake they turned toward the mountains. In minutes all signs of civilization had thinned out. They wound around and traveled over a few places where the road was nearly washed out. They stopped on an old wooden bridge. Dmitri pulled out an automatic pistol and checked the load.

"We're close," he said.

They slowly drove around a corner. The white pickup, high-centered on a big rock, sat in the middle of the road.

"Wait here," Dmitri said.

"Not gonna happen," Nort replied.

Dmitri grinned, and then shrugged. "It's your ass," he said.

With the weapon pointed at the truck, Dmitri moved forward cautiously. There was no movement in the truck's cabin. After arriving at the driver's side window, Dmitri leaned over and peered in. He tapped on the window with the gun. Charlie started and looked out with wide eyes. He rolled down the window.

"I'm really glad to see you," Charlie said. "I'm in trouble."

Nort peeked around Dmitri and wrinkled his nose.

"What's that nasty smell?"

"Thirsty," Charlie said. "I'm really thirsty. Could I have some water, please?"

Dmitri clicked the safety on his pistol and stuffed it into his belt. He reached in and pulled out the ignition key and slipped it in his pocket.

"You heard the man. There's water in the back of the Hummer. Please go grab a couple of bottles." Nort stared at Dmitri with wonder. "Go," Dmitri said.

Nort shrugged. "Okay."

When he came back, he handed the bottles to Dmitri, who held them up to the window. Charlie looked at the water and licked his lips. Dmitri handed them back to Nort.

"Charlie," Dmitri said. "Can you hear me?"

"Yes," Charlie said.

"I'm going to ask you to do a few things. Okay? Then you get the water."

Charlie nodded eagerly.

"I'm dying of thirst."

Dmitri grinned. "Right," he said. "I'm going to push you off the rock with the Hummer and move you ahead a hundred yards. See up ahead? Under the trees? That's where we're going. Is that okay?"

"Yes, sure," Charlie said.

To Nort he said, "I'm going to drive really slowly. You reach in and help Charlie with the steering wheel if he needs it. Okay?"

Nort nodded. "Okay," he said.

Dmitri walked back to the Hummer and pulled it forward. The Hummer had huge, curved bars on the front. Dmitri eased the massive truck forward and pushed the Toyota. Once it was hidden under a thick patch of trees, he stopped and got out. Shiny chrome handcuffs dangled from his fist. He walked to the truck.

"Charlie?"

Charlie nodded.

"I'm going to put this handcuff on your left wrist, but I'm not going to cuff both hands. You'll be able to drink your water with no problems. Okay?"

"Yes. Okay."

To Nort, he said, "Go around to the other side and get your phone out of the truck. Let's not leave anything Charlie can use to escape or anything that can be traced back to us."

Nort nodded. He went around to the passenger side and fished around behind the driver's seat until he found his phone while Dmitri clicked the handcuffs closed.

"Got it," Nort said.

"Give the man his water."

Charlie worked the lid off one and guzzled the water. It ran down his chin.

"Thank you," Charlie said. "That's really good. Now, my gut really hurts. I don't think I can walk. Will you guys help me out? I need to get to a hospital."

Dmitri grinned and gestured to Nort. While Nort walked

back to the Hummer, Dmitry, with the butt of his pistol, smashed out the truck's rear window. He walked back to the idling Hummer and got in.

"That's it?" Nort said while fastening his seatbelt.

"That's it," Dmitri said while looking over his shoulder and working the Hummer backwards on the narrow road.

"The handcuffs?"

"I go back for them in a couple of days."

"What was the deal with the water?"

"He'd be dead in a couple of hours without water. With water, he'll last a day, maybe. It won't be the best day of his life."

"Ah," Nort said. "What about the broken window?"

"Nature doesn't like to let protein go to waste. If we're lucky, his body won't be found until spring and there won't be anything left but bones and gristle. No evidence."

After that, they drove the hour back into town without speaking. Dmitri pulled the car into the detailing area at Discount Auto and gestured for the Mexican lot boy to wash it. They walked back to Viktor's office. Viktor, wearing reading glasses, was looking at a thick sheaf of contracts. He took off his glasses and leaned back in his chair.

"Done?" he said.

"Done," Dmitri replied.

"Did we get Fairhaven's car?"

"It wasn't convenient."

Viktor shrugged. "Okay." He looked at Nort. "You're young, so I'll spell this out clearly. The way I see it, you owe us a favor."

"I'm young. What can I do?"

"Your grandfather used to be a cop. Your stepgrandmother

works at the police station. You might be useful to me someday."

"My grandfather might not make it and he hasn't married Maureen yet."

Viktor shrugged. "He'll be fine. They'll get married."

"He had a heart attack. How do you know he'll be fine?"

Viktor sighed. "Did you catch the doctor's name?"

Nort thought. "Dr. Valenko?"

"Dr. Valenchenko. He's a friend of the family. Now, it's time for you to go."

Nort reached his hand across the desk. Viktor looked at it a moment before grabbing it and squeezing it. Hard. Nort squeezed back.

"There is one more thing," Viktor said.

"What?"

"My nephew, Adamik. He likes to ride on the skateboard. When he and his friends go to your shop, you give them a fair deal. Wholesale price. Okay?"

"Done," Nort said.

"That's the way the world works."

"I understand."

He extracted his hand and rubbed his knuckles, then walked out the back door to get in the Buick. When the gate rolled out of his way, he backed out.

At the hospital, he checked in at the reception desk. Jake was out of surgery and had been moved to Room 29. In the room, Maureen sat by Jake's bed. He looked pale, but he was conscious.

"What's the deal?" Nort said.

"He was completely blocked," Maureen said. "Bypass

surgery. Pig valves and they put in a couple of stents. With a new diet and exercise program, he'll be fine. They move patients out of here quick. If everything stays on track, he'll be out of here the day after tomorrow. We decided not to wait or take any other chances. The Chaplin will be here any minute. We're getting married."

"What about Fairhaven?" Jake whispered.

"The Russians helped me. We don't have to worry about Fairhaven anymore."

"The Russians?"

"Yeah. Viktor says we owe him a favor."

Jake's face twisted into a grin.

"Okay," he said.

The hospital Chaplin ushered Talon into the room.

"I'm sorry. We're all here, so let's go. I don't mean to rush, but I have Viaticum[7] to give and there is no time to waste." He glanced at a sheet of typed paper. "Do you, Jake?"

"Yes," Jake whispered.

"And you...Maureen?"

"I do," she said.

"Let's call that good, shall we? I hereby declare you, et cetera. I'll leave the paperwork for everyone to sign. I'm sorry to do it this way, but I really must go or a man will die without spiritual food for the journey. May God bless you and keep you."

With gown rustling, he dashed out of the room.

Maureen leaned over and kissed Jake on the lips.

"How do you feel?"

"Hitched," Jake said. "Which is fine. I'm not complaining,

---

[7] Catholic last rites.

but you can still click the morphine up a notch if you like."

Charlie Fairhaven

For the fourteenth time, he checked the water bottles. They were dry—not even a drop to wet the tip of his tongue. It didn't matter, the water did not help. He was still thirsty. Beyond thirsty. His belly was swollen and the puncture wound seeped no matter how he tried to block it. The skin of his stomach was hot and stretched like a balloon, but the evil smell did not bother him anymore.

Through the trees, he could see the stars—they were blinding-bright. They were supposed to be flaming balls of plasma, but Charlie knew the ancient Greeks were right; the sky was like a colander and starlight poured through round vents. He was going into the welcoming light.

He realized that his mother's voice…the constant cacophony between his ears…was *not* immortal. As the starlight swelled, her voice faded…replaced by yipping and keening. Like a ghost, a little gray dog ran across the road. Then another.

He stomach felt like it would split open. He moaned. Then the flesh *did* split open and his lap filled with hot coils of pain.

No. This is not right.

Something jumped in the back of the pickup. Then another something. He could hear the scratch of claws on the truck's bed. Snuffling snouts. The dogs.

"Puppy," he said. "Get help."

The stars stared down, but the light did not seem so warm and pleasant anymore. Cautiously, a dog put its head through

305

the back window. Its breath was foul. It smelled like death.

Wild dog. Coyote.

He remembered a TV documentary...coyotes were called American jackals and he remembered what they ate. Carrion.

No.

No.

This is not right.

25

Jake Mosby

JAKE WAS NOT moving very quickly while he dressed in his black suit and silver tie. Maureen adjusted the knot.

"You look really sharp, Jake," Maureen said.

The nurse opened the automatic door and rolled in a wheelchair.

"I already told you. I'm walking out of here," Jake said.

"Hospital rules," the nurse said. "No exceptions."

"Leave the chair," Maureen said. "I'll take care of this." To Jake, she said, "Here's your bear."

The stuffed bear was designed for people recovering from heart surgery…to be clutched to the chest as a cushion when coughing.

"I like the bear," Jake growled. "I don't like you."

Nort's mother, Eileen, came in. She was dressed in a long sheath skirt covered with an ultraviolet cardigan sweater.

"Hey, Dad," she said. "You look great for a dead man."

"Hey," Jake replied.

She gave him an awkward hug.

"Did you know Nort got his general equivalency diploma?

307

How did you do that?"

"I didn't do anything," Jake said.

"Hayward says Nort can come back home, but Nort wants to go to community college here in Skagit County. I knew you guys would either kill each other or Nort would come around. Hayward sends his regards, but he's doing a clinic in Mexico. He won't be able to make it to your reception. Ellen is in town. She's meeting us there."

"Reception?" Jake said. He turned to Maureen with a stern look. "What reception?"

"Don't worry about that right now," she said.

"All I want is a simple life with zero complications."

Eileen laughed. "He's been saying that since I was a kid," she said to Maureen.

Maureen picked up Jake's overnight bag.

"Ready?" she said.

Jake stuffed the teddy bear under his jacket and put his arms across the shoulders of the women.

"Yeah, I'm ready," he said.

The Wedding Reception

Maureen plucked the glass of wine from his hand and replaced it with another glass.

"No alcohol for a while," she said. "You can have sparkling cider."

Jake looked at the glass with disgust and put it on a table.

"I need some air," he said.

He slipped out through the 'Employees Only' door and entered the workshop. Bill, wearing a pair of greasy overalls, was maneuvering a chain around the back gears of a bicycle.

Fairhaven

"What a mob," Bill commented.

"Yeah," Jake replied. He walked through the shop and out the back door. Outside, wispy clouds drifted over the building and trees. It was cold. He walked to the river boardwalk and flicked most of the water off a bench before sitting down to watch the river flow by.

His daughter, Ellen, sat down beside him. Her hair was whipped up into a French roll and she wore a long sable-fur coat.

"Mom sent a note. She's glad you're happy."

"I'm not happy. Things are noisy around here and I'm never going to get any peace and quiet."

"You and Maureen should come visit us. We have a nice place with lots of room. Ocean view."

"It sounds nice for you."

Ellen laughed. "If you ever changed, I wouldn't know what to do with myself. Why did it take a heart attack and a marriage to remind us we're family?" She looked down the boardwalk. "Who's this coming?"

Jake glanced. "I don't know," he said.

"Come back inside when you get cold, Dad."

Jake grunted.

Ellen got up and brushed water from the back of her coat, and then walked back across the parking lot to the skateboard shop.

Jake didn't look up when a girl approached. She wore a short, gauzy dress whipped by the wind—and dark brown UGG sheepskin boots. She stopped directly before him.

"You're going to freeze your ass off," she said.

Jake looked up. "Talon? What did you do to your hair?"

She ran her fingers through short, feathery locks.

309

"I decided to be pretty," she said. "You can call me Krista. I'm not going by Talon anymore."

"I'll try to remember."

"I'm glad you're letting Nort stay."

"I'm not letting him stay. I told him to go home to his mother."

"You're letting him build a bedroom and a kitchenette in Party Central."

"That's got nothing to do with me."

"Right. It's just your place and your money."

"Right."

They sat in silence. A seagull wafted by.

"It's too cold out here. I'm going back inside. Can I bring you something? Coffee?"

"Yeah, you can bring me a couple of beers."

Krista laughed. "Maureen would have my head on a platter."

She got up and looked at him for a moment. Then she leaned over and kissed his forehead.

"If I marry Nort, then you'll be my grandfather."

"If and when that ever happens, I'll be an in-law. Your grandfather-in-law."

"Same thing. I love you, Jake."

He turned his eyes up river and pulled the lapels of his jacket tighter around his neck. He opened his mouth, but didn't trust himself to speak, so he said nothing.

She smiled and smoothed his thin hair against the wind before walking back to the wedding reception.

A motorized wheelchair whined down the boardwalk.

Now what?

It was Mrs. Bradley—covered in quilts and blankets with

only her jowly face exposed.

She stopped directly in front of him and worked the joystick until she faced him.

"I've been looking for you," she said.

Jake sighed.

"How have you been, Eleanor?"

"We have no time for 'have a nice day' and 'how have you been'. Mrs. Caldwell's daughter is missing. She comes every Tuesday, but this Tuesday? She didn't come. Mrs. Caldwell doesn't make things up. She thinks her daughter's ex-husband did something bad to her."

"What did the police say?"

"The creep has an alibi for when Mrs. Caldwell's daughter went missing."

Jake leaned his head back against the bench and closed his eyes.

"If I promise to look into this, will you leave me alone?"

She pulled her hands free of the heap of blankets and handed him a paperback book of Sudoku puzzles.

"I think the Japanese are making these things harder so Americans will feel stupid," she said.

She worked the joystick and rolled down the boardwalk.

He was cold. The wind found every gap and seam of his clothing and drove icy fingers into his old bones.

For a long time before giving up, he shivered and tried not to think about how warm it was inside. Then, slowly, he got up and walked back toward the building and his friends and family.

Ken Coffman

Epilogue

Jake Mosby

THE AFTERNOON SUN broiled the sand along the river.
Jake sat on a towel wearing only long skateboarder shorts and a
floppy straw hat. The sun soaked into his brown, scrawny body.
The scars from gunshots, the stabbing and heart surgery were
puckered dents in his body. Across the river, a bald eagle
perched on top of the tulip-painted smokestack and stared at
him with ugly malice.

A volleyball rolled up to his feet and the willowy brunette
wearing her tiny brown bikini top over teacup breasts ran up
to retrieve it. He kicked the ball toward her.

She lifted her sunglasses.

"I remember you," she said. She bent over to pick up the
ball. She gestured with the ball. "Thanks."

Jake nodded.

"But you're still a miserable prick," she said.

Jake smiled and leaned back on his towel.

"That's me," he muttered.

CPSIA information can be obtained at www.ICGtesting.com
Printed in the USA
LVOW041031260312

274786LV00005B/16/P